THE PRICE OF DECEPTION

THE PRICE OF DECEPTION

The Legacy Series – Book Two

Vicki Hopkins

ISBN: Softcover 978-0-9832959-1-4

To order additional copies of this book contact:

Holland Legacy Publishing
www.hollandlegacypub.com

Table of Contents

Prologue 9
Chapter 1 12
Chapter 2 22
Chapter 3 34
Chapter 4 43
Chapter 5 53
Chapter 6 65
Chapter 7 71
Chapter 8 80
Chapter 9 91
Chapter 10 101
Chapter 11 111
Chapter 12 122
Chapter 13 133
Chapter 14 140
Chapter 15 155
Chapter 16 165
Chapter 17 176
Chapter 18 187
Chapter 19 200
Chapter 20 208
Chapter 21 216
Chapter 22 224
Chapter 23 232
Chapter 24 241
Chapter 25 248
Chapter 26 258
Chapter 27 265
Chapter 28 275
Chapter 29 283
Epilogue 288
The Legacy Series 292

DEDICATION

To my Holland ancestors in England, who taught me that success in business begins with a good foundation, a ton of bricks, plenty of mortar, and the audacity to triumph in spite of obstacles.

Prologue

"Oh what a tangled web we weave, when first we practice to deceive." Sir Walter Scott (1771-1832)

"Gentlemen, you may choose your weapons. Monsieur Moreau, because this duel is your challenge, you will have first choice."

Philippe studied both pistols and grabbed the gun on the right. Robert reached over and retrieved the gun on the left. Pelletier snapped shut the lid of the case and shoved it under his arm.

Robert's heart pounded in his ears as he waited for the instructions to stand back-to-back with Philippe Moreau and then pace off, turn, and shoot. For a quick moment, he thought himself quite insane for agreeing to accept the challenge. He had put his life on the line to win his cherished Suzette and the son he loved. The stakes were high. In the next few minutes, he could very well be dead.

He held the pistol in his right hand and looked at the maker's engraved name on the stock, feeling the weight, and gauging its handling. Made by a French gunnery, it felt somewhat different than the English pistols he had been accustomed to holding. He prayed the use of a foreign weapon would not hamper the accuracy of his aim, even though he was a first-rate shot.

Pelletier announced the conditions to them both in a gruff, loud voice.

"Monsieur Moreau has requested that the duel be to first blood, in which case the matter will be settled upon one man being wounded. However, if one man is severely wounded, and that wound leads to death, Monsieur Moreau will receive full and complete satisfaction of the disrespect done to his name."

Robert knew then his nemesis intended to shoot to kill. His gut turned into a hard knot, as the moments slipped precariously toward battle.

"Gentlemen, please proceed to the clearing, stand back to back, with pistols in hand. I shall count to twenty paces, upon which you will stop upon the number twenty, turn, and fire your weapons. Do you understand my instructions?"

Robert nodded affirmatively. Philippe called out a confident "yes" in response.

"Very well then."

Quickly, Robert glanced over at Giles who stood on the sidelines watching. The man looked pale as the moon, and Robert lifted his lips in a forced smile. He gave him a quick wink for an ounce of reassurance that all would be well.

"One, two, three . . ."

Robert moved his booted right foot in front of him and stepped in cadence with the numbers that were spoken. Twenty paces—it seemed like such a long distance, which would indeed make it a more difficult aim. He wondered why Philippe hadn't chosen a lesser number to do him in at point blank range and be done with it.

"Seven, eight, nine . . ."

Robert faced his countdown to eternity. He focused upon Suzette and his beautiful son, who looked so much like him.

"Twelve, thirteen, fourteen, fifteen . . ."

In a few more seconds, it would be over. One way or the other.

"Eighteen, nineteen, twenty . . ."

Robert turned on his heel, lifted the gun to aim, and heard Philippe's pistol discharge. He pulled the trigger almost instantaneously in return, and waited for the bullet from Philippe's pistol to lodge in his heart.

Chapter 1

Surrey, England – Spring 1884

Robert studied his appointments in the leather-bound journal. Since he had taken over the title of duke upon the death of his father five years earlier, his life had filled with duties that he found both monotonous and burdensome. Nevertheless, the tenants upon his lands merited his attention and respect. His father had been a good landlord, fair and equitable. Robert believed they deserved no less under his watchful care and management.

As he twirled the quill around in his hand, he glanced up at the clock on the fireplace mantel. The day had not even reached noontime, and Robert found it impossible to concentrate. The regrets of the past arrived to plague him once more. Their onset made him anxious and impatient in his tasks.

Remorse, an emotion he experienced often, became increasingly difficult to dismiss. He admitted, with some difficulty, that he had indeed squandered his younger years on drinking, gambling, and the brothel beds of enticing women. Of course, his choices were merely the rebellious streak that most privileged, titled young men his age experienced on their road to maturity. Even some of his closest comrades from his university days were prone to their share of indiscretions. It had been easy to justify his own foolish activities, when others he knew played the rogue, as well.

He hadn't expected, though, through the course of his frivolous days, to meet a woman who completely and utterly captured his heart. Robert's life had certainly not been absent of single ladies seeking his attention. Many, who he termed social leaches, desperately clung to him as an ideal potential catch. Robert routinely ignored them all, because the taste of forbidden pleasures had been far more succulent and to his liking. The regal, stuffy women of society, bearing the title of "Lady" due to their father's aristocratic status, bored him to no end.

Suzette had come into his life at the peak of his carefree idealization of young manhood. He made a habit of visiting Paris often in order to escape from home and the dull instruction of his father regarding estate matters. Like a lad running away from responsibility, Robert found solace in the arms of various women at the local brothel that catered to aristocrats. Had he been in England, he would have never been able to play the cad so openly.

The Parisians were far less condescending toward men of title who sought pleasure. In fact, they offered the rich the best they could afford in the way of entertainment—women, fine wine, and delicacies at high-end restaurants and casinos. His time spent in Paris invigorated Robert; it fueled and fed the raging hormones of a man his age.

One mystery purchase at the Chabanais drastically changed him for the better. A homeless woman without a Franc to her name, or a title of honor from a decent family, had instantly captured his heart. He saved her from a life of prostitution in a brothel, and she offered her love and body in thankfulness. Robert spirited her away to England and regularly visited her bed as his mistress.

He frequently pondered why he loved his petite French mademoiselle so deeply. Perhaps, she represented the freedom and innocence he yearned for in his existence, in comparison to the duties that chained him to a life of propriety instead.

Suzette, on the other hand, had been born a simple commoner, untainted, and unpretentious. She brought balance and completion to his world. After they parted ways, his life turned into an empty shell. He felt void of love and passion, even though there was another woman.

His parents had plans for his future. Marriage had become an obligation. To this very day, he grieved over his final obedience to his father's dying wish to wed a woman of his parents' choosing. He thought that he could satisfy both the requirements of the obedient son and retain a lover at the same time. His arrogance proved him wrong.

In foolish desperation to keep Suzette, Robert continued to use her for sexual pleasure without telling her the truth of his marriage to another woman. He had been selfish and grievously regretted his behavior.

When the death of his father occurred, so did the death of his former ways; but not necessarily the demise of his former desires. With Suzette gone, he had been denied comfort. In order to fulfill his needs, he still held some pleasures neither his mother nor wife knew about. Whenever he visited Paris he treated himself to slight indiscretions, for old times' sake, in the arms of a prostitute whose bed he had shared before.

Robert stood from his desk in his dark-paneled study and wandered over to the window. He had been cooped up for hours trying to dodge the cackling voices of his mother and wife, who were the busy-bodies of the estate household. He found their never-ending need to redecorate the estate irksome, but it kept them busy and out of his hair. Their hobby demanded little of his attention, except for money.

The gardens outside were in full bloom after a rather harsh winter that had finally passed. His eyes darted toward the stables and his neglected Arabian mare that probably wished for him to take her reins and run her in the meadows.

"Perhaps tomorrow." Robert sighed. He hadn't the heart to do much of anything after wrestling with regretful ghosts of the past.

His thoughts drifted to and fro, like the wind that moved the limbs of the tree outside his window. A distinct sadness washed over his soul thinking of Suzette. She sauntered through his mind and invited him to remember each moment they shared.

He did love her, though he never told her in so many words. How could he? If he did, she would have expected marriage. No, instead there were non-committal nuances of adoration and expensive gifts in order to keep her hopeful he'd one day offer an engagement.

Robert would have kept her as his mistress even after his ill-begotten union to his wife, Jacquelyn Spencer. At least he would be in the arms of a woman he loved and who loved him in return. Instead, he let her go.

Robert narrowed his eyes as he remembered her words when they parted. Even now, they possessed the power to sting his heart.

"You see, I have a confession to make. I've been a bit naughty while you were away so long. I spent quite a bit of time with Philippe Moreau, and I . . . well, I have discovered that I still love him."

"Love him," he mumbled under his breath with a unrelenting jealousy. "She lied. I'm sure of it. She loved me, not him."

In the end, Suzette had punished him for his dishonesty when he wed another in secret. He had come to tell her that he was leaving in order to give her an honorable life. Instead, she pushed him away first before he could get the words out of his mouth.

Robert closed his eyes and remembered the first night

they met. Scared and petrified like a mouse before a cat, she entered the Louis XV Chambre at the Chabanais brothel with a slight push from Madame Laurent. The scene returned a smile to his face, which eased the heaviness in his chest.

When the door closed, Suzette took baby steps in his direction. His heart couldn't help but be touched by her beauty and innocence. He had purchased her virginity and would have gladly taken it with his sexual appetite, but discovered he could do no such thing.

She appeared far too pure and innocent to touch. He hungered to possess her soul, more than he ached to taste her flesh. Robert had not the heart to introduce her to the life of prostitution, and in doing so carried out a ruse to bide time.

During his last night in her company, all changed in a matter of moments. Their little deception had backfired, and Madame Laurent played her own game of revenge by selling Suzette to another. Had he not arrived when he did, she would have been violated by the fat pig, Marquis Barone, who squashed her petite frame underneath his mass. Each time he thought of the scene, anger rose in his heart as fresh as the night it transpired.

Robert walked back to his desk. He pushed around the mounds of paper that needed attention. His index finger shoved sheets left and right, and he admitted he had not the heart to do any work. He needed to get away.

It had been nearly six months since he visited Paris. Springtime afforded a perfect season to travel to their townhouse in Arrondissement de Passy. The Seine would be at its peak with the runoff, and the parks and gardens brimming with budding flowers and trees. The thought of traveling alone appealed to Robert, but a stab of guilt told him that his wife needed a respite too.

Determined to act upon his urge, Robert exited his study and walked down the corridor toward the main parlor. The high-pitched voices of his mother and spouse filtered down the hallway as he approached. The two were probably orchestrating a new project that would cost him money.

As he drew near, he stopped for a moment and inhaled a deep breath for fortitude. He rounded the corner of the doorway and strode into the center of the room. Both women eyed drapery fabrics for their next redecorating enterprise.

"I like the emerald green," he chimed in just to give his opinion. "The color of a forest is indeed soothing, don't you think?"

Jacquelyn wrinkled her nose in disapproval. "Oh, Robert, how awful and dark it would be. Mother and I just agreed that puce is a much better match. Especially since we've ordered a new settee with matching arm chairs. The unique flower pattern contains splashes of puce throughout and will undoubtedly show well in this dull room. Perhaps, if there were more westerly daylight, green might work; but as you know, the morning rays soon fade. The sitting room looks quite grim afterward."

Robert wanted to roll his eyes over Jacquelyn's usual long justification of the perfect choice. Everything he suggested had to be discarded as inconsequential in her thoughts. Each opinion he gave fell upon deaf ears, and every suggestion she made had to be accepted without disagreement.

He glanced over at his mother, who sat quietly, taking note of the conversation. Finally, she spoke her opinion in an attempt to bring some agreement between the two.

"I do concur with Robert, because I know that green is his favorite color. But, unfortunately," she exhaled, as she glanced at her daughter-in-law, "I have already ordered the furniture and puce will match perfectly. Green will clash." She looked at Robert and continued in an emphatic tone. "It is the color we shall choose, Robert, and it will be delightful. You'll see."

"Delightful, indeed." He surrendered to the ladies of the house and would lick his wounds from this latest defeat later. Irritated, he had almost turned to leave, but he had purposely come there for a reason.

"Paris," he announced. "Springtime in Paris. Does that intrigue anyone here?"

Jacquelyn quickly lifted her head and dropped the fabrics in her lap. She looked at Robert's mother in wide-eyed astonishment and then back at him.

"Are you serious?" She jumped to her feet and approached Robert with a broad smile. "The spring fashions will be released in the next few weeks, and you know what that means to me Robert. Fashion shows, new designs, hats, and special fittings."

"Yes, I know." He held out a carrot to entice her further. "You want money to buy another wardrobe for the summer, no doubt, and as your husband, I shall provide." Robert calculated in his mind how much this new endeavor would cost him.

Jacquelyn spun around quickly and looked at her mother-in-law. "But what of you, Mary? The furniture is due to be delivered and the drapes must be installed."

"Oh, don't worry about me." She waved her hand at Jacquelyn. "Go! Just bring me an outrageous hat, my dear, and I will be very content."

"When, Robert? When shall we leave?"

"In a fortnight," he said, thoughtfully. "I have some estate matters to attend to, but you can write ahead to our staff at the townhouse and have them ready our residence for arrival. Will that do?"

Jacquelyn smiled and then stepped closer to him. He braced his stance in anticipation of her show of affection. A moment later a kiss met his cheek. "Thank you," she whispered in his ear. "I need this."

Robert grasped her hand and gave it a slight squeeze. "I

know. We both do, frankly."

The trip had been arranged, and Robert found no need to linger with the women of his household. He turned and left them alone to talk of colors, patterns, and draperies. In two weeks' time, he would be back in Paris where his real love resided.

As Robert strode down the hallway, he pondered if Suzette found happiness and contentment after she married her former fiancé. He probably would never know. Perhaps it remained better that way, so he could cherish the memories instead. Why torture himself with the thought she had found something superior to their love? It was too depressing.

In the years he had periodically returned to Paris on holiday, their paths never crossed. Of course, there were millions of residents in Paris, why should he think they ever would? Yet, the possibility of seeing her never left him as soon as his feet landed upon French soil.

Robert felt the need for a breath of fresh air. He walked to the foyer, opened the front door, and stepped out to view the emerald green hills in the distance. The English countryside unrolled like a breathtaking oil canvas. The artist of Heaven had splashed a pallet of brilliant colors wherever Robert's eyes roved.

The deep blue sky accented the green. He loved the rich color of the grass and trees. The leaves had sprouted from their limbs and dangled down, swirling with the gentle breeze that passed by. The flowers shoved their heads up from the ground, and life renewed itself after the dead of winter. The sight brought a smile to Robert's face, stimulating his love of country and the legacy of the land his father left him.

As beautiful as the scene happened to be at that moment, the gray cloud of his life pushed its way into his thoughts. Jacquelyn's whisper a few minutes ago haunted him with worry. He knew her mentality. She had been seasonally depressed during the winter months. Each year, the dark months with rain, snow, and lack of sun covered her mind with a cloak of despair. This past season had been unusually harsh upon her psyche. It sent her moods soaring into deeper depths.

Thankfully, beautiful days like today would help to turn the tide of her melancholy. He noted her spirits had lightened up and took encouragement that she would recover more quickly if he took her to Paris, or so he thought.

Not long after their marriage, Robert learned that his wife's downhearted moods were frequent. Her mind tended to wander, making her unresponsive when engaged in conversation. Jacquelyn's ability to socialize with others suffered. The only person she seemed comfortable with on a daily basis happened to be his mother, Mary, who pampered her like a daughter. As the years continued to pass with no sign of pregnancy, the frequency of his wife's misery increased exponentially.

Robert soon discovered, in his role as husband, his unpreparedness to handle the emotions of a woman—especially one such as Jacquelyn. There were moments in the depths of her despair that he believed she needed the help of a physician. However, when he suggested that medical counsel be sought in the course of her depressed phases, she adamantly refused to comply. As a result, Robert bore it silently, accepting it as his lot. To compensate, he avoided her as much as possible.

On the other hand, Jacquelyn portrayed a beautiful and gracious woman in spite of her negative traits. Her gorgeous blond hair and fair features were pleasant to look at, and her curvaceous body would appeal to any man.

She had been raised in an aristocratic family of wealth and privilege and bore the title of duchess, which she assumed upon their marriage, extremely well. Intrigued with her when they first met, Robert swiftly courted her due to his father's ill health.

Locked into a union of convenience in all respects, Robert possessed no endearment toward Jacquelyn, as hard as he tried. When feeling well, Jacquelyn portrayed an extremely poised and well-mannered woman. In contrast, though, when her spirits fell low, Robert noted a distinct change in her behavior. She would turn into an argumentative shrew and badger him verbally, until he would give into her demands. If anyone deserved the title of expert in the art of manipulation, it would be Jacquelyn Spencer.

The trip would hopefully bring Jacquelyn a sense of happiness. Fashion and new frocks seemed to be her single fountain of joy. He'd give her a generous allowance and let her shop to her heart's content.

In the meantime, he would visit his old friends for drinks and card games, and other acquaintances that he never failed to see when in Paris. Robert determined to have a good time of it, no matter what. While away, he would put aside troublesome thoughts of his poor decisions of the past and find some comfort elsewhere. Paris, known as the city of love, had its pleasures. Robert intended to enjoy them all.

Chapter 2

Robert pulled off his black leather gloves and handed them to his butler, along with his cane. The maid attended to his wife. She unpinned her hat and then placed it inside a box in the hall closet. The trunks were unloaded from the carriage and footmen busily carried them up the grand staircase to their private chambers.

They had arrived in Paris for their holiday. The journey across the channel had been blessed with pleasant weather, and the train ride from Calais to Paris uneventful. Jacquelyn, however, remained quiet through the course of the trip, and Robert hesitated to ask her why.

As he stood in the foyer and made a quick glance about the stately rooms, everything seemed to be in order. The staff had readied the residence for their arrival. The interior smelled clean, the furniture dusted, and the tiled black floors gleamed from fresh polish.

"I've taken the liberty, Your Grace, of ordering a tray of hot tea and cakes for you in the parlor. Is there anything else I can do for you?"

"No, that will be all, Gerard. Needless to say, the duchess and I are a bit tired after the long journey. Thank you for the kind gesture of tea upon our arrival."

"Of course." He bowed at the waist. "If you need me, please do not hesitate to ring."

Robert offered his arm to Jacquelyn who remained unresponsive. For some reason, he anticipated a more jovial response over their arrival in Paris. Instead, a miserable countenance captured her face.

He surmised she felt exhausted from travel and gently helped her to the nearby settee. The maid poured them both a cup of tea from the pot, giving Robert his cup with a usual dash of white milk. Jacquelyn received her brew with her usual two cubes of sugar.

"Thank you, Rosalind. That will be all."

She curtsied, left the parlor, and closed the double doors on her way out. Robert looked over at his wife and patted her arm tenderly with the palm of his hand.

"You look exhausted, Jacquelyn. Are you all right?"

She picked up the spoon from her saucer and began to swirl the sugar cubes around and around until they were totally dissolved. Her actions appeared to purposely delay her response. Robert waited. He watched her thoughtfully with each movement of her hand.

"Well, I'm exhausted," he finally offered. "I think I'll drink this tea, have a piece of cake, and then ask Giles to draw me a hot bath." He made sure that his personal attendant traveled with him as usual, and Jacquelyn's lady's maid, Dorcas, accompanied his wife.

"I'm off to bed. You should—" Robert abruptly stopped midsentence as he saw a tiny tear trickle down Jacquelyn's cheek. He looked at her for a moment and wondered why the display of tearful emotion. It wasn't long before she articulated the reason for her distress.

"I've bled."

"You mean—?"

Jacquelyn bitterly interrupted. "Yes. When we stopped in Calais before boarding the train and I excused myself to the powder room, I . . ."

Jacquelyn didn't need to say anything else. She pulled her gaze away and lowered her head. Tears freely poured over her lower eyelids and spotted her lace bodice below. Robert knew exactly what she inferred. Her menses had arrived, and another month passed without conception. The scab, which had healed on the wound of disappointment a month ago, had been cruelly ripped open. Discouraged once more, he felt nauseated. He slowly put his teacup down on the side table.

He had consulted their family physician privately some time ago to understand the process of conception. The doctor explained to Robert that even if she skipped her menses on a regular basis, they could never be sure of a viable pregnancy until five months passed without the sign of blood. On the other hand, if she bled it meant no pregnancy or possibly a miscarriage.

The complex female body operated mysteriously, and Robert felt uncomfortable with the term of menstrual blood. However, he understood the consequences of its occurrence—it meant no child had been conceived. He collected his thoughts and looked at his broken wife. Her disappointment mirrored equally his own.

"I'm sorry." He choked the words from his hoarse throat. What more could he say? It would be the same *sorry* he had uttered every month for years—a never-ending disillusionment that left him cold and empty inside.

Jacquelyn wept silently. She stared at her cup. Robert knew she needed more than tea. Perhaps a hot bath and tender care would ease her pain. He stood to his feet and pushed apart the wood-paneled double doors and headed down the hall. He found Dorcas and called her aside.

"Your mistress needs pampering, Dorcas. I believe there are female matters to attend to."

Dorcas remained silent. She lowered her eyes and curtsied, understanding exactly what he meant. All the servants knew of their dilemma. Both staffs in London and Paris had followed their lives for five long years. His wife's barrenness had been spoken of throughout the household, and each cycle the entire staff waited for word that this would be the month of good news. It never arrived.

Robert allowed her to assist his wife. She would remain in bed for a few days while she passed her menses in depression. Dorcas would do as she always did on a monthly basis for her mistress. Jacquelyn would be escorted to her bedchamber, assisted with a warm bath, and then put to bed. Thank God for a tender lady's maid, who knew exactly how to deal with such female matters. Robert could handle no such task, for he too often fell into a few days of despondency after he heard the news.

He left Dorcas to tend to his wife, turned to the stairway, and made his way up to his own suite. When he entered, he saw Giles standing by his armoire unpacking his trunks and hanging up his clothes. Robert remained silent but instantly spied a full decanter of brandy on a side table. He needed a strong drink—to hell with tea and cakes.

Swiftly, he pulled the stopper from the crystal and dispensed an ample amount. He brought the glass to his parched lips and downed the liquid in a few gulps; then he poured another. Giles noticed his rapid consumption and raised his brow over his employer's behavior. Robert saw him out of the corner of his eye.

"I need it, old man, to drown the disappointment once again." He looked up at his trusted assistant and waited for words of solace in return.

"Am I to assume, Your Grace, that the duchess has no good news to bring this month?"

"None," he bitterly spewed.

He picked up the decanter and poured one more. "There will never be any good news, Giles. When will she accept it?" He took another swig from his glass. "When will I accept it for that matter?" he moaned, as he wiped his mouth with the back of his hand.

Robert swirled the left-over liquid around the bottom of the glass and lost his thoughts in the pool of alcohol. He wished he could drown in a sea of brandy to ease the pain.

"I'm destined to produce no heir," he said, emphatically convinced of his future. "I shall be without a son of my own. This blasted estate of mine and its fortune will pass to my cousin, Roger Dawson, the black sheep of the family. The man is a total ass and unworthy of a shilling of my family's inheritance."

Robert huffed and pointed his index finger at Giles. "I shall toss in my grave after I die, knowing that my estate did not go to my own immediate flesh and blood. It's a bloody damn shame!" His voice bellowed through the suite.

"One never knows, Your Grace, what tomorrow will bring. I cannot ever encourage you to give up hope. You should always cling to it for comfort, if nothing else."

Robert dismissed Giles' words as rubbish. *Hope? Hopeless,* he countered bitterly. He had quit counting the number of times he attempted to impregnate his wife. When he made love to her, she felt like a cold brick. Her body lay rigid underneath him, unresponsive and void of passion. He despised it, but only performed to deposit his seed to produce a child. Somewhere in the back of his mind, he hoped that each child conceived would bring continual comfort to his burdensome, duty-filled life, and awful marriage.

Robert finished the glass and set it down on the silver tray with a *clang*. The alcohol coursed through his veins, which soon brought relief to his anxiety.

"I need a bath," he commanded, untying his cravat. He pulled it from his neck and threw it on the bed. "Ready one for me and bring me a lit cigar to puff upon while I soak. I'm going to drink, smoke, bathe, and then sleep. It's all I care to do at the moment."

"Of course, I shall draw it immediately."

Robert took off his suit coat and unbuttoned his white linen shirt. With each button that slipped through the eyelet, he wrestled with his disappointment.

"I came."

The words echoed in his mind. His thoughts wandered into a mire of gloominess. For five years, he heard the same two words—he damned their existence.

The fact that Jacquelyn could not conceive posed a conundrum. The unanswered question remained—who was to blame? Women were delicate creatures, with workings that only a physician understood. His doctor explained the various reasons why wives often did not conceive, or if they did, the grounds behind miscarriages and stillbirths.

He knew that syphilis could be one reason, but he had checked and received a clean bill of health. The risks of infection were prevalent in Paris. He had been assured that the prostitutes in the brothels he frequented for aristocrats, received examinations every 15 days. Robert knew that men became infected regardless of how careful they were in their sexual exploits. Luckily, he had been spared in spite of his risky behavior.

Convinced that no disease prevented him from impregnating his wife, it had to be Jacquelyn's body that refused his seed. Why?

Although he wasn't a religious man by any means, Heaven had closed his wife's womb for some reason. Occasionally, a rare prayer would escape from his lips to entreat his creator for the gift of a child. He'd confess his sins of his earlier days, in an attempt to appease God for his prior reckless behavior. It mattered not. His prayer went unanswered.

He finished his contemplation, after liberating his body of clothes, and stood naked and ready for his bath. While Giles discreetly averted his eyes, he climbed into the water. Robert reclined in a comfortable position and took the lit cigar from his assistant's hand.

"Pour me another drink, Giles, and bring it to me."

He puffed the cigar and blew smoke rings into the air above him. Giles returned with the alcohol, and Robert continued to anesthetize his disappointment.

What a damnable situation, he thought. He had no solution for the quandary.

❋ ❋ ❋

"Now, now, Lady Jacquelyn, you must control your weeping. You shall make yourself ill."

"I don't care," she wailed harder. "I'm already ill. Can you not see by the blood in my bloomers?"

Jacquelyn glared at Dorcas, who took a deep breath for fortitude. Her lady's maid had been with her since she came of age at 16. She cared for her needs in her father's house and followed her to the Holland estate upon marriage. Though Jacquelyn maintained strict lines between mistress and servant, she knew Dorcas to be an empathetic woman. She could release her frustration and despair without danger of condemnation.

While Dorcas took off her mistress's clothes, Jacquelyn's body shook with sobs. Her fingers quickly unbuttoned her dress, then shoved it down off her shoulders. When it pooled at Jacquelyn's feet, she stepped out of the circle of fabric. Dorcas slipped the strings of her corset through the eyelets to free her from the soiled undergarments.

Jacquelyn flinched when she saw the bloody stain on her bloomers. As she glanced at her feet on the carpeted floor, it felt like she stood upon the edge of a precipice. One wrong move and she would tumble into a pit of everlasting shame. She'd be branded with an eternal mark of disgrace. Any wife who failed to produce children bore dishonor, especially one with the title of duchess.

Dorcas pulled her chemise over her head and gently pulled her bloomers down. Jacquelyn tilted her gaze and beheld the trickle of red crimson that made a pathway down her inner leg toward her knee.

"Your bath is drawn, my lady. Freshen up from your trip and then I will prepare the rags for this month's flow while you relax."

Jacquelyn took her hand and followed her maid obediently to the bath chamber. Tears of grief flowed silently down her flushed cheeks.

She approached the claw-foot tub that held comforting warm water and dipped her toe into the pool of liquid. After sliding into the bathwater, she observed the trickle of blood on her leg dissipate. Her heavy flow would begin in the morning as it always did.

"Lavender, Lady Jacquelyn, or do you prefer primrose?"

"Pardon?"

"Your bath fragrance. Shall I put in lavender or primrose?"

Numb with emotional pain, it mattered not to Jacquelyn. "You chose for me, Dorcas. I do not care."

"Very well, my lady."

She poured a generous amount of lavender into the water. The mixture filled Jacquelyn's nostrils with a relaxing scent. Dorcas left to prepare her pads. Jacquelyn slipped deeper into the waters, and then laid her head back upon the rim of the tub.

Her eyes fixated on the ornate plaster treatment above with its swirling decorations. She followed the lines and decorative curves and made a conclusion it had been silly to decorate a bath chamber ceiling. Jacquelyn understood such ornate treatment in a bed chamber or parlor, but not here. *What a waste of the architect's efforts*, she thought, *such unneeded Parisian opulence.*

For quite some time, she stared blankly at the pattern. Jacquelyn waited for the emotional pain to drain from her pores into the tub of water. No matter how long she looked at the ceiling, the ache in her heart would not leave. When she realized how pointless her little exercise had been, her emotions exploded.

"How stupid can you be?" she blurted out over her silly thoughts. "You lay here judging useless ceiling decorations when it is you who are useless. A barren nobody unable to conceive life."

Rage burst from her soul. Jacquelyn balled both hands into a fist and pounded the water in the tub where she lay. *Splash, splash, splash.* The water sloshed back and forth in the midst of her tidal wave of anger.

"Stupid! You're nothing but stupid and useless!"

The water recoiled from the invasion of fists. Waves breached the sides of the tub and spilled onto the floor. Tears of frustration and self-loathing poured down her face. She glanced down into the water and noticed a bloody clot had released between her legs. Terror spewed from her mouth.

"Dorcas, get me out! Get me out!"

Dorcas dropped the clothes in her hands and ran to the door. Quickly, she slipped her arms underneath Jacquelyn and lifted her up out of the water.

"Now, now, Lady Jacquelyn, it will be all right. Calm down. I'll have you in bed shortly."

She wrapped her mistress tight in a fluffy towel and took the liberty to put her arms around her sobbing body. Jacquelyn took no offense over her maid's intimate response. After all, Robert's nonattendance created a void in her life. Why shouldn't she rely upon a servant to show an ounce of sympathy?

Hastily, Dorcas dried her body, clothed her in a nightgown, and prepared her undergarments with clean menstrual rags to catch the flow. She helped Jacquelyn crawl between the sheets and covered her with the blanket.

"There, now get some rest, my lady. You'll feel better in the morning."

The next few days Dorcas would wait upon her in the privacy of Jacquelyn's quarters. After her emotions settled back into semi-normalcy and the menses subsided, she would emerge from confinement and return to her duties. Then, as she had done for years past, she would proceed to beseech Robert to visit her bed and try again.

❋ ❋ ❋

Jacquelyn's quiet seclusion afforded Robert time to spend with his usual male comrades at the Jockey Club de Paris, located at 2 rue Rabelai. Originally established as a society for the encouragement of the improvement of horse breeding in France, it had evolved into a rather exclusive club of aristocrats and men of the bourgeoisie. When Robert visited, he enjoyed intelligent conversation with fellow peers of similar background and title.

Along with the dialogue, of course, came the candid banter about the finest in alcohol, cigars, women, and the brothels in town. Although five years had passed since he darkened the door of the Chabanais, Madame Laurent's popularity had not waned in her ability to offer the best of prostitutes. Her competition, Rue des Moulins, had been given rave reviews too by a few of Robert's acquaintances. He had tasted its treats on one other occasion in Paris and found a welcome partner that filled his need for an unbridled romp between the sheets.

After a few days, he had caught up with old friends and turned his attention back to Jacquelyn. When she had left her chamber from her morose depression and monthly illness, as Victorian women often termed those times, he knew that soon she would begin her shopping for the latest fashions. He, however, had another idea that he thought might brighten her spirits.

The weather had been perfect since their arrival, with comfortable temperatures and no rain. He felt the urge to take her on a stroll in the nearby Parisian gardens. Many locals promenaded in their parks, which seemed a sensible pastime. To that end, he suggested his idea over breakfast.

"Why don't we take a walk when the sun is a little higher and it's pleasantly warm? The bright outdoors will return a rosy glow to your cheeks. It's sorely missing."

Jacquelyn, still a bit withdrawn, looked at him. He had to admit his actions were uncharacteristic to offer such kind attention to his wife. More often, he neglected her needs, but this time he felt compelled to show pity over her recent disappointment.

"I think that's a fine idea, Robert," she replied, with a faint smile.

They finished their late breakfast, and Jacquelyn asked Dorcas to fetch her jacket and a hat that matched her dress. Robert watched as she helped her pin it upon her head and slip her arms into her outer garment. Jacquelyn always dressed in impeccable attire, which enhanced her striking appearance. However, what Robert sought beneath her beauty did not exist. When he looked into her eyes, they were void of the womanhood he craved.

Robert played the role of the genteel husband and offered his arm in escort. They exited the door and proceeded to walk in a leisurely stride. Robert headed for their destination—the Tuileries Gardens, where a significant number of Parisians meandered in the morning hours.

Jacquelyn clung to Robert's arm tightly but remained silent. She held her tongue, and Robert held his. Whenever alone in each other's company, simple conversation between the two came with considerable difficulty.

They entered through the gate and began to stroll past the blooming flowers that lined the pathway. The budding cherry trees created a canopy of pink, both fragrant and pleasing to the eyes. Robert deeply inhaled the fresh air.

"It's a fine day for a walk," he chimed, with a slight smile. "I'm glad I suggested we take one."

"Indeed," she responded, in a lazy drawl. "The weather is comfortable."

Unbeknownst to either of them, their innocent walk through the gardens on a perfect spring morning in Paris had placed them on a course of unforeseeable change.

Chapter 3

Philippe had spent years building his new life with the woman he adored. After a long and terrifying search, he had recovered Suzette in England. He had rescued his precious fiancée from a life of degradation and immorality at the hands of Robert Holland—a vile Englishman with no scruples. Now, they were married and bound together, far from his touch.

For years he brooded over the audacity of the man, and each time it caused his blood to boil. Philippe tried not to mull over the past, but the little hand that clung to him made it impossible to eradicate the monster from his thoughts. Especially, when everyday he looked into the face of the scoundrel's offspring.

The aristocrat had used his beautiful wife for sexual pleasure without an ounce of remorse. Perhaps he did owe the jaded lord a morsel of thanks, since he rescued Suzette from a life of prostitution. However, he made her his private mistress afterward, which was a shameful act. All the while, he fully intended to secretly marry another woman. His actions remained an unforgiveable sin in Philippe's eyes.

Thankfully, Suzette agreed to leave the insufferable man after she discovered his deception, along with her unfortunate and untimely pregnancy. Philippe merely wished to shield Suzette from further harm and keep her hidden. It seemed the wisest course of action at the time. After all, a man of power and title would do anything to protect his reputation or fortune. He could have very well taken the baby from Suzette, sent the child away to an orphanage, and continued to degrade and use her without a shred of guilt.

Of course, Suzette had tried to tell him that she loved Robert and didn't believe him capable of such cruelty. Philippe convinced himself that she had mistaken love for gratefulness. Her naivety merely duped her into believing him a man of honor. His innocent Suzette had been blinded by the rich aristocrat. Foolishly, she had clung to the hope that he would one day marry her in spite of her lower station in life.

Philippe refused to believe that she had truly loved him. After all, she agreed to marry him instead and leave London. She had been his first love—his first innocent and pure love. Philippe had asked for her hand in marriage from her father, who willingly gave him the right to be her husband. They had joyously planned their wedding upon his return from a tour of duty.

Smugly convinced Suzette rightfully belonged to him in every possible way, he mourned over the one gift that had been denied him—her virginity. His rival for her affections had selfishly taken it instead.

As Philippe's feet walked along the pebbled pathway of the gardens, he attempted to pull his thoughts away from the memories that weaved through his mind with infinite chords of hatred. Nothing could be done about the past, so he determined not to spoil the brilliant spring day. He glanced down at the boy that clung to his hand and smiled.

The gardens were ablaze with pink and white cherry-tree blossoms dangling from limbs. The outdoor air was filled with the fragrance of new life. A walk in the park seemed the perfect choice for the two to take alone. They often enjoyed time together as father and son, and Suzette needed time alone to recuperate.

Deep within the park, Philippe noticed in the distance the figure of a couple. Both were dressed in rich finery and appeared to be enjoying a leisurely stroll like many others.

When they drew closer, the man's striking blue eyes met Philippe's. Instantly, the two recognized one another. The chance encounter thrust Philippe's heart rate into a pounding drum within his chest.

Had he not just cursed the sod approaching him? Why in God's name did their paths have to cross today, after all these years?

His jaw clenched tightly, and his eyes narrowed when he contemplated the potential confrontation. For the sake of Suzette, Philippe drew in a deep breath and attempted to maintain composure. They came face to face and stopped, and Philippe tipped his hat, as a matter of manners, rather than honor. He greeted the cad in an even tone.

"Lord Holland, good to see you. What brings you to Paris this time of the year?"

Philippe watched Robert Holland stop and examine the pair for a brief moment before he responded. His curious eyes darted between the two.

"It's duke now," he clarified, unemotionally. "Holiday—just a holiday."

Philippe frowned as he watched the duke's wife nudge him with her elbow to gain her husband's attention. Robert responded with a slight look of annoyance over her pointed jab.

"May I introduce you to my wife, monsieur? This is Jacquelyn." Robert looked at his wife and added, "Jacquelyn, this is Philippe Moreau, who is an old acquaintance I have not seen for many years."

Robert's wife reached forth one hand in his direction. Philippe hesitated, but then kissed it reverently, lightly brushing his lips against her white glove.

"Your Grace, it is a pleasure to meet you."

"And you, monsieur," she replied, with a warm smile.

The two men entertained an awkward moment of silence. The duke fiddled with the top of his cane, and Philippe tightened his grip when Robert's keen eyes inspected his companion. To his surprise, the duke suddenly knelt down on one knee and addressed the boy.

"And who are you, might I ask?"

Robert's soft and surprisingly kind voice spoke to the small face with big blue eyes and blond hair. The young lad's countenance brightened over the attention.

"Robert Philippe Moreau," he recited, with pride. The child stood tall and raised his chin toward the stranger to display a bold confidence.

Obviously shocked at his response, Robert slowly rose to his feet. With a distressed look across his face, he asked another pointed question. "And how old are you, Robert Philippe Moreau?"

"I'm five," he said, holding up five little fingers to confirm the announcement.

"How charming," Jacquelyn spoke in a fascinated drawl. "He has your first name. Isn't that adorable?"

"Yes, charming." Robert suspiciously eyed the boy.

Philippe could see both individuals had latched upon little Robert, and he hoped they witnessed no concern in his own face. He feared Robert would inquire further.

"And how is your mother?"

The child immediately looked up into Philippe's eyes and displayed his hesitancy to answer the question. He bent down and scooped him up in his arms to grant him the assurance needed, as he spoke the response to the duke's uncomfortable inquiry.

"I'm afraid that Robert's mother passed away last winter," he feigned, with a sad voice. He leaned over and kissed his son's cheek. The lad turned his head and gazed with curious interest at the duke's blue eyes.

The color drained from Robert's face. He looked intently at the boy. Immediately, Philippe wondered if he saw his reflection in the lad's countenance that gave way to doubt.

"Oh, I'm sorry to hear that." His voice choked with emotion. "May I ask how?"

Philippe, somewhat pained over the duke's obvious sorrow, replied with sadness. "Influenza—the influenza epidemic."

"Yes," Robert nodded his head. "It was quite severe in England, as well."

A few moments of silence passed between the four individuals, and then finally Robert turned his gaze back to the young boy. "Your mother was a good woman."

Robert reached out and touched the child's cheek with his fingertips. Philippe frowned and stepped backward, irritated over his show of affection.

"Have you any children of your own?" he interjected tersely, in an attempt to divert his attention. Robert's wife interrupted before he could answer, as if she needed to spare her husband embarrassment.

"Not yet, I'm afraid."

Philippe noted the anguished appearance on Robert's face. He hugged little Robert tighter and wished the two would leave. Apparently, his sour expression had been noted.

"Shall we go, dear?" The duchess tugged on her husband's sleeve. Robert's gaze would not leave the little boy, and Philippe feared more questions.

"Yes, we should go," he finally sighed in reluctance.

Philippe bid him goodbye and offered his hand in parting.

"I'm sure if Suzette were here, she would have much to say." He nearly choked on his words.

Robert strongly grasped his hand and shook it in return, which somewhat surprised him. Philippe felt no remorse over his boldface lies.

"Goodbye." Robert took a painful, last glance at the boy. He offered his arm again to his wife and then continued their stroll toward the opposite end of the park.

Philippe set his son down on the pathway and walked toward the exit. With his palm, he wiped away the beads of nervous sweat that had formed on his forehead.

"Who was that man, Daddy?"

"He is a man, who once helped your mother through a very difficult time. That's all."

A small stab of guilt pricked him as he led the child away from his real father. However, he had sworn that Robert Holland would never know his son, if he had anything to say about it. His heart had tied affectionately to him for Suzette's sake, in spite of the child not being his own flesh and blood.

He grasped Robert's tiny hand, and Philippe quickened his step. While his heart continued to pound like thunder in his chest, he couldn't help but glance over his shoulder one more time during his hasty departure. As he did, he met Robert's cold stare and quickly glanced away. Philippe darted around a corner and headed back toward the gated entrance of the gardens.

"Daddy, did I do all right?"

"Yes, you did fine."

The child struggled to keep up with the long-legged strides of his father. Philippe picked him up in his arms and held him tight to quicken his pace. His tiny legs dangled from Philippe's arms and bobbed back and forth with each step. The boy clung tightly to his neck.

Philippe raised one arm and hailed a hansom cab to take them home. He climbed inside, settled back in the seat and held Robert in his lap. The whip cracked, and Philippe glanced over his shoulder out the rear window toward the gated exit. He let out a sigh of relief when no one pursued.

As he held the boy close, his thoughts grew rampant

with questions and fear. *Why now, after all these years, had their paths crossed?*

He glanced down at Robert once more, overcome by a sense of protectiveness for his wellbeing. Philippe had always wanted to be a father. The liberation of Suzette, pregnant with another man's child, seemed to be of little consequence to him five years ago. He loved her. He wanted a family. Nothing could have made him happier than to be a father, and even more so since a newborn child had recently arrived from their union.

Philippe hoped the duke didn't suspect the boy's identity, but couldn't convince himself that danger did not exist. Though Robert said nothing, Philippe knew the man must have entertained questions. The lad bore a spitting image of his biological father. Certainly, he saw his likeness—blond hair, blue eyes, fair complexion, and the same square jaw.

Today had upset the apple cart of his idyllic existence. As the cab bounced toward its destination, he agonized over telling Suzette. Everything in his married life up until that moment had been perfect.

Minutes passed while Philippe fumed over his encounter. Finally, he collected his thoughts. The horse trotted onto the stone drive, which elicited delight in his modest estate. He had done well, even though no title of nobility attached to his name. Philippe's measure of success only recently began to decline with difficult trials and a turn of bad luck.

His half interest in the shipping business, which he had purchased before he married Suzette, had proven to be a wise investment. He possessed a home comfortably staffed with a cook, two maids, and a governess.

When the cab slowed, Philippe couldn't shake a sense of unwelcome change in the future. The driver pulled back the reins on the horse until they came to a complete stop. Philippe didn't wait for him to open the door. He flung it wide, pulled Robert into his arms, paid the fare, and headed for the front stoop.

Once inside, the maid greeted his arrival. Philippe set Robert down in the foyer.

"Monsieur, you look a fright! Is everything all right?" His maid creased her brow in a worried fashion over his obvious frantic state.

Philippe fidgeted with his gloves and tore them off his hands in nervous frustration. "Yes, yes," he mumbled. "Just in a hurry."

He glanced down at Robert and noted his worried gaze too. Clearly, he sensed something odd in his animated behavior. Philippe took a deep breath to calm his jitters and knelt down in front of the boy.

"Run along now and go play in your room for a while, Robert." The lad clutched his father around his neck and gave him a tight hug. Philippe smiled over the gesture and with a small pat on the behind gave him a friendly scoot.

He watched Robert run up the stairs to his room, with the knowledge that he had stolen something that belonged to another man. A pang of misgiving over the wisdom of hiding the child's existence made him shuddered. His gut churned as the worry of his deception loomed like a mountain before him. The strong, determined man that Philippe Moreau had evolved into a few years ago, suddenly felt weak and vulnerable.

He turned to his maid. "Where is my wife?"

"In the parlor, monsieur."

Robert handed his gloves and hat over to her, and then walked down the hallway to the right and entered a small parlor ablaze with the afternoon sun. As his gaze rested upon his wife, the air sucked from his lungs at the vision of beauty that met his eyes. The rays danced off her auburn tresses in the sunlight. *Beautiful as ever*, he thought. Nothing had changed, except for one small addition—their newborn daughter.

He stood in silence, afraid to speak his next words. Slowly, he stepped inside and embarked on a most unpleasant task.

Chapter 4

Suzette spent her time alone as a welcome reprieve. Her husband had an uncanny sixth sense when it came to her needs to recuperate on certain days. He probably noticed that morning she felt out of sorts.

Only two months earlier she had given birth to their first child, a baby girl named Angelique. The delivery had been extremely difficult, with long, tedious hours of labor, and the loss of more blood than the physician cared to see in the afterbirth. It had drained Suzette physically and mentally.

On this particular morning, Philippe decided to take little Robert on a walk. Their son had exhibited a short temper lately, and Suzette and Philippe attributed his rash behavior to a bit of jealousy over the new arrival in the home. Perhaps some undivided attention between father and son would help with his feelings of neglect.

After morning tea and toast, she put on an apron and headed outside to enjoy the fresh air. Even though they had a gardener to tend to the grass and trees of their upper class residence, Suzette wanted to nurture a small plot of flowers by herself. Lilies reminded her where she had come from and the trials of her past. They held in their beauty the hope that life would ultimately bring her the contentment she sought.

After a half hour in the morning sun, she went indoors, washed her hands, and asked for another cup of tea. Suzette headed to the parlor and a delightful book, written by her favorite English author, who treated her to times of female fantasy. She took a seat by the window to soak up more sun and opened the volume to the placeholder and began reading.

"How is my beautiful wife?"

Philippe's voice startled her, and she looked up at him. He stood in the doorway with an agitated look upon his face.

"What are you doing back so early?" she asked, annoyed. A few more hours to enjoy before the house became busy again would have been diverting.

"Suzette, I need to speak with you."

Suzette sighed and closed her book. Philippe looked pale. Immediately, she knew by his unusual demeanor that something had to be wrong.

"I need a word in private."

Philippe closed the sliding doors to the parlor until they met tightly together. Suzette looked at him in confusion.

"I don't understand why you're acting so strangely, Philippe." She stood to her feet and walked toward him. He remained silent and pulled her into his arms and held her tight. Afterward, he released her with a frown upon his face.

"Come sit with me a moment," he beseeched.

"Philippe, what is it? You're frightening me."

They settled on the divan, and Philippe picked up her hand and stroked it tenderly for a few moments before he answered. Finally, he spoke with considerable difficulty, sputtering words from his nervous lips.

"I saw—I saw Robert today."

He looked into her amber eyes with a solemn

expression. Suzette's head tilted in puzzlement as she tried to make sense of his declaration. The only name of Robert spoken for the past five years represented her son. It took a few moments to grasp the meaning behind his words.

When the reality sank in, her eyes widened. Suzette seized Philippe's lapels with both hands and pulled him toward her in desperation.

"Where is little Robert?"

Philippe held her hand in reassurance. "He's in his room. He's fine, Suzette."

Her lungs exhaled a sigh of relief, but her heart pumped ferociously in her chest.

"Did—did—" Suzette couldn't form the words. She wanted to scream the question, but nothing would come out of her mouth.

"Everything went fine," he assured. "He asked about you. Robert did as we instructed. He said nothing and looked to me for guidance. I picked him up, held him tight, and then told the duke and duchess you died last winter from influenza. He believed me."

"Are you sure?" she begged, with her grip tightening.

"Yes. I hate to admit it, but he looked quite pained when I told him. I'm sure he believed my words by the way he acted."

"What about Robert? Did he talk to Robert?"

"He knelt down and asked him his name and age."

Suzette gasped as her fears rose from the depths of her heart.

"My God, Philippe! He knows!"

"No, no." Philippe quickly dismissed her worries. "I don't think he suspects. Really, I don't."

"He's not stupid!" Suzette flung in his defense. "Surely, he suspects after seeing his blond hair and blue eyes."

"Perhaps," Philippe responded bitterly, clearly irritated over his wife's comment. "But there is no way for him to prove that Robert is his child. It's my word against his. As far as he knows, you are dead and cannot confirm any suspicions lingering in his heart." Philippe paused and added, "I'm surely not going to tell him and neither are you!"

Suzette looked warily at Philippe over his bold command. "Of course, I won't tell him." She pulled away from him. "I don't want to lose my—our son," she corrected herself.

"I care about the boy," Philippe countered, as he reached out and pulled her back into his arms. "Don't be angry with me, Suzette. I only wish to protect what we have together."

He drew her to the warmth of his chest and held her tight. His palm gently stroked her silky hair while words of encouragement left his lips.

"Suzette, I promise it will be all right. Robert will return to England when his holiday has ended, and that will be the end of it. You have two children that need your attention—a wonderful son and our beautiful new baby daughter."

Suzette pushed her fears aside as Philippe's comfort covered her like a warm blanket. His levelheadedness and logical thoughts brought calm to her life. He had, after all, taken her back unconditionally. She often felt as if she didn't deserve his kindness after her affair with Robert.

They quickly married after he had spirited her away to Paris in her pregnant condition. He settled into work, and Suzette assumed the role of wife and mother. At first loneliness shrouded her life, as she often thought of Robert.

The months preceding the birth of her son had been extremely difficult. When she left England, under the ruse of loving Philippe, it broke her heart. She had only done so because she could not bear to hear Robert's declaration that he wanted to leave her instead. It would have torn her to shreds. Undoubtedly, she would have relented and told him about her pregnancy to keep him at her side had he pressured her for answers. She loved him deeply, and her heart mourned the breakup for many years afterward. Eventually, Suzette buried the past and locked away her emotions.

Philippe, on the other hand, seemed driven to give her the best of everything. If truth be told, Suzette appreciated it. Her experience of homelessness on the streets of Paris had left her with fears of poverty. It wasn't long before Philippe prospered in his business, and he purchased the house where they currently resided. It gave Suzette a sense of extreme security, which she clung to with tenacity. As Philippe held her, she knew she had to trust in his words. Robert would return to London and all would go back to as it had been before. Yet Suzette struggled over the possibility of a different outcome.

"You're right. I've always feared this day would come, Philippe. Something inside told me one day Robert would find us, and now it has happened."

"Perhaps then we should not been seen on the streets or in public places together for a month or so until we are sure he has returned to England," Philippe counseled.

"Yes, that would be wise." Suddenly, she felt the need to see her son. "I wish to see Robert."

Before Philippe could say another word, Suzette rose and sprinted out the door leaving Philippe alone to deal with his own concerns. Her actions were perhaps selfish, but she needed to leave and look in the eyes of the child that resembled his father.

Suzette climbed the staircase of their estate. Once upon the second floor, she passed the nursery and stopped for a moment. Madame Dubois sat in a rocking chair holding their newborn, Angelique.

Amazed she had finally conceived again, she believed her daughter, Angelique, had been a symbol of God's long-awaited forgiveness. She blamed her years of an empty womb as just punishment for giving birth to a baby out of wedlock.

Suzette could not be convinced otherwise, except for one other factor. Philippe rarely visited her bed, not being a man driven by passion, like Robert who couldn't keep his hands off her body. On the contrary, cold logic drove Philippe Moreau. He relegated intimacy to occasional gratification, but not one of necessity for a close marriage. Whenever he needed a release, he would roll over for a quick performance.

Suzette walked into the nursery and gazed affectionately upon the face of her daughter. She had obviously inherited Philippe's genes in tone of complexion and hair color. Her eyelids fluttered open, and a yawn escaped her petite pink lips.

"Madame, do you wish to hold her?"

Suzette smiled. "No, you keep her. She looks as if she's drifting off to sleep."

She blew her baby girl a kiss, and then turned back into the hallway that led down to her son's chambers. Suzette stood in the open doorway and saw him sitting in the middle of the room.

Robert busied himself surrounded by blocks of colorful, painted wood cut into squares and rectangles. Suzette watched with amusement. His little hand placed one more square upon a tall wall erected in front of him. He carefully set the block down, but its uneven placement caused the entire structure to crash into a heap. Robert's face grimaced and turned red. He kicked the tumbled mound with his foot and scattered the blocks across the floor.

"Stupid blocks!"

Suzette walked in and knelt by his side. Her son seethed with frustration, and his innate lack of patience protruded its ugly head.

"Robert," she said, giving him a hug. "It was a fine wall. Perhaps just too tall and that last red block a bit too heavy."

"I hate stupid blocks!" he spat. He jumped to his feet

and stomped across the room in a huff.

Suzette sighed and wondered how one small child could express so much fury. A frown crossed her face, and she stood up and approached him.

"You needn't be so annoyed, Robert. It's just a wooden block."

Robert looked up at his mother's critical scowl. Suzette felt relieved to see the irritation dissipate from his face. She put her arms around his tiny body and gave him another hug.

"Tell me about your walk in the park with father today. Did you have fun?"

Robert's eyes sparkled. "Yes, we did, Mommy."

"You did?" She grasped his little hand and led him over to the window seat where they both sat down. "What did you see? Did you find any birds you like?"

"There were ducks in the river. Father brought some bread in a paper bag, and we fed the ducks."

"Quack! Quack!" Suzette made the sound of a duck, and Robert laughed hysterically.

"You're funny, Mommy." He looked up at her with childlike glee. Then suddenly, as if a spark of inspiration entered his tiny mind, Suzette witnessed a change in his eyes.

"We saw a man and a lady today, too."

Suzette kept a smile across her face and tried not to show any outward concern. "You did?" she replied nonchalantly.

"He asked, 'How's your mother,' and I did like you and Daddy told me. I was quiet."

Suzette reached out and stroked the side of his head. "You did very well, Robert."

"I don't understand, Mommy. Daddy said you passed away. What does passed away mean?"

It never dawned on Suzette that her son would not know what Philippe's answer meant. She debated whether to tell him, and then decided not to elaborate on the word's meaning—at least not now.

"It means that Mommy is somewhere else." Robert's face looked confused while he tried to understand her explanation.

"Why, Mommy, must I be silent when people ask about you?"

"We talked about this before, didn't we?"

Robert shook his head. "Yes, but I don't know why."

"Sometimes, Robert, people just want privacy for many reasons. When you are older, you'll understand." Suzette hesitated and tried to clarify her words.

"It's just a game." Philippe's voice came from the doorway.

"Yes!" Suzette exclaimed, supportive of his explanation. "It's just a game."

Philippe glanced over at the pile of blocks strewn across the floor. "It looks as if a catastrophe occurred. Was there an earthquake?"

Robert giggled.

"Well, we had an incident where everything tumbled down, I'm afraid," Suzette interjected. "One block too many on the wall was the culprit for the disaster."

"Hum," mused Philippe. He knelt down and gathered all the blocks with his arms. He piled them into a big group in the center of the carpet and glanced up at Robert.

"Well, are you going to help your father build the Great Wall of China or not?"

Robert jumped off the window seat, plopped on the floor on his knees and started his first line of blocks for their Great Wall of China. Suzette watched the two play together. The scene touched and warmed her heart, which calmed the last few stressful minutes.

"Well, then, I'll leave you two men alone to construct your latest design."

"Yes, please do." Philippe flashed a smile at Suzette.

She left them alone. Suzette could not think of any other picture she wanted in life. Philippe had fathered little Robert as if his own. She believed that he cared for the boy and would protect him at all costs. There would be no cause for worry, she concluded with each step down the hallway to her bedchamber. None whatsoever.

Surely, Robert must have sired his own children by now, she assumed. Even if he suspected Robert to be his son, there would be no reason for him to set his eyes upon the lad. An illegitimate son born out of wedlock with his mistress could destroy his aristocratic social life, or so Suzette thought. Regardless, Robert Holland had believed Suzette died, and life would go on as it had in the past.

Suzette passed her bedchamber, and a sudden rush of memories washed over her like warm oil. She had committed to remembrance his tenderness, touch, kisses, and their first time together. Suzette had chosen to give him her most prized possession—her virginity. After all, he had paid for it, and she felt the need to repay him for saving her life.

He rescued her from a lifetime of prostitution and certain rape by that horrible Marquis who had pinned her to the bed. She shuddered when remembering his knee prying her legs open and the screams that came from her throat pleading for mercy.

"Robert," she whispered, stopping in the doorway.

Vivid memories of his toned body, blond hair, and blue eyes that she loved to look into, made her smile. Suzette blushed as she reminisced over their intimate ways, which far surpassed the bed she shared with her husband. For years, she resisted the thoughts of their passion and their unbridled behavior together. Robert had showed her ways to please him that she by no means dared to practice upon Philippe.

She glanced at their marriage bed. Sadness engulfed her as she struggled with her lack of contentment. She had tried to resurrect the former affection that she held for Philippe as young and naïve girl but failed. She could feel only one emotion—gratefulness that he concealed the shame of her illegitimate pregnancy.

Suddenly, the last words that Robert spoke to her floated through her mind like a gentle, refreshing breeze. She closed her eyes remembering the deep, velvet quality of his voice and his entreaty spoken to her in French the day they parted.

"Never forget I was your first, oui?"

Forget? How could she ever forget? She could only bury her sentiments deep within her heart. Her love for him remained.

"I still love you, Robert. I always have and always will."

She finally admitted her adulterous emotional sin, which she harbored every day since her marriage to another man. Guilt stabbed her conscience and fate whispered in her ear the haunting phrase of Sir Walter Scott.

"Oh what a tangled web we weave, when first we practice to deceive."

"Someday I'll pay for this," she declared. Her eyes stared at her bed while she lost herself in the imagination of her lover's arms. "There will be a price to pay for not telling him the truth. I know it."

Chapter 5

Robert peered over his shoulder one more time. His eyes met Philippe's, and the nervous expression upon the man's face disturbed him to the core. Robert watched with a dark glare as Philippe's steps quickened around a corner. His wife tugged at him again until finally he turned back to the path that lay ahead.

Oblivious to the tight grip Jacquelyn exerted on his forearm, his mind relived the last few minutes. His heart broke with bitter grief over the passing of Suzette. Philippe's words echoed like the beat of a morbid death march.

"I'm afraid that Robert's mother passed away last winter."

Robert's endearing Parisian mademoiselle had died. Forever his dreams of her charm and their lovemaking would haunt him until he passed to a place where he hoped to see her again. The loss crushed him, and Robert felt his chest tighten with emotion.

"Robert. Robert!"

Jacquelyn demanded his attention with a screech and pulled his thoughts back to the present.

"Yes, what is it?" He hoped the conversation would not

focus on recent events. His wishes were quickly dashed.

"Who was that man?"

"An old acquaintance, like I said before. Nothing more." Their walk continued deeper into the gardens, and Robert wanted to turn his prying wife toward the exit.

"Well, I find it quite curious that little boy was named after you."

"Me?" Robert quipped back in defense. "Are you so naive as to think every boy in the city named Robert is named after *me*?" Robert sighed at the utter stupidity of her comment.

"Well, no," Jacquelyn replied meekly lowering her head like a scolded puppy. "I thought perchance the man chose the name to honor you in some manner, since you apparently know one another."

"I can assure you, the child was not named after me." Robert wondered why Philippe had even allowed Suzette to do such a thing. Didn't the child's name torment him with the remembrance of the bed he and Suzette shared as lovers?

"Well, I just thought it curious, that's all. The boy even looks . . . "

Jacquelyn's words trailed off, and Robert's heart stopped cold. He halted their walk through the gardens and turned to face his wife. The conversation needed to cease before it went further.

"That's enough, Jacquelyn. There is nothing there besides a young lad named Robert—a common name and nothing more." Robert reached for her forearm, grabbed her, and gave her a little shake. He raised his voice, "Nothing more!"

Jacquelyn's eyes darted away from her husband and fell to the path beneath their feet. "Of course, Robert. You know how I am about children. I just wish we—" Her voice quivered.

Pained for his aggressive stance and unnecessary

roughness, he saw the familiar disappointment in his wife's eyes. Her face turned flush, and her green eyes brimmed with tears that threatened to spill down her cheeks.

"I know." Robert softened his harsh tone. "Believe me, Jacquelyn, I know. I wish we had children. You know I do."

He released his firm grip and gathered his wife into his arms. Robert kissed her gently on the cheek and then whispered in her ear. "It will happen. Be patient." He wanted to say that her prayers would one day be answered, but something in his spirit told him it was a lie.

She wrapped her arm around his, and he patted her in return. Their stroll continued in silence until he suggested a change of plans.

"When we return to England, I'll invite Marguerite and Lord Chambers to stay for a few weeks. They can bring their two children, and we'll let them run the estate and make a ruckus. Would you like that?"

"Yes, that would be nice," Jacquelyn responded with renewed enthusiasm. "I miss your sister. We have much to catch up on and having children in the household would be a welcome sight indeed."

"Good," Robert concluded. "Then it's done. I'll pen a letter to Marguerite before we sail home and ask that they meet us upon our return to Surrey."

Convinced he had patched things up for the moment, Robert directed his wife back toward the exit of the gardens. Their outing had emotionally drained him; he had much to think about.

The vision of the young boy, who held up his five fingers and proudly announced his name of Robert Philippe Moreau, brought a smile to his face. Robert struggled with the similarities of name, appearance, and date of birth. He could very well be the boy's father. He wanted to believe it, though he had no proof.

His existence eased the loss of Suzette, but he realized Philippe Moreau would never allow him to know the truth.

The thought that he could be educating his son, shot a vulgar flurry of curses through his troubled mind.

"Robert, I'm tired. Can we go home?"

Surprised at his wife's request, he willingly agreed. "Yes, of course."

They meandered their way back toward the exit of the gardens. Robert glanced around watching for signs of Philippe, but saw nothing. They had disappeared into the streets of Paris, probably never to be seen again. For now, he would let the matter go.

❋ ❋ ❋

Jacquelyn clung tenaciously to Robert's hand to steady her weak legs upon their return. The walk in the park had done nothing to revive her spirits or her body. Perhaps a nap would help instead.

She noted Robert's pensive face and forced smile his way hoping to change his apathetic disposition. "Thank you," she spoke, batting her eyelashes at him in a flirtatious tease. He remained unmoved and said nothing in response.

After they arrived home, Jacquelyn handed her jacket to Dorcas, who greeted them at the door. Her lady's maid unpinned her feathered hat. Jacquelyn watched her husband out of the corner of her eye wondering what he would do next. The usual gloomy demeanor had returned.

"I'll be in my study if you need me." Jacquelyn's eyes followed him as he disappeared down the long hallway of their Parisian townhouse. A moment later, Robert retreated from sight, and Jacquelyn heard the latch of his door click shut.

A sneer of disgust curled her lip, sick of the multiple times he fled from her presence. He spent more hours behind closed doors while in Paris than he had the past whole year in London. Jacquelyn wondered why.

It seemed a pattern had emerged over the years. They

had lived comfortably in their Surrey estate, but Robert maintained his townhouse in London and the one in Paris. Jacquelyn adored Paris thinking it the most beautiful city in the modern world. The shopping—well, the shopping for any woman of title offered the best in Europe. Fashions were at their pinnacle, and Jacquelyn loved to amass the latest styles of gowns and hats from a world-famous haute couture.

Yet the fact remained that each holiday abroad, Robert's behavior changed. He became a recluse and preferred to hide during the day. His suggested walk that morning tremendously surprised Jacquelyn. Even if they spent the night out for dinner or the opera, nothing differed. His mind drifted elsewhere.

Occasionally, he would disappear for an evening with the declaration he needed time alone at the Jockey Club for drinks and poker with old friends. Jacquelyn doubted every word that fell from his deceitful lips. She had her own suspicions, though she could prove nothing.

Robert's Parisian male acquaintances would comment in her presence about their outings. They sounded purposely spoken for her benefit to corroborate his whereabouts. Like a sixth sense God gives every wife about her husband's fidelity, she knew something had to be amiss. Indisputably, he bedded others for entertainment while in Paris.

"Will there be anything else?" Dorcas asked.

"Perhaps a cup of tea in the sitting room. I could use a moment alone."

Jacquelyn dejectedly walked into the parlor. She sat in an oversized chair near the window and stared blindly into the adjacent garden. Instead of children playing amidst the green grass, the gardens lay bare except for budding roses and hedges.

Her empty arms throbbed like a chronic disease eating away at her soul. She felt cursed by God and abandoned by her husband. Today, like so many others, she despised life. Even to take a mere breath, proved an unpleasant task.

For five years, they had tried to have a baby, but Jacquelyn's menses repeatedly arrived to wash away any hope of conception. There were a few times when she would be late or skipped her monthly discharge. Those instances raised her hopes to the heavens, only to be dashed later by the first sight of blood.

More than anything in the world, Jacquelyn wanted a baby. Her whole character had been bred to marry an aristocrat. Part of her duty as a faithful wife included producing an heir to the Holland name.

Every woman possessed a natural yearning to be a mother. Jacquelyn had played the role with dolls since childhood. She loved rocking babies in her arms, nurturing, cooing, and nuzzling her nose against their soft skin. Nothing in the world exhilarated her more than the scent of a newborn.

When her sister-in-law and friend, Marguerite, bore children, she fussed over them to such an extent that her husband reprimanded her behavior. Apparently, she had become an embarrassment to the family. Marguerite didn't appreciate her constant handling of her children. But what did they expect? It satisfied her innate desires being able to touch a child and fantasize the baby came from her womb.

As she sat quietly, waiting for her tea, she mused over the emptiness of her life. She had been deeply depressed for years. Jacquelyn tried to hide her anguish from Robert, but it proved difficult. Her soul, void of any contentment and happiness, aggravated her mental state. Jacquelyn's existence had been relegated to a loveless marriage, a husband who frequented the bed of others, and a home empty of children.

Why bother to breathe when there is no purpose to life? She asked herself the same question over and over when engulfed in seasons of deep despair. *Why bother to breathe?*

Could she stop breathing? Could she hold her breath long enough to make her heart stop? Perhaps she could smother herself with a pillow one night and leave her tormentors and mental anguish behind in her dead body. Would there be peace? Would Heaven embrace her in mercy or would Hell torment her for eternity?

"Madame, your tea."

Jacquelyn flinched and broke her thoughts away from her hopeless predicament. She glanced up at Dorcas and retrieved the cup and saucer.

"Thank you. Please close the door on the way out."

"Yes, ma'am," she replied, with a quick curtsy before obeying her command.

As she watched her back out of the room and close the door, Jacquelyn felt envious of her uneducated and simpleminded lady's maid. Dorcas, a middle-aged woman, plain and unpretentious, had never married. Short in stature, her eyes unmemorable, marked her with drab plainness. Irrespective of her lack of attractiveness, Dorcas' personality possessed an extraordinary kindness that Jacquelyn admired.

Even as a maid the woman has purpose, she thought to herself. Jacquelyn envied her uncomplicated subservient life with little worry.

She turned her gaze out the window to the empty gardens void of the laughter of children and mumbled under her breath again, "*Why bother to breathe?*"

Jacquelyn took a sip of tea. A tiny tear rolled down her cheek and then another and another, until they doused her fair complexion in a river of sorrow. There were days she felt as if she would go mad, if God did not grant her a baby. Perhaps today she would.

❋ ❋ ❋

Robert's antsy manner followed him the entire way

down the hall to his private quarters. He needed time alone to think and sort out his volatile emotions. If he stayed in the presence of his bothersome wife, it would afford no peace whatsoever.

He removed his coat, flung it upon a chair, and embarked on a frantic pace the width of his study. Clearly agitated, he needed to calm down, so he walked over to his favorite decanter of brandy and poured a glass.

After a few quick gulps, he emptied the contents and poured another. The liquid burned down his throat, and Robert knew soon its alcoholic effects would flow through his veins and deliver relief. His dependency upon spirits had increased to a worrisome degree. He'd face that another day. Right now, he needed a drink.

He sat in his leather chair, lifted his booted heels on the desktop, leaned back, and closed his eyes. Robert purposely drew in a few deep breaths until he felt his heart rate lower and the relentless pounding in his chest dissipate. The past hour had been absolute torture.

Robert pondered the last time he saw Suzette, and the vision of her beauty lingered fresh in his mind. When he had parted her side years ago, he did so because he wished to do the right thing for her sake. He needed to be a man of honor. Philippe's words were brutally true. He had made her his personal whore. Suzette deserved better.

He returned to his wife that day and settled into a routine as a dutiful son. As the doctors had predicted, his father's health, after his marriage to Jacquelyn, made a speedy decline. Heart failure, they told the family. Robert painfully witnessed his father turn into a weakling before his eyes. The illness progressed excruciatingly slow, until the end finally arrived. Bedridden and unable to draw a simple breath, Robert's father slipped into eternity while he stood at his bedside. Though crushed and devastated, he held back any external emotions of grief for the sake of his mother and sister.

The dowager duchess, Mary, did not handle the death of her husband well. They buried his father in the family plot alongside his ancestors on their estate. Because of her loss, his mother turned into an inconsolable, depressed, and demanding woman who gave him no rest.

She turned the entire household into a blackened state of bereavement. As soon as the funeral ended, she insisted that Robert, his sister, and every one of the staff observe the full respectable time of mourning dictated by society. She would have carried it on for years had Robert not put his foot down.

Newly married and joined to a wife, who clung to him like a leech, Robert felt stifled by her and crushed by his mother's demands. Jacquelyn required his constant attention and bemoaned her barrenness as the years progressed. She became obsessed with the state of pregnancy, so much that she insisted on decorating a nursery for the baby before its arrival.

Presently, the chamber remained empty, like a monument to the unborn. Robert hated its existence. He allowed her to proceed with the decorations. It proved to be a foolish act that only fed her obsession. Often he would find Jacquelyn sitting in the rocking chair by the window pretending to hold a child in her arms. She'd rock back and forth and blindly stare into the distance at only God knows what.

When his sister gave birth, a new kind of obsession entered his wife's way of life. She became an aunt that overstepped the boundaries Marguerite tried to maintain. He constantly worried over Jacquelyn's sanity.

His sister married shortly after their father's death. Lord Chambers, who always gave Robert an uneasy sense, had proposed to Marguerite. Reluctantly, he agreed to the match after his sister begged and confessed her undying love for the rich and handsome Lord of Yorkshire.

Robert struggled with jealousy that his sister had the

opportunity to marry for love, while he, on the other hand, had married for duty. The couple quickly bore two children—a boy named Geoffrey, and two years later, a girl named Nora.

Robert found their children to be well behaved. His sister had hired a talented governess who had done well, and he held no hesitation in inviting them to the estate. Nevertheless, he had committed himself to the invitation upon return to England to give his wife an opportunity to play with their children.

To keep his earlier promise, he picked up his pen and wrote a request to Marguerite to join them upon their return in a fortnight. Fourteen days. It seemed like such a short amount of time. Robert feared he would not have an opportunity to look thoroughly into the matter of his accidental encounter.

He took a few more sips of his brandy and contemplated his intended visit to Rue des Moulins. He decided against another private mistress, but he had not given up his occasional trips to the brothels of France. Robert justified his actions simply. He deserved the comforts of a passionate woman to pacify his dreary sexual life.

His marriage to Jacquelyn had proven physically frustrating, to say the least. He held no passion for his wife—none whatsoever. He had tried to teach her new ways of ecstasy, but to no avail. On his wedding night, Jacquelyn presented herself as a woman committed to fulfill her wifely duty and nothing more. Lately, she only lay beneath him for one thing—his seed. It frustrated the hell out of him.

He finished the note and inserted it into an envelope, addressed it, and set it aside to give to his butler to post in the morning. Satisfied he had fulfilled his promise, he sat down to relax for a moment when he heard a knock.

"Come in." The door opened, and his wife sheepishly

stood in the threshold.

"Dinner is served in the dining room, Robert."

He had no appetite whatsoever for food. "I don't think I'll dine this evening, Jacquelyn. Do so without me." He anticipated her reaction with disdain.

"Why, might I ask? Are you not hungry?"

He pulled out his watch from his vest pocket, flipped the golden lid open, and glanced at the time. "Six o'clock. I'm late for a poker game at the Jockey Club with some friends."

"We've barely arrived in Paris and already you are off with your men friends?" Jacquelyn questioned in anger. "Why must you go out nearly every evening when we are in Paris?"

Robert observed the ire in his wife's eyes and returned his own gaze of disapproval. "I come to Paris to relax, Jacquelyn. I've told you that before. We spent the day together. Must I spend every waking hour of my life with you, as well?"

"No doubt you spend it in the arms of some Mademoiselle," she flipped back in his face.

"And what is that supposed to mean?" He hurriedly slipped his arms into his jacket.

"You know what I mean," she spat. "If you spent more time in our marriage bed, perhaps I would get pregnant. Instead, you choose to play poker games and God knows what else every evening!"

Robert's jaw clenched. He hated these moments of confrontation with Jacquelyn, but he knew if he didn't smooth things over, she'd make his life hell for the next few weeks. He straightened the suit coat on his tall frame, and then walked over and stood in front of her.

"I'm on holiday, Jacquelyn. My duties at home strangle me. When I come to Paris you should know after all these years I use the time away to relax." He reached out and took her hands into his gently. "I'm merely going for a game of poker with Vicomte de Rieux—nothing more."

Jacquelyn stood silent before him, and Robert saw her relent in response to his tenderness.

"You blame me for my barrenness. I know you do."

"I blame you for nothing," Robert said emphatically. "There is no way of knowing who is responsible, and I have not the mind of God in this matter." *Whatever that may be,* he thought.

The stark reality of whose fault it had been looked at him in the face. Jacquelyn unquestionably carried the guilt of their childless marriage. The young boy he met earlier in the day could actually be his. If that were the case, it wasn't his defective seed by any means. He had married Jacquelyn for one reason, to give his father an heir to the Holland line. The precise purpose he had chosen her as his wife would never be fulfilled. As he stood and held her cold hands in his, he knew it to be truth.

He kissed her softly on the cheek and then ran his hand down the side of her face. "I'll try not to be overly late this evening." Robert hesitated. "Would you enjoy an evening at the Garnier tomorrow night?"

Jacquelyn's eyes rose from the floor and widened with excitement. "Oh, Robert, I'd love to spend an evening at the opera."

"Good then. It's done. The opera tomorrow evening."

He gave his wife a hurried kiss on her lips. Robert headed for the door. Giles helped him on with his overcoat, hat, and cane.

"There is a posted letter on the corner of my study desk. See that it is mailed tomorrow morning."

"Yes, Your Grace."

Jacquelyn stood nearby. He smiled and then exited their residence. His booted feet couldn't carry him fast enough to the cab that waited at the curb.

Chapter 6

Robert grunted in pleasure and rolled over next to the curvaceous blonde-haired woman next to him. He felt relaxed, spent, and immensely satisfied. As usual, his purchase for the night paid off. She never disappointed him, with her lively foreplay and lack of inhibitions.

He turned on his side, leaned on his elbow, and propped up his head in the palm of his hand. Robert smiled at the Nordic beauty. Unable to keep his hands off her bulging breasts, he fondled them with teasing desire.

"You haven't changed one bit, Nadine!" He paused for a moment. "I don't know what I would do without you. Thank God you left the Chabanais and came here."

Nadine watched the hand of her patron playfully roam her flesh. She enjoyed his fondling touch.

"Well, after all, Robert, you're my favorite," she cajoled, with a twinkle in her eye. "Besides, Rue des Moulins offered me more for my seasoned professionalism than that greedy Madame Laurent."

She took a lock of his blonde hair and twirled it with her finger. Teasingly, Nadine licked her lips while looking into his blue eyes.

"You poor Englishmen. Every one of you that I bed is so starved for love. Don't your English wives know anything about sexual pleasure?"

Robert smiled. "You should be thankful they don't; otherwise, your French brothels would go broke."

Nadine let out a hearty laugh and then settled down into a blissful moment of hair twirling, while he played with her flesh.

"I had a stressful day," Robert confessed. Unable to let go of the luscious body, he found comfort in Nadine's breasts and refused to withdraw his hand or gaze from her hard nipples.

"How so?"

Robert struggled for a few moments and wondered whether he should speak of the matter. He liked Nadine for sexual pleasure, but he felt no love for her either. She embodied convenient entertainment but nothing more. He contemplated the wisdom of becoming too personal with the gorgeous prostitute beyond the bed they shared. Weakened over the day's stress, he didn't fight the urge to spill his soul.

"Remember Suzette?" he queried pensively.

"How could I forget the little virgin you purchased," she said, annoyed. "What happened to her, anyway?"

Robert finally released her breast and heaved a sigh. He rolled over onto his back and stared at the canopy cover overhead.

"I took her to England with me."

Nadine sat up next to Robert and peered downward into his face. "You did what?"

"I took her to England with me," he moaned. "She was my mistress for a while. Then her old beau happened upon her and took her away from me." Robert swallowed and looked into Nadine's curious eyes. "I found out today that she died last winter." The statement tore his soul, and Robert experienced a profound sense of loss wash over him once more.

Nadine leaned her back against the headboard of the bed.

"You made her your mistress? Well, it sounds as if you got what you paid for—her virginity."

"I could not marry her, Nadine. My father and station in life would not allow it, and Suzette—well, Suzette, you know how naive her thoughts were. I'm afraid I wasn't as honorable about the situation as I should have been." Robert inhaled a deep breath, astonished over the pain that had surfaced. "Besides, she left me for another, and now she's dead. No reason to mourn what never could be, is there?"

Robert yawned. He glanced at the clock on the fireplace mantel and cursed over the late hour.

"Damn! It's almost midnight."

He swung his legs around the edge of the bed and stood up. "The wife calls."

"Did you love the Queen of the Chambre?" Nadine's face soured in her expression.

Robert picked up his clothes and started dressing. "Love? Do men love their mistresses?"

"You loved her. I can tell by the look on your face."

Robert said nothing and continued to dress. The conversation brutally assaulted his emotions. He glanced at the naked Nordic beauty lounging seductively on the bed. Her long blonde hair cascaded in curls down her chest and pink nipples peaked out from behind the strands. He smiled.

"You're a pretty sight for a man in need, Nadine."

He opened his wallet, pulled out a hundred francs, and approached her body propped up against the headboard. "I already paid my dues to the brothel mistress downstairs, but here—this is for you. Go buy yourself a new frock."

Nadine smiled as her hand curled around the crisp bill. In the flash of her eyes, Robert saw more than sexual desire. He worried that her affections were becoming deeper than he wished to engage. As a prostitute, she should know better than to get involved with her customers; but Nadine had been sexually involved with him for a long time.

"I don't know if I'll be back before I return to England." He pulled on the last glove over his long fingers. "Hopefully, the next time I come, I'll be able to leave my wife in London."

Nadine rose from the bed and sauntered over to Robert. She wrapped her warm arms around his neck, pushed her breasts against his chest, and bestowed upon him a long deep kiss that filled his mouth with her tongue. Her actions thrust him into another arousal.

"What a vixen you are, Nadine."

"Thanks for the tip, sweetie."

Robert grasped her naked derrière, gave it a playful squeeze, and then left the room.

A carriage starter procured a cab, and Robert instructed the driver to take him back to his townhouse. The thought caused a knot to form in his stomach, and he hoped his late arrival home would not end up in a battle. Tomorrow night he'd be at the opera; and though he enjoyed the arts occasionally, he truly wasn't in the mood for shrieking sopranos or tragic love stories. He had felt enough tragedy for one day when he learned of Suzette's death.

The bothersome matter of the little blond-haired boy with blue eyes holding up five fingers, as he proudly announced the name of Robert Philippe Moreau, didn't help either. He concluded the child must be his, because he saw in Philippe's eyes worry—not that of an assured father.

"Damn him!" Robert roared, banging the leather seat with his fist. Anger rose inside, as he thought of the man who stole his beautiful Suzette. He played a ruse to make him feel guilty about his moral obligations, when all along he planned to take not only the love of his life, but his son.

Robert's eyes narrowed. He turned and glanced out at the streets lit with gas lamps and saw that they neared his residence. A moment later, the horses' gait slowed, and then halted. The driver opened the door, he paid the fare, and Robert warily climbed out and headed for the entrance to his townhouse.

He slipped inside, and all appeared to be quiet. The staff probably had retired, as well as his wife. He laid his hat and gloves on the side table, then swung off his top coat and hung it on the hook of the hall coat tree. He tiptoed into the parlor and illuminated a small electric lamp in the darkened room. He gasped, startled to find Jacquelyn sitting in a chair. Their eyes met, and Robert saw trouble.

"My God, woman!" he exclaimed, reacting to her unexpected appearance. "Why are you not in bed?"

"I was waiting for my husband to return home," she answered in a sarcastic tone.

Robert cleared his throat. "The poker game went far longer than I anticipated, as well as the drinking. I apologize for the lateness of the hour."

Jacquelyn rose to her feet and slithered across the room until she stood in front of him clothed in her night garments. Her robe revealed a sheer nightgown underneath. In a brash move, she kissed Robert forcefully on his lips. Afterward, she drew away and wiped her mouth from her sloppy kiss with the back of her hand.

"I taste and smell no alcohol on your breath, darling."

She leaned into his neck and sniffed the collar of his coat. "I do smell the scent of perfume, however." She curled her lip as she inquired. "Does Vicomte de Rieux wear perfume?"

Robert stood astonished at the brazen assault from his usually docile wife. Jacquelyn's eyes darkened like the chambers of Hell.

"This is ridiculous," Robert flung. He stepped backward to put distance between them.

Jacquelyn refused his spurn and returned to stand in front of him. She seized his hand and forcefully placed his palm upon her breast.

"Well, then, if my suspicions are ridiculous, perhaps

you'll show me by bedding me for the evening. Perchance tonight I'll conceive."

Robert's blood ran cold. He looked at his wife's hand that forced his own against her breast. He felt no arousal or desire for the madness in front of his eyes.

"You're tired, Jacquelyn. It's making you irrational. Go to bed."

Jacquelyn dropped her husband's hand and then glared into his blue eyes. "Apparently visiting the comforts of two women in one night is a bit too much in the way of performance for the infamous duke?"

Robert's anger rose as he watched her storm from the room. He heard her footsteps run up the stairs and the door to her suite bang shut with a loud *thud.*

He fell into a nearby chair and held his head in his hands. He utterly despised his life. No, he despised his wife, even more so, now that Suzette lay in a cold grave. To deepen his sorrow further, he probably had a son that he would never know or be able to acknowledge.

Tired and weary, he finally stood and climbed the staircase to his quarters. He had stopped sharing a room with her years ago. Once inside, he locked the door to keep at bay the thorn of his life. Without fully undressing, he flopped on the empty bed and fell asleep.

Chapter 7

Robert stood in front of the full-length mirror and adjusted the lapels on his suit. Dressed in his finest apparel, he braced himself for an evening at the opera with Jacquelyn.

He had managed to somewhat patch the difficult night between the two of them by playing upon Jacquelyn's neediness for attention. Robert had become a master of appeasement when it came to his wife, which brought peace to the household. A few tender touches, embraces, and feigned words of love always melted her to his whim.

However, Robert noticed lately that Jacquelyn had undergone a dramatic change in her conduct. His tender tactics had become less effective. Her behavior the evening before, lying in wait amidst a dark room, displayed a prime example. It appeared the tables had turned, and she began to show her frustrations in a more aggressive manner.

He made a mental note to visit Jacquelyn's bed after the opera. She had asked to try again. He'd oblige her request. Certainly, it would be another unsuccessful attempt to conceive, as he pictured his seed swimming around a barren womb finding no egg to fertilize.

After one final adjustment to his ascot, he left the room and found his wife being pampered by Dorcas. Her lady's maid struggled with a latch on a sapphire necklace.

"Here, let me."

Robert approached his wife, who sat on her vanity chair, and gazed at her in the mirror. She had not lost her beauty outwardly. Inwardly, though, Robert perceived ugliness. He took the small clip, hooked the latch in the eyelet of the necklace, and arranged it perfectly center. He smiled at his accomplishment, and then bent down to kiss her on the cheek.

"You look stunning, Jacquelyn. Are we ready?"

"Thank you for the compliment, Robert." Jacquelyn rose and smiled in response to Robert's approval. "I am looking forward to this evening."

"As I am," Robert confessed, lying between his teeth.

He held out his arm and escorted Jacquelyn down the staircase to the foyer. Dorcas waited with her white fox shoulder wrap. Robert donned his top hat and overcoat and then led his preened wife to the waiting carriage outside their front door. A moment later, the hooves of the horses clapped against the stone pavement and headed for the Théâtre National de l'Opéra.

Robert scrutinized the pleased expression upon Jacquelyn's face. She expressed a look of love he had not seen in some time that caused him to shift uncomfortably. From disdain to love to disdain. Her moods changed daily like the ocean waters.

At that thought, Robert's mind drifted back to the moment of levity he had shared with Suzette in the small café in Calais. He distinctly remembered his words and her response.

"Frankly, I love the sea. I find great comfort in its beauty and its ever-changing nature. One moment it can be peaceful as Heaven, and the next stormy as Hell itself. Just like a woman."

He looked at his wife and smiled. His mind spoke to his departed love.

"Yes, Suzette, I think women are that changeable from

one extreme to the other."

Robert chuckled.

"What's so funny?" Jacquelyn asked with a curious expression over his behavior.

"Nothing. Just an odd memory, which popped into my mind, that's all."

"I haven't seen you smile in some time, Robert. You should have odd memories more often."

Robert didn't respond as the carriage had slowed and came to a halt in front of the entrance to the Garnier. The area choked with activity as arriving patrons pulled up in various modes of transportation, dressed in their expensive evening apparel.

He glanced up at the majestic building and realized it felt good to get out for the night. Perhaps it was what he needed—a night out with his wife to provide an escape from the pressures that weighed upon his heart.

After they entered the impressive lobby, Robert escorted his wife slowly up the wide staircase to the corridor that led to their box for the performance. Robert recognized very few faces, but he wasn't surprised, as most the men he knew found companionship in the presence of their mistresses at night.

They reached the assigned box, and a uniformed attendant handed them a program. He pulled the velvet red curtains apart that led to the interior. Robert escorted his wife to her chair and then sat at her side. He glanced over and saw the distinct pleasure written across her face. He leaned in and made a comment.

"You must admit, The Royal Opera House cannot compare to the opulence of Paris."

Jacquelyn agreed, "Yes, it is beautiful."

They both surveyed the 2,000 seat interior laden with rich velvet, gold leaf, and classic Baroque decorum. Overhead the many cherubim and nymphs smiled down upon their location.

"It's quite breathtaking."

Robert opened his program and turned his attention elsewhere. As the house lights dimmed and the stage lights illuminated, the curtain pulled back. In the darkness of the box, Jacquelyn reached over to Robert's hand and grasped it firmly. He made no attempt to resist her touch and held her hand in return. He forced a smile and settled in for the first act hoping the performance had no tragic ending.

Intermission arrived, and the lights rose in the interior. He needed a breath of fresh air.

"Do you wish me to bring you a glass of champagne, or do you prefer to rise and walk with me?"

"I'd like to walk," she responded, standing to her feet. "After sitting for such a long period, I need to move too."

He offered his arm and pulled back the curtain and Robert directed his wife to a large hall. Patrons mingled together in a buzz of chatter. Champagne floated by on silver trays held by servers. Robert plucked two flutes and handed one to his wife. He took a quick sip while glancing over the crowd. A dreaded voice called his name, and he jolted.

"Why, Lord Holland, is that you?"

Madame Laurent sauntered toward him in a dark purple gown with a brown mink fur around her shoulders. At her side stood a tall, unrecognizable gentleman, no doubt her escort. Robert sucked in a breath and braced for all of Hades to break loose. She stood with a broad, sly smile on her face and glanced at his wife.

"Lord Holland, don't be rude, who is this lovely woman?"

She fluttered her long black lashes at Jacquelyn. Robert felt like a cornered animal. He loosened his tight grip on the champagne flute, which was about to shatter from the pressure exerted by his hand. Robert cringed as he proceeded with the introductions.

"It's duke, and this is my wife, Jacquelyn."

He brandished a look and a raised brow at Madame Laurent that screamed *keep your mouth shut*, before proceeding with the remainder of the introductions.

"Jacquelyn, may I introduce to you Madame Laurent. She is a member of The Jockey Club. I've not had the pleasure of seeing her for many years. How long has it been now, five?"

"Yes, five years I imagine," Madame Laurent replied, her eyes filled with questions and curiosity.

Robert hoped the woman would keep the real nature of their acquaintance secret and her painted red lips tightly shut.

"It's a pleasure to meet you." She turned to her escort and apologized for neglecting his introduction. "Please forgive me, Your Grace. May I introduce Monsieur Belafonte, a close business associate of mine."

Her companion nodded his head in acknowledgement. "It's a pleasure to meet you, and of course, your lovely duchess."

Jacquelyn stood curiously silent throughout the entire exchange and then abruptly spoke. "Robert, will you please excuse me while I visit the ladies' parlor?"

"Yes, of course, dear."

He set her flute of champagne down on a table along the hallway, and Jacquelyn retreated leaving the threesome alone. Robert watched her departure with concern and then turned to Madame Laurent.

"I appreciate your discretion in the matter."

"Of course, Robert. Did you expect me to tell your English wife you were my investor and patron at the brothel? I dare say that would have caused a scene, wouldn't it?"

Robert heaved a sigh.

"So what happened to your purchase the last we met? Did you get your money's worth?"

"And then some," Robert replied snidely. A deep

agitation rose when he remembered her traitorous action of selling Suzette to Marquis Barone behind his back. His jaw clenched as he spat out his final words. "I don't believe that is a topic I wish to discuss in depth. Now, if you'll excuse me, I'll take my leave."

Robert walked away and left the dejected Madame Laurent with her escort. He did not intend to inform the witch what happened to Suzette—none whatsoever.

As he reached the end of the hallway, he saw Jacquelyn emerge from the ladies' powder room. Her face looked distraught.

"I hear the orchestra tuning their instruments, Jacquelyn. Intermission is nearly over."

He offered his arm to his wife but noted a hesitation on her part. She remained silent. Her suspicious eyes roved over him searching his soul for secrets untold. Robert felt an extreme embarrassment that surprised him. It remained one thing to be unfaithful to an unsuspecting spouse, but quite another to be unfaithful to a wife who knew all of her husband's escapades.

"Yes, of course. I don't wish to miss the second half," she finally responded.

Robert escorted Jacquelyn back to their private box, relieved to see that Madame Laurent had disappeared. He sat next to Jacquelyn as before, only this time he reached out and picked up her hand that lay lifelessly in her lap and held it throughout the performance.

Unable to concentrate on the operatic display, Robert relived each moment of the past two days in horror. An occasional glance over at this wife's face spoke the same, as she showed no interest or enjoyment on the stage below. Had she sensed the identity of the outrageously dressed Madame Laurent or perhaps knew of her reputation?

Robert hoped to salvage what remained of the evening. The performance ended, and the couple remained aloof and quiet while they returned home. After their arrival, both retreated to their upstairs suite. Robert made it a point to close the door behind him. He had promised himself earlier to attend to his wife.

"You needn't stay with me tonight, Robert. I'll understand." Jacquelyn's words fell from her lips as a confession of defeat.

Robert approached her from behind and turned her around to face him. "No, I wish to spend the night with you." He hesitated then forced a tender touch on the side of her face. "Perhaps tonight will be the night."

He softly kissed his wife and slowly unbuttoned the back of her gown. She accepted his advances, doubtless yearning for his seed rather than him.

Robert knew it would not be the night she would conceive nor would there ever be a night she would conceive. He had finally accepted the terrible truth of the barren womb that would never be filled. He felt as empty when he touched her flesh.

He closed his eyes and took her to their marriage bed. It would have been easy to lose himself in such a gorgeous creature, if she would only respond to his touches. All he wanted was an ounce of desire for the satisfaction he could give her body.

Instead, Jacquelyn lay cold and unresponsive. Her usual aversion of an intimate touch that would give him pleasure continued. How in the world did she ever expect him to ejaculate when she lay so impassive underneath him?

Frustrated and losing interest, Robert found it impossible to perform. The encounter had drained every ounce of sexual arousal.

"I cannot," he groaned. He rolled off her and flopped onto his back. Frustrated, he ran his fingers through his hair wiping away the beads of sweat on his forehead—apparently the only thing he could work up to at that point.

"Why must you be so unresponsive, Jacquelyn? A man needs more than a piece of frigid flesh underneath his body! You exasperate me!"

In anger, he sat up in bed, swung his feet around, and grabbed his trousers from the floor pulling them up to his waist.

"What do you expect from an unloved woman? Passion? Response? I'm nothing to you, so why should I try to be anything to you!" she yelled, as she threw her pillow at him and slammed him in the back.

Robert spun around and looked at her in disdain. She continued to rant and rave.

"Why do you think I want a child so badly? I need to love a baby, and I need a baby's love in return. You give me nothing, you unfaithful bastard! No doubt the whores you bed in Paris keep you in prime performance!"

"I've had enough," Robert seethed.

"How much seed have you spread about Paris and wasted, Robert? What whores have aborted babies they've given you without your knowledge? Hum? Do you even know or care?"

Her sour statements broke his restraint. "I doubt my seed is the problem, Jacquelyn, so don't blame me for your empty womb. If you were half as beautiful inwardly as you are outwardly, perhaps I'd find an ounce of desire and love for you in my heart!"

His words cut cruelly like a knife. Robert had never been so vocally malicious toward Jacquelyn before. She had hit a raw nerve that pushed him over the brink and out of control.

"You son-of-a-bitch!" she screeched. "Get out!"

"I'll gladly get out," he spat. "I'll stay out, too. Who shall fill your womb then with precious seed, Jacquelyn Spencer?"

Robert hastily grabbed his remaining clothes and boots from the floor then flung open the door to the suite. It banged loudly against the wall. Jacquelyn continued to scream curses at him, while he walked down the hallway, waking the entire household staff.

He flew into his own room and locked the door behind him, then threw his things onto a nearby chair. At that moment, he felt like bellowing at the top of his lungs and shoving his fist through the wall. Instead, he wandered over to the decanter, poured a full glass, and determined to drink himself drunk until he passed out.

Robert's situation proved impossible. His trapped existence and loveless marriage would be the end of him. *If only Suzette was still alive—if only,* he cried inwardly. He'd move Heaven and Hell just to spend another moment in her arms and confess his love he never articulated years ago. He had been a foolish ass indeed.

Chapter 8

The days passed, and Jacquelyn and Robert barely spoke to one another. She had decided to treat her sorrows to a lavish spending spree on the newest fashions and kept her promise of buying a new hat for her mother-in-law.

Robert spent his evenings drinking and playing cards with friends, and made one last stop to Nadine's bed before he departed back to England. He had told her he would not return, but decided after further spurning from his wife, he damn well deserved a good lay. He enjoyed the Nordic beauty and tipped her generously once more for the heated comfort.

It seemed as if time flew by, and the day approached for their return home. Robert attended to some business, in the early morning hours, before they were to leave. He knew that every unanswered question swirling around his mind would haunt him until he discovered the truth. After obtaining a recommendation from friends, he sought professional assistance from a Parisian solicitor.

"Your Grace, please have a seat," he motioned to the leather chair across from his desk.

"Thank you, Monsieur Girard," Robert said as he sat down.

"Cigar?"

"No. No, thank you." Robert sighed and adjusted

himself comfortably in the seat. "I do appreciate you agreeing to meet on such short notice, monsieur. I'm due back in England shortly but have matters I wish to discuss."

"Yes, of course."

"One of your clients, Vicomte de Rieux recommended you as a resource, stating that you had an excellent staff that might do some private investigation on my behalf."

Monsieur Girard's brow raised above his left eye as he sat behind his desk. He slowly folded his hands and rested them on top.

"Yes, he is quite right. My staff is very seasoned, shall we say, in searching out matters."

He leaned back in his chair, and Robert noted his curious eyes that waited for an explanation as to his visit. He attempted to formulate his words carefully before speaking of the delicate subject, which could very well ruin him socially if leaked.

"I demand that what transpires between us here be held in the strictest of confidence."

"You have my professional word, of course. Everything you say to me will be kept confidential."

Robert had no qualms over his professional integrity and took him at his word. "I wish to have a certain individual investigated, by the name of Philippe Victor Moreau."

"Philippe Moreau?"

He noticed a glimpse of familiarity in the solicitor's eyes. "Do you know the man?"

"Only what I have read of his shipping company in the Parisian business news lately regarding Duval & Moreau."

"And what have you read?" Robert inquired leaning forward with interest.

"Well, Your Grace, it's been reported that Duval & Moreau is on the brink of bankruptcy. The newspapers have accounted their financial difficulties in the business section."

"Really?" Robert sat on the edge of his seat.

"Yes. The business has been struggling for some time, and the elder partner, Monsieur Jacques Duval is terminally ill."

Robert sat speechless while he thought of the consequences of the news. If this were true, then the boy that could be his son, may be on the brink of destitution along with his stepfather. The solicitor interrupted his thoughts with a conclusion of the obvious outcome.

"It has been speculated that once the elder partner dies, the business will undoubtedly close due to financial difficulties."

Monsieur Girard studied him with curiosity before asking further questions. "What is it that you wish to know about Monsieur Moreau?"

"As much as possible. His finances, business affairs, family, background—anything you can give me." Robert hesitated. "I believe he has a son, and I'm not sure of his current marital status either." It never dawned on him until that moment that perhaps Philippe had another woman in his life that could be a stepmother to Robert.

"That should not be a problem," he answered, with a confident air. "How shall I provide this information to you?"

"By post will do," Robert replied frustrated. "I'm afraid I must leave for England straightaway and do not know when I shall return." Robert drew from his vest pocket a calling card with his address. "Send the report by post to my attention, marked confidential, as soon as you can gather the information."

Monsieur Girard took the card and examined it.

"Do you require a retainer?" Robert inquired.

"Five hundred francs, and the remainder I will invoice when I forward the information. We will charge you at an hourly rate of 100 francs. Is that agreeable?"

"Yes, yes, fine." Robert retrieved his wallet, counted out the correct number of bills, and handed them to the solicitor.

"Of course, and if there is anything else you may need as a result of the information obtained, please do not hesitate to contact me again. I'm happy to see to your legal affairs while here in Paris."

Monsieur Girard took out his register and wrote a receipt for the retainer handing it over to Robert. He slipped it into his vest pocket.

"I appreciate your help."

It only took a few moments after leaving before the news began to grate upon Robert. Philippe Moreau had failed financially. As much as he secretly disliked the man, he felt somewhat concerned over his current state of affairs. He would have to wait for the full report before he even dared to think of any further action.

He climbed into his hired carriage and gave directions to be taken home. The face of the little boy that he met in the park haunted him. Reluctant to leave, he struggled over the return to his estate and his sister's visit. He had no choice in the matter, now that he had committed to the affair.

As soon as he arrived, Robert exited the carriage and headed for the door. Upon entering, his anxious wife stood waiting for his return.

"Robert, where have you been? We are nearly packed and ready to leave."

"Business," he replied, walking past her. "I had some last minute business to take care of." He glanced around the foyer and noted the stacked trunks. Giles stood nearby awaiting further orders.

"Go ahead, Giles, you may load the carriage now." He brushed past Jacquelyn and then strode down the hall to take inventory.

"Everything is done, as usual, Robert. The furniture is covered and all is packed."

Jacquelyn approached him and put her arms around his

neck. "Robert, I'm so anxious to return home. Please promise we won't return until next year."

Robert bit his lower lip in an attempt to hold his tongue. His wife made an outward show of affection. For the first time since their spat, a civil comment flowed from her lips. She wanted something.

"I can make no such promises. There may be times I need to return on business, but you needn't accompany me."

Jacquelyn pulled away. "Nonsense." She approached Dorcas to get her hat and gloves. "Why would I do that?"

Robert curiously viewed his wife as she donned her latest flashy, Parisian monstrosity on her head. She slipped her fingers into her purple gloves, which matched her gown, with an air of conceit.

"Yes, why, would you do that?" he countered curtly, as they walked toward the door. "God forbid you'd ever let me travel alone."

❋ ❋ ❋

Jacquelyn felt relieved the moment her foot set down upon the estate grounds. Robert's mother met them at the door.

"Finally!" She rushed toward the couple. "You are back." She gave Robert his usual hand pat upon the side of his face and smiled endearingly.

"Hello, Mother." He bent near her cheek and gave it the ceremonial kiss of respect.

Jacquelyn hugged her mother-in-law tightly and immediately brought her attention to the newest purchase perched upon her head. She twirled around and flashed a smile.

"What do you think? Isn't it gorgeous?"

Mary gave the purple silk, netting, lace, feathers, and flowers resting on top of her golden locks a keen inspection. "Gorgeous," she complimented, with jealousy.

"Well, you needn't be jealous," replied Jacquelyn, with pleasure. "I brought you one back from Paris with red silk."

Jacquelyn relished the moment of acceptance received from Mary. It often contained more attention than her own husband afforded her. She wrapped her arm around her mother-in-law, while she made her way inside. With great care, she unpinned her prize possession and handed it to Annette, a housemaid, with instructions.

"Make sure nothing is crushed when you store it with my others."

One finger at a time, she pulled off her gloves. Robert's attendant took his hat and cane.

"If you'll excuse me, ladies," he said, briskly walking away. "I have matters to attend to."

Jacquelyn shot him a dark glance over his hasty exit.

"Annette, get us some tea and bring it to the drawing room for Jacquelyn and myself," Mary ordered.

Jacquelyn turned to Dorcas with instructions to manage the footmen as they delivered the trunks. "Make sure my new dresses are out and hung up speedily, Dorcas. I want to show my mother-in-law the wonderful fashions."

Mary sauntered down the hall, and Jacquelyn followed. "Dear, you must tell me everything about your trip," she entreated, as she walked over to a new chair and sat down.

Jacquelyn rested on the settee next to the window. A moment later, it finally dawned on her they were the new pieces that had been ordered for the room.

"Oh look, Mary! The draperies match wonderfully, and the cushions are very comfortable."

"Yes, indeed," she agreed. "I was quite busy supervising the hanging of the draperies while you were away."

It felt delightful to be home, but she hesitated to tell her mother-in-law everything about the trip. The maid arrived with tea and set two cups and a china pot on the table nearby. She poured both a cup, adding their usual amount of sugar and cream, then handed one to the dowager duchess and the other to Jacquelyn.

"Close the door on your way out, Annette," instructed Mary. With a curtsy, the maid retreated and closed the double doors. "So, tell me all about your holiday."

"Our trip went well," Jacquelyn answered, a bit hesitant. After a few quick sips of tea, she continued. "I am glad to be home though."

"And Robert, did he enjoy the time away? He seemed so stressed before leaving."

Jacquelyn glanced down at her skirt that had been wrinkled from the long ride in the carriage and thoughtlessly stroked it to collect her thoughts. *Robert always enjoyed his evenings out*, she mused to herself. She glanced back up at her mother-in-law and wondered if she had any sense of her son's behavior.

Mary's eyes narrowed over Jacquelyn's hesitancy to respond. "No different, I take, it. Still the sullen, serious, reclusive son." She paused momentarily and heaved a frustrated sigh. "And no doubt husband."

Jacquelyn felt obligated to defend him. "Well, you know how stressed he becomes over matters regarding the estate and such." Her mind wandered to the day they took a walk in the garden park. Suddenly, she heard her own voice blurt out the incident.

"He was doing fine until he ran into an old friend."

"Old friend? And who might that be?"

"Philippe Moreau. Do you know of him?"

The duchess shook her head. "No, the name means nothing to me. A Frenchman, no doubt?"

"Yes, with a little boy."

"Well, I'm afraid I know nothing of Robert's acquaintances in France," she said nonchalantly, before taking a sip of tea.

"His little boy was quite adorable. A little blond haired, blue-eyed child named Robert."

The china cup met the saucer with a loud *clink*, and Mary raised her widened eyes to Jacquelyn. Her reaction startled her, and she wondered if she suspected the same.

"How delightful." Her lips pursed tightly together. "Might I ask how old is the child?"

"Five, I believe." A blush burst upon her cheeks.

The room fell silent between the two women as they both sipped their tea and pondered the meaning of it all. Finally, with a nervous tone, Mary changed the subject.

"What other Parisian fashions did you return with, my dear? You must tell me of the newest rage from the haute couture."

Jacquelyn's eyes brightened, thankful the conversation turned elsewhere. She set her teacup down on the tray and stood to her feet.

"Come, you must see! I'm sure Dorcas is unpacking them as we speak."

Jacquelyn and Mary proceeded upstairs to inspect the latest styles from Paris. *Thank goodness for frivolous pleasures,* thought Jacquelyn. Fashion diversions happened to be the only avenue of sanity in her life.

❋ ❋ ❋

Mary finished her visit with her daughter-in-law after looking at the dresses one by one. She had to admit, a trip to Paris for herself would be entertaining one day. After her days of mourning, a closet full of new gowns and hats could help pull her out of the doldrums once and for all.

Afterward, she headed for her son's study, itching to inquire further about the conversation shared with Jacquelyn over the odd encounter. Fully aware that her son would probably not admit to anything, she still wished to discuss the mention of a five-year-old boy who possessed his features.

Mary knew of Robert's indiscretions with a French

mademoiselle years earlier. His father had spilled his secret prior to passing away for fear that he had sired a bastard son. The thought troubled her deeply. Her deceased husband had worried for years that one day Robert's roguish behavior would come back to bite him in the ass. She wondered if that day had arrived.

Mary adored Jacquelyn in many ways and felt terrible over her inability to bear Robert children. It seemed as if everyone's prayers had gone unanswered for an heir to the Holland legacy. The situation brought immense sadness upon the entire household.

She arrived at Robert's study, inhaled a deep breath, and rapped on the door with her knuckles. "Robert, it's your mother. Let me come in." Mary waited for what seemed like an eternity before the door slowly opened to reveal her disheveled son on the other side. As soon as she saw his glassy eyes, she knew he had reached his third or fourth drink.

"Don't you think it's a bit early to be hitting the bottle, Robert? She pushed past his body and walked inside. Robert closed the door behind her.

"Can't a man have a drink in his own house?" he grumbled.

"A drink yes, but not the entire decanter. It's barely afternoon."

"What do you want, Mother?" Robert plopped down in the chair behind his desk piled high with papers.

"Neglecting your business affairs, again," Mary noted, while she pushed a few pieces of paper around with her fingertips. "Your father did much better when it came to running the estate. Why you cannot live up to your responsibilities is beyond me."

"I've been on holiday," he slurred. "I've just returned, so stop badgering me. I'll get around to the matters at hand." Robert took a swig of the last drop of cognac in his glass. "Besides, I haven't bankrupted the estate yet, now have I,

Mother? You're well cared for."

"Huh," she said, in a huff. "Yes, well cared for, but you neglect your husbandly duties toward your wife."

Mary narrowed her eyes at her son. He brought great disappointment and grief to her heart. Robert's duty to embrace his title and maintain honor stood paramount in her mind. Now she feared that honor had been tainted by the past. *I'll get to the bottom of this*, she thought, as she glared at him in a half stupor.

"Jacquelyn tells me that you ran into a man and his son while on holiday. What can you tell me about them?"

"There's nothing to tell," Robert answered annoyed. "We transacted a business deal five years ago."

"A business deal? You probably got that vernacular from your father coaching you on how to hide illicit affairs."

Like every other aristocrat, Mary had been quite aware that her dear, departed husband bedded a few mistresses of his own during their many years of marriage. However, he at least had the decency not to father any bastard children or cause shame to come to the Holland name. Mary accepted her role as duchess. Men strayed, and nothing could be done about it.

Robert jumped to his feet in anger. His eyes glared at his mother, who in his opinion had just crossed the line with her persistent pestering. Unable to hold his tongue, he spat back his defense.

"Almost certainly father had many business deals due to your constant nagging. Whatever I choose to do in order to find entertainment in my dull life is my business—not yours."

"Is the child yours?" she pressured, posturing herself at his side.

"The child is not mine," Robert growled and pushed his chair away from the desk. "In fact, if you care to know, the mother of the boy is dead and buried. Satisfied?"

"You do Jacquelyn a great injustice visiting the bed of

other women. You're just like your father—an unfaithful and sordid man whom I'm ashamed to call my son!"

Mary picked up her skirt, swirled around, and headed in a huff for the study door. "Mark my words, Robert, if that child is yours it will destroy the last ounce of happiness your wife possesses. The fact that you have a bastard heir when she cannot give you a legitimate heir in wedlock is scandalous!"

She flung the door open and banged it shut behind her, then proceeded to tread heavily down the hallway. Mary determined not to shed a tear over her irresponsible son. The consequences of his behavior could very well damage the family's position in society.

In a hurried huff, she stormed upstairs to her room. "Men and their mistresses," she spewed loudly, as she passed Jacquelyn's suite. It felt good to discharge her frustrations over Robert. Being the mother of a man with no sensibility or propriety saddened her deeply.

Mary's little outburst brought enormous release; but unbeknownst to her, it carried to the ears of another. Jacquelyn heard her venomous complaint when she passed her door.

Chapter 9

Suzette felt the need for a sense of security, so she rested her head in the corner of Philippe's shoulder as they lay in bed. He must have sensed it, because he gently stroked her hair with the palm of his hand but remained silent. Fear, longing, confusion—they wrapped Suzette tight in a blanket of uneasiness.

Two weeks had passed since the chance meeting in the park, and Suzette fretted over numerous possible outcomes. Philippe seemed unscathed by the encounter with Robert and confident nothing would come of it.

He's right, I shouldn't worry, she thought in an attempt to allay her fears. A voice from her past resonated in return. *"The man is going to be duke! He has a reputation to protect, and he will not acknowledge a bastard child in his lineage."*

Perhaps the wisdom of her former maid, Madame LeBlanc, rang true after all, in spite of the fact she despised the woman. Certainly, Robert wouldn't pursue the child, even if he suspected it was his. It would be impossible to prove, as long as he thought her dead. It would be Philippe's word against Robert's speculations.

She had done as Philippe suggested and secluded

herself in their home. The little walks she took with Robert were put aside, until they were assured Robert had returned to England. Yet, even with Robert's return, Suzette knew he would come back to Paris again. What if sometime in the future he saw her on the street? It could happen, just like it happened in the park with Philippe. If Robert discovered her existence, then he could pressure her for the truth about their son.

The more Suzette thought of the consequences of her deception, the more nauseated she became with anxiety.

"Philippe, is there any way that we can determine if Robert returned to England and we are safe?"

"Safe?"

"I'm afraid he might see me somewhere. Perhaps I shall stay close to home until we can be assured he has left France. How horrible it would be if he saw me!" Suzette waited for Philippe to answer, but she sensed a slight hesitation on his part.

"Yes, that is prudent. I'll make inquiries, if I can, on his scheduled return to England."

"How?"

"I'll see what I can find out, Suzette, about his stay in Paris and schedule. I don't know how, but I'll find a way if it makes you more comfortable."

"Well, I'm not looking forward to being a prisoner in my own home with our son. That reminds me, as well, Philippe. I think you and Robert should forgo any more strolls in the park? We should be cautious."

"If that is what you wish, Suzette."

"I do!" she forcefully replied, leaving no room for discussion. "I cannot bear to think what would happen should Robert . . ."

"I doubt he will do anything, Suzette. Truly I do."

"I hope you're right." She snuggled her head again into the corner of his shoulder. His arm tightened around her. "I'm sorry I worry about so many things, Philippe. You're more than patient with me."

"You are a bit of a worry wart," he said, with a chuckle. "But I understand your fears. I, for one, do not wish for him to find out the truth."

He released Suzette, sat up and swung his legs around the edge of the bed. "Will you join me for breakfast?" he asked, while fastening the tie of his robe about his waist.

Suzette stretched and yawned. "Yes, of course. In a moment." She flashed him a pleading glance for a few more minutes of rest.

Philippe smiled and retreated to the bath chamber, and Suzette watched as her husband left the room. She wanted to feel love for him. Being an honorable Christian man, he acted mercifully in the way he accepted little Robert as his own.

Regrettably, though, whenever she beheld her son, she saw Robert in his face and eyes. At times, his memory proved unbearable. To compensate, she had settled upon his likeness as a warm reminder of the man who saved her from a life of degradation, a path less painful than to remember a lost love.

Interrupted by a knock on the door, Suzette's chambermaid entered and offered to help her with her morning bath. Time had arrived to put away her worries for the day, or at least she would try.

❋ ❋ ❋

Philippe entered his office to settle in for a day of work. He sat at his desk and studied the business ledgers. Each time he calculated the totals, the results were the same. The quill in his hand shook from nervous jitters realizing bankruptcy loomed around the corner. Nothing could be done about the grave situation.

He laid down the pen, lowered his head to the desktop, and rested it upon the palms of his hands. The weight of responsibility crushed his shoulders. For the first time in years, he wrestled with fear. He hadn't succumbed to such emotion since his naval days and the war. A battle loomed on the horizon for survival, and if he lost, the casualties would be heartbreaking.

Philippe didn't wish to jeopardize Suzette's security. He had learned early in their marriage that she often needed reassurance of their financial wellbeing. Those weaknesses never existed beforehand. She had been such an innocent, unspoiled woman, who trusted him implicitly during their youth.

His mind drifted back to the days when both were untouched by the cruelties of the world. Life had altered them equally in character. He had grown into a hardened and determined male from years of war on the high seas. Being a Lieutenant in the French Navy and commanding men below his rank had molded him to a man of control and absolutes. His circumstances, surroundings, and the people in his life had to conform to his wishes and desires, or anxiety and anger crept into his heart.

Suzette had been flung from innocence into maturity through her experiences on the street after the death of her father. Her struggle to survive and her illicit affair had unquestionably altered her personality, as well. She had been destitute and used, which resulted in her need to cling to him for security.

"Damn," he muttered aloud, as he rose from his chair. He walked over to the window and looked out into the active business district streaming by his office—hansom cabs, growler carriages, individual horse riders, and citizens going about their day. Humanity passed by without a care in the world. He, on the other hand, existed as an unknown behind a window. No one cared whether he succeeded or failed, except perhaps one, who would soon be lost.

Jacques Duval, his business partner, lay at the brink of death. Bedridden and gravely ill, Philippe daily waited for word of his demise. Together they were a formidable team of two enthusiastic businessmen. The past five years they built a sound shipping company, until recently, when everything began to unravel like a ball of yarn. The business hung by one frayed thread, which would soon break; and when it did, he would tumble into financial ruin.

When Philippe had purchased his half interest in the company years ago, it stood stable and thriving. Then their luck turned sour, and a run of unfortunate happenstances took over instead. It seemed the sea gods were hell-bent on their destruction.

The original shipping fleet consisted of three fine vessels, captained by good men and faithful crews transporting goods from exotic countries to Europe. Everything ran smoothly, until a monsoon had destroyed one of their ships and the entire cargo sank to the bottom of the ocean.

The tragedy resulted in extra expenses and a damaged reputation. Their insurance failed to cover all the losses, so they made restitution to their customers from business profits. Accounts cancelled one by one, as others yielded to superstitious nonsense that they would share in their string of terrible luck. The recent news of Duval's terminal illness added to the stigma that Duval & Moreau Shipping had fallen under a curse.

As the orders dwindled, they were forced to lay off crew members and sell the second ship in the fleet of three. Philippe could barely keep things afloat with one vessel transporting goods.

When he returned to his desk, he sat down and picked up the ledger once more. The stark reality of his situation made him feel like his business would be lost in the depths of the ocean. He'd be going down with the ship and forced to declare bankruptcy to avoid the creditors that demanded payment.

His personal assets were in jeopardy. He had purchased

a home far too expensive for his earnings in order to give Suzette the best in life. As a result, he now reaped the consequences of his foolish spending during times of profit.

If matters didn't change soon, he'd have to sell their home and live less expensively. The servants would be let go, as well as the governess. The household and rearing of their children would need to be solely upon Suzette's shoulders, while Philippe found work elsewhere. No other choice remained.

Only one last desperate chance to salvage the company existed—find an investor. With their recent failures, it would be a monumental task to attract a wealthy infusion into a dying venture; but he could think of no other course to survive.

"Excuse me, monsieur, but a courier has brought you a note." Philippe's clerk, Roland, entered and handed him an envelope, which he immediately tore open. Word from Jacque's family had arrived. Last rights had been administered, and if he wished to say his goodbyes, he had to come now.

"Watch the office," he ordered, as he stood to his feet. "I'm afraid this is it. Monsieur Duval is very grave. I must attend him."

"I'm very sorry to hear, that sir. Please, I beg you, give my condolences to his family."

"Of course," Philippe replied. He took his top hat and headed for the door.

Philippe left and hired a cab that soon brought him to the Duval residence. He worried about Mrs. Duval and their ten-year-old daughter. When Jacques passed, there would be little left for each of them, since his estate would pass to a nephew.

"Oh, Philippe, you've come." Grace Duval took Philippe by the hand and led him to her husband's room. "The priest has given his last rights, it won't be long now." Tears streamed down her face.

"I shouldn't be here. This time belongs to your family to be at his side." Philippe felt like an intruder upon an intensely private moment of final goodbyes, but Grace insisted.

He entered the chamber and saw Jacques's face white as a sheet. His partner took short, shallow breaths with great difficulty. Jacques looked semi-conscious but then stirred. Philippe warily walked to his bedside.

"I'm here, Jacques," he whispered. He touched his hand briefly, but swiftly pulled away after feeling his cold flesh. Philippe, painfully aware only moments remained, nervously fiddled with the rim of his hat between his fingers.

Jacques opened his eyes and shook his head, acknowledging Philippe's presence. "Take care of them . . ." he begged in a raspy voice. Philippe knew exactly what he meant.

"Of course, Jacques, be at peace. I shall watch over your family with ardent care." He nodded a few times and then closed his eyes. Philippe turned to see his wife standing in the doorway crying, with her daughter by her side.

"Please," he pleaded, "these last moments should be yours—not mine."

As they approached Jacques' bedside, he drew in a deep breath, and then slowly expelled his last ounce of earthy air from his lungs. His wife and daughter sobbed and clung to his body.

Philippe, upon seeing the scene, released his own tears of grief and turned to leave the room. He refused to observe the private grieving of immediate family. More than a business partner had been lost. A good friend had passed into eternity. Philippe felt dreadfully alone and deserted.

Perhaps he should have returned to the office, but he had not the heart to do so. His chest tightened with emotion. The time had arrived to tell Suzette of their current affairs, as much as he despaired doing so. If he didn't take care of it quickly, he would hide the truth from her as long as possible. She needed to know, so he could make the necessary arrangements to scale down their life into a manageable financial state.

When he arrived home, he found Suzette playing with little Robert in another game of blocks. For a few moments, he stood in the doorway beholding the child that looked nothing like him. He bore his father's light features and blue eyes. At times, he wished he could dye the boy's hair to match his own.

Even though in times past Robert's appearance hadn't bothered him, lately it irritated and reopened a wound he thought had healed. An ounce of resentment had crept back into his heart amidst other troubles. He cared about the little boy, for Suzette's sake, but now he saw in his face a new threat—another mouth to feed.

"I see you're block building again. What are you two up to this time?"

Suzette rose to her feet from her sitting position on the floor. The palm of her hands smoothed her wrinkled skirt, as she walked over to him in surprise.

"Philippe, you're home early."

He accepted her peck on the check and returned one upon her forehead. "Yes, I need to speak with you."

He knelt down before little Robert, who feverishly built his next creation. "Do you mind if I take mommy away for a few minutes?"

Robert shook his head no. Philippe stood back up, grasped Suzette's hand, and led her downstairs to the parlor. When they arrived, he closed the door behind them and motioned for her to sit in the settee.

"What is it?" she demanded impatiently. "You're worrying me. Is everything all right? Has Robert returned?"

Philippe sat next to her. His face noticeably displayed the strain of the past few hours.

"I'm afraid I have some bad news, Suzette. Jacques Duval passed away not more than an hour ago."

Suzette gasped and brought her hand to her mouth. "Oh, my God, no! His poor wife and daughter! What happened?"

"He's been ill for some time now." He lowered his eyes to the floor and waited for her reaction. "I didn't tell you, so you wouldn't worry."

Suzette touched Philippe's hand, which lay limp in his lap. "What will you do? The business is now yours, is it not?"

"What's left of it." He swallowed the thick lump in his throat. "I don't want you to be concerned, Suzette, but things have not gone well with the business for the past year. We were struggling. There have been losses."

"Losses?" A confused look came across Suzette's face, "I don't understand, Philippe. You never said anything." Her faced turned angry, and her voice rose. "Why haven't you said anything?" Suzette pulled her hand away and jumped to her feet. A sense of dread crawled across her face.

"We've had a few setbacks," he continued. Philippe walked toward her for reassurance. He placed his hands on her shoulders. "Everything will be all right. I'll find a new investor, and things will turn around. In the meantime, we will need to cut back on expenses, and I may need to travel in the future to search out new customers."

Suzette's countenance fell, and the familiar crinkled brow of worry came upon her face.

"I want to know what you mean. What are you proposing?"

Philippe sighed. His gaze crawled dismally to the floor, and his shoulders drooped low. "We'll need to sell the house, Suzette, and let go of the staff until I can recoup some of the losses. I also promised Jacques I would look after his wife and child, which means I need to help support them until I can return Jacques' share of his business for his family to have something to live upon."

He committed himself to the difficult job of caring for two families, but what choice did he have? Philippe worried whether Suzette would understand his obligation to the Duval family, but Jacques had suffered financial loss too. Philippe watched tears spill down his wife's cheeks as she processed the gravity of the situation.

"I'm afraid, Philippe." She laid her head upon his chest. Philippe encircled her with his arms and held her shaking body.

"I swear, Suzette, I shall take care of you. Do not fear. We'll get through this."

At that moment, Philippe felt like an utter failure. His only recourse to find another investor in his business had to be done quickly or file for bankruptcy. If it ended up being the latter, then he would need to find other work immediately.

"Suzette, I need to return and make arrangements to meet with our solicitor regarding these matters," he announced, when he released her from his embrace. "I need to tell the office and crew of Jacques' passing too." He looked at her sympathetically. "Please, my love, do not worry."

Easy to say, he thought, as the empty words left his mouth. The concern over the future pushed down upon his shoulders, and his strength waned under the pressure. He felt as if his legs would give way at any moment; but for the sake of his wife and his pride, he struggled not to show his fears.

Chapter 10

Robert's patience wore thin. It had been an entire month since he hired the investigator and returned to England. Nothing arrived by post. As he pondered another trip to Paris to take matters into his own hands, a courier finally delivered a communication, which contained the information he anxiously awaited.

He quickly snatched the letter from his butler and promptly made his way to his study. He closed the door behind him, shoved his finger underneath the seal, and tore the lip of the envelope open. His hands trembled when he pulled out the paper inside.

Robert fixed his eyes upon the words, but his mind could not focus on the writing. The letters blurred in his vision, which sent his anxiousness soaring to new heights. He needed a drink. Robert placed the document on his desktop, and quickly walked to the decanter, pulled the top, and poured a glass of brandy.

He slowly turned around and faced the communiqué. Robert held the crystal in his hand and stared at the letter lying on the desktop. Why did he stand there with foreboding hesitation? It contained the answers he sought. Perhaps he feared the truth after all.

After a few sips of alcohol, he finally returned to his

desk and sat down. He chewed on his lower lip as he lifted the letter and read the report.

Your Grace,

As requested, I am writing to you with our findings regarding Philippe Moreau. Below is a chronological record of what we have discovered.

In July 1878, Lt. Philippe Moreau resigned his commission, with honors, from the Royal French Navy. On August 12, 1878, he entered into a partnership business with one Jacques Duval, registering a shipping business in the name of Duval & Moreau Shipping. Three ships were originally purchased; one has since been lost at sea, one sold, and the remaining is heavily mortgaged.

Monsieur Moreau's partner recently died, and the company is on the brink of bankruptcy. We have noted in the business section of the Paris news that Monsieur Moreau is actively seeking a new business investor. It appears that financial affairs are grim. His current residence is up for sale. Our investigations with his employees reveal he has given them notice that they will be let go at the end of the month, except for one housemaid.

As far as his personal life, Philippe Moreau married a Camille Rousseau in November of 1878, two children have been born of the marriage. Robert Philippe Moreau, birth date May 2, 1879, and Angelique Juliet Moreau, born March 21, 1884. His wife and children currently reside at his current residence of 82 rue . . .

Robert's grip slipped from his glass of brandy, which sent it flying to the floor. It hit the tile beneath his feet and shattered.

"*Camille . . . Camille . . .*" he repeated, refreshing his memory. Confused over the name, he strained to put the pieces of the perplexing puzzle together. Philippe's voice spoke in the recesses of his memory, as it had years ago over lunch.

"I wish to know your intentions, monsieur, regarding Suzette Camille Rousseau."

Robert recalled his answer as if it just left his lips that moment. *"Camille. I didn't know that was her middle name. Yes, a virgin when I met her."*

When he realized the deception, he bellowed aloud, "The bastard lied to me!"

His boot crunched the broken glass underneath his foot, when he stomped across the room in a heated rage of anger. A knock came at the door, and Robert took the papers from his desk, shoved them into a drawer, and slammed it shut. "Come in," he barked.

"Are you all right, Your Grace? I heard something shatter." His butler stood in the doorway surveying the mess beneath his feet.

"I dropped a glass. Nothing more. Clean it up."

Robert could barely push the words from between his clenched jaw. He felt his heart choke the breath from his lungs. Rashly, he pushed past the butler and out of his study. He strode heavily down the hall with his heels clicking upon the tiled floor. He seized the door handle, flung it open, and walked outside into the fresh air.

Robert headed straight for the stables. Without a word to the groomsman, he grabbed a saddle and bridle and readied his horse. Within minutes, he sped down the tree-lined drive and crossed the fields, deep into the countryside. He wanted to get far away from his estate, prying eyes, and ears that would eavesdrop over the words he needed to spew from his mouth.

With each hoof that beat the ground with loud thumps, Robert's heart beat in rhythm, *"She's alive . . . she's alive . . . she's alive . . ."*

He galloped at full speed to rid his body of the adrenalin that gushed through his veins. Robert pushed Adara to the limit, frantic to release his emotions. Unable to think beyond the shock of the moment, he galloped miles before he finally slowed his horse to a trot. The animal's coat dripped with sweat.

Robert spotted a large oak tree with plenty of shade and came to a halt and dismounted. He let his horse graze nearby, while he plopped down at the base of the tree trunk and leaned back. Out of breath, he rested his head against the rough bark and closed his eyes. Robert's fury boiled beneath the surface.

Philippe had lied. Suzette had used her middle name on their marriage registration rather than her first. There could be no other reason than to hide and disappear, though it undoubtedly had been a poor attempt on both of their parts.

Of course, if Robert hadn't happened upon his son and Philippe in the park, perhaps he would have never bothered to investigate the matter. He hadn't done so in the past. In fact, there had been plenty of trips to Paris where he had successfully wiped Suzette from his memory—at least he thought he had.

Robert's emotions teetered dangerously at the breaking point. He clearly remembered the day he decided to let Suzette go, while lunching on a plate of roasted duck. Yes, he had done the honorable thing, but she had turned and abandoned him before he even spoke the words. Had they planned their deception all along? Did Philippe know she carried his child?

A flurry of curse words escaped his lips, and his knuckles balled into fists of rage. Suzette's womb held his baby when she left—his child! Why didn't she tell him? Why lie to him? *Why, why, why?* The question echoed in his mind like an unanswered prayer.

Robert stood. His body shook. He wanted to scream, yell, or punch something to release his emotion. For years, he had tried to have a child—a son to continue the Holland line. His soul had cried its tears of disappointment. The days that should have been his, filled with joy and pride in raising a son, had been enjoyed instead by his rival.

After the rash thoughts had spoken their mind, a broad smile burst across his face. *I have a son—a fine, handsome young lad.* At that moment, Robert knew he would travel to Hell and back to raise him as his own and quickly decided he needed to involve himself in their lives—all three of them in one way or the other.

The words of the report came back to him. "*We have noted in the business section of the Paris news that Monsieur Moreau is actively seeking new investors for his business.*"

The perfect opportunity had presented itself. Robert decided to invest in the business anonymously. He would own half of their lives to do with as he wished. At least it would keep a roof over their heads. That was his major concern now—to provide for his son and Suzette when her useless husband had failed to do so.

At present, he could not acknowledge the child as his, but someday the boy would know his true father. It would only be a matter of time. Robert vowed it as he inhaled a deep breath and felt peace blanket him in a mirage of hope.

❋ ❋ ❋

Philippe met with his attorney to talk about his options after Jacque Duval's funeral. Arrangements had been made to sell the Duval residence and relocate the family to a smaller and more affordable flat in Paris. Thankfully, Jacques' nephew felt some compassion upon his uncle's relatives and gave to his widow and daughter a reasonable stipend to live upon. Though their living conditions had been substantially reduced, they were not homeless.

Philippe felt enormous relief that their care had been undertaken by another and turned his attention to his own pressing financial matters. He determined to rebuild the shipping business and pay back to Jacques' family the half interest in the firm for the sake of their continued welfare.

Arrangements were made with the company creditors to bide more time before any foreclosure occurred on his remaining ship. Drastic measures on a personal level were ready to be put in place regarding his outlay of expenses at home. The majority of his staff would be released, and Suzette would pick up more responsibilities with cooking and cleaning.

The beautiful home they had purchased had already been put up for sale, but no offers were forthcoming. Philippe made a difficult decision that if it did not immediately sell, it would be rented out instead. His family would take a smaller flat in the center of town to compensate until things turned around.

To his relief, there had been no further word of Robert. He had passed his residence located in the exclusive area of Paris and noted that it had once again been closed. Another small secret, which he had kept over the years, had to do with the knowledge of its location.

Philippe confirmed Robert's departure and told Suzette all was safe. After hearing the news, her worries of discovery melted away.

After Philippe decided to employ his financial recovery plan, he received word from his solicitor that he needed to speak with him immediately. He feared that rumors had spread around town and creditors began calling in their loans. It would only be a matter of time now before total ruin knocked on his door.

The mere thought drove his nerves to the cutting edge. He anxiously arrived at his solicitor's office to hear what would certainly be miserable news. The clerk announced his arrival, while Philippe sat in the waiting room fretfully rubbing his fingers around the rim of his hat. He glanced annoyingly at the clock on the wall, which played its tick tock tune adding to his jitters. Finally, after a ten-minute wait, the door opened, and Monsieur Benoit invited Philippe into his office chambers.

"Ah, Philippe." He greeted him with an unexpressive face. "Come in and let's talk."

Philippe reluctantly entered and found a chair in front of his solicitor's desk and sat down. Monsieur Benoit shuffled a stack of papers across his mahogany desktop.

"I have here a letter," he began, taking the paper into his hand. "I'm afraid the news will be quite shocking to you."

Philippe raised his eyes and gulped the lump down his throat. "Does someone wish to foreclose upon a loan?"

"Oh, no, no, Philippe. Our meeting here today is not to give you bad news, but frankly I'm here to tell you some rather surprisingly good news."

Philippe couldn't help but lean closer.

"Someone responded favorably to the advertisement we placed in the business classifieds for an investor. I'm here to tell you that you've received a positive and rather generous offer."

Benoit adjusted his spectacles that had slipped down his nose, pushing them up with his index finger.

"The individual has gone so far as to send me the investment funds in good faith." Monsieur Benoit picked up a check from his desk. "I've been instructed by the investor to give you this money; however, it does come with some conditions."

Philippe's eyes bulged from their sockets. He could hardly believe the news that an investor dared to find an interest in his failing business. He scooted forward and leaned over his solicitor's desk to ask a question.

"Conditions? Exactly what do you mean by conditions?" Philippe furrowed his brow in concern.

"Well, first off, the individual who wishes to invest, insists on total anonymity. I have strict instructions to deposit this money directly into your account without your knowledge of who signed the check that I hold in my hand." Benoit set the check face down on his desktop and picked up the letter once again.

"You are to be given total control of the business, but are required to write monthly reports and give a strict accounting of your earnings and expenses. In addition, a detailed business plan must be submitted within the fortnight outlining the efforts you plan to take to bring the business from the red into the black. You have six months in which to turn the circumstances around, and if the investor is not happy with the results, he will withhold further funds."

Philippe sat somewhat dumbfounded over the news. "May I ask how much the check is for?"

"15,000 Francs, based on the current valuation of your customer base. Frankly, I think that is a rather generous sum in light of your company's recent performance."

"My recent performance," Philippe mumbled. "I had a thriving business until a string of bad luck and my partner died. It wasn't entirely all my fault." He raised his voice in defense.

"I'm not accusing you of anything, Philippe. However, as you can see, these conditions are rather strict. It may take you some time to comply with your investor's wishes. That is, of course, if you decide to take his offer." He hesitated for a moment and then continued. "The investor has one further requirement."

"And what is that?"

"He requires that if he finds suitable accounts that are worthy of your pursuit, you are required to take his recommendations and procure those accounts to the best of your ability."

Philippe considered the conditions. The anonymous investor wanted to insert his advice and exercise power over certain business transactions. Though Philippe wanted total control over all aspects, he had been pushed into a corner of take it or leave it.

"Based on that further requirement, will you take the offer?" Benoit looked at him in hopeful earnest.

It didn't take long for Philippe to reply. He blurted out, "You think me a fool? Of course, I'll take his offer. What choice do I have? Shall I relegate my wife and children to living upon the streets? I'll lose everything if I don't turn things around."

He wanted to grab the check from his solicitor's possession and see the name penned across the signature line. It was frustrating not knowing who was behind the investment.

"Very well then," Monsieur Benoit replied. He slowly folded the letter and laid it down. "I shall communicate with the gentleman that you have accepted his offer. He has asked that I be the intermediary in this arrangement. All correspondence, reports, etcetera, are to be funneled through me to pass onto the investor who offers these funds. I shall without delay deposit the money into your business account. When the check has cleared, I will notify you so that you may access the money immediately."

"Thank you," Philippe breathed in relief.

"Be careful with the funds Philippe. Use each Franc wisely to get yourself back on your feet. I'd hate to think of the alternative."

"And I," he wholeheartedly agreed.

Philippe watched Benoit stand to his feet and reach out to shake his hand. He stood and grasped it in return. "Thank you for the good news. I was expecting the worst, I'm afraid."

"Not today," he replied. "Today you've received good news."

As soon as Philippe left the office, he let out a loud sigh and wiped from his brow the beads of nervous sweat with the back of his hand.

Whoever this mysterious sponsor happened to be, he

owed him his life! He would be eternally grateful for the infusion of funds. The peculiar fact that he wished to remain anonymous shaded the offer, but it wasn't unusual.

Philippe shrugged off the uncomfortable aspects of the terms and focused on the positive. One day he hoped to meet the man who saved him from bankruptcy and profusely thank him for this second chance.

Chapter 11

Robert discovered the perfect avenue into the lives of Suzette and his son—through the weakness of her husband. When the correspondence arrived a week later from Philippe's attorney regarding the acceptance of his offer, a smug smile spread across his face. Unquestionably, if he really knew where the money came from, he'd refuse it in a heartbeat and bring his family down to destitution through his pride. Robert had to protect Suzette. He had cared for her since he met her at Chabanais, and he determined to care for her until the day he died, now that he knew the truth of the matter.

The check had been cashed, and Robert used his connections to further his infiltration into their lives. Of course, like any shrewd business investor, he wanted a return for his money. In order to make certain he received a profit, he turned to Marguerite's husband, Lord Chambers, to secure that future.

As promised, though slightly delayed in occurrence, Marguerite and Lord Chambers arrived at their residence for a visit with their two children. Suddenly, the household filled with the activity of a rambunctious four-year-old boy and a two-year-old toddler, who seemed to get into everything. Marguerite brought their governess, whose extra set of eyes kept the little ones in line.

As soon as they walked through the front entrance, Jacquelyn swooped down upon both children like a hungry eagle out to rob another's nest. Marguerite could hold her tongue no longer. He could tell that his sister was on the verge of giving Jacquelyn a piece of her mind, so Robert pulled her into her study for a heart-to-heart talk.

"Give her an opportunity to get it out of her system, Marguerite. She desperately needs it," he pleaded.

"Needs it? The woman takes over every time she's with them. I really think she'd steal them away, if she could do it. It's rude, Robert. Terribly rude."

"I know. I know," he agreed, with a sigh. "She's getting worse in many ways as the years pass and no child is conceived. I have no answers to the dilemma."

He wanted to tell her Jacquelyn's stability was a concern, but worried it would fuel fears in Marguerite's mind that she might do something harmful to her children. Robert thought the idea ridiculous, but his sister had a way of blowing things out of proportion.

"Well, I do feel for her, Robert. Every woman wants a baby, and I assume you do too, though you don't articulate it very much."

"Of course, I want children. A son in particular would be nice," he added, with the knowledge of one already. "Just let her play with them. It makes her happy. If you scold her like a child over the matter, she'll only sulk and then I'll suffer for her miserable moods." Robert chuckled, trying to make light of the situation.

"I will try and be tolerant," Marguerite conceded. "Though I find her somewhat overbearing in many ways. She completely occupies my children's attention when they are here." She paused for a moment as she thought of the past.

"I suppose, Robert, you could very well blame me for your predicament. I am the one, after all, that told father and mother of her family. When I first met Jacquelyn, we were close friends. She was quite different in personality years ago. I thought her a good match, and so did mother and father."

"Well, I don't blame you, if that's what you're worried about. I answered father's bidding. What's done is done, isn't it?"

Robert walked toward the study door and opened it for Marguerite. "Now, do me a favor, little sister, and send your husband in here. I have business to discuss with him."

Marguerite raised an eyebrow. "And what kind of business might I ask?"

"Business," Robert insisted. "Money matters, which would bore you to death. Now go get him."

Marguerite raised her right hand and patted Robert on his cheek. He knew she did it specifically to provoke him, because he hated the patronizing practice of his mother.

"Of course, dear, whatever you say."

He rolled his eyes, and she laughed gleefully as she left the room. Robert walked over to his desk and sat down. A few moments later, Lord Chambers stood at the door.

Edmund Chambers did not receive any deep respect from Robert. Though he had given in to Marguerite's cries to marry him, he found the man of questionable character. His father apparently had no objection to the match, so to honor his dying wishes, he relented to the marriage.

Edmund's wealthy family had made their fortune in generations past through, what Robert thought a despicable means—slave trading. Lord Chambers' father had been a ruthless man with no mercy for the plight of Negros. He transported men, women, and children from Africa, the West Indies, and elsewhere to the Americas during the heyday of purchased workers and servants. Though they had, since the abolition of slavery in the Americas, ceased business, Robert knew the money that now cared for his dear sister had been earned by the sweat and torture of other human beings. It disturbed him to the core.

Edmund, though, had continued commerce in the West Indies by maintaining a sugarcane plantation that his father had owned. Though he lived in England, his shrewd land managers took care of the business for him and merely forwarded his profits. Occasionally throughout the year, Edmund would travel to the plantation on business and leave Marguerite at home.

As much as Robert hated the question he would soon ask Edmund, he knew that the man had to be used to further his less than honorable purposes.

Edmund walked through the door and greeted him with little civility. The man's demeanor brought a spirit of darkness to the atmosphere. Tall and commanding, his dark hair and eyes added to the mystique of his appearance. The two rarely talked one-on-one in a situation such as this, and no doubt Edmund wondered about the sudden need for a private conversation.

"Ah, Edmund. Come in. Would you like a drink?"

Edmund glanced about the study and spied the decanter of alcohol. "Is that brandy?"

"Brandy it is." Robert walked over and poured him a glass. He took one as well, and then returned to sit behind his desk after he gave the spirits to Edmund. He watched as he swallowed it rather quickly and then took a seat in a nearby chair.

"You wanted to talk?"

"Yes, I have some business matters I'd like to go over with you."

"Well, this is a rare occasion," he sarcastically replied.

"Yes, rare indeed," Robert chimed back. "I've recently made an investment in a shipping company."

Edmund nearly choked on the alcohol in his throat. His eyes narrowed. "You invested in a shipping company? Pray tell, why?"

Robert took a drink. "Let's just say it's for personal reasons. An old friend from Paris fell on hard times and needed help. I offered to invest so his company wouldn't go bankrupt."

"Nice of you," he drawled. "But what's that got to do with me?"

"Well, I need to procure a rather large account, Edmund. You ship your sugarcane from your plantation to Europe, do you not? Who is your shipping company?"

Edmund laughed aloud. "Oh, I see where this is going," he said, with a look of superiority on his face. "You wish me to drop my current carrier for your new business?"

Robert smiled in response. "You've concluded correctly. Can we talk business?"

"Refill my glass and we'll see."

Robert reached over and took the empty glass from his hand and walked to the decanter. He poured enough into the glass to loosen up his brother-in-law and handed the brandy to him. Robert sat down and sported a smug look upon his face.

Edmund took another sip. "Willingham Brothers Shipping is my current carrier. If I were to drop them, it would have to be worth my while. I am after all a business man as well, Robert."

Robert watched Edmund mull over the possibilities of savings in his mind. Instead of waiting, he decided to make the first offer.

"Ten percent discount off your current terms with Willingham."

"Fifteen," he pompously countered, "or we have no deal."

"Fifteen it is then." Robert extended his hand across the desk. He knew he had just procured for Philippe a large account, but one more thing had to be done before the deal concluded.

"I need another favor," Robert said, as he shifted his eyes to the desktop thinking how to formulate his words.

"This sounds serious," Edmund replied.

"Well, not serious, but rather odd. The business I've invested in belongs to Philippe Moreau. It used to be under the name of Duval & Moreau Shipping, but the elder partner passed away a few months ago leaving the company close to bankruptcy. Even though we've made our deal, I want to send Philippe to the West Indies under the ruse he's to try and close a deal with your manager. Can that be arranged?"

Edmund eyed Robert up and down suspiciously, and then pulled his mouth to one side before asking a snide question.

"What are you up to, Robert, you bastard? You've got something up your sleeve, now tell me."

"Nothing," Robert replied, with a shrug of his shoulders. "I just need to remove his presence from Paris for a month or so to take care of some other matters."

Edmund looked surprised over his comment. He thought for a moment and then put two and two together.

"If I didn't know you better, I'd say there's some woman behind this whole set up. You know, I can get to the bottom of it by myself," he threatened, with dark eyes.

"Don't try to intimidate me, Edmund Chambers. I already know of your indiscretions regarding my sister and the mistress you have on the side." He brought his fingers to his chin and stroked them thoughtfully. "Let's see, what's her name—Miss Arlene Dorothy Graham from London? I think she lives in that little townhouse that you gave her on Dorsey Street, correct? She travels with you on your trips to your plantation."

Edmund's jaw dropped wide open. He set his glass down on top of Robert's desk.

"Very good, brother-in-law. Very good. I shall not speak of your little scheme, and you shall not speak of my private social arrangements. The account is yours. Send your Mr. Moreau to the West Indies, and I'll write ahead to my manager to close the deal within a few days of his arrival at our agreed price. Will that give you enough time to pursue your interests?"

Robert smiled. "Make him linger there for at least two weeks."

Never before had Robert considered himself a man who could devise underhanded schemes. However, for some strange reason he felt quite pleased at that moment. He had rid Suzette of Moreau and procured the deal with Lord Chambers.

"Your private matters will remain silent, Edmund, as I request that mine will, too."

Though Edmund's unfaithfulness irked him, at least Marguerite had her children and was well cared for in every way. Whether she knew of his indiscretions, he did not know. Regardless, he wished to protect her from the truth.

Edmund reached across the desk. "A gentleman's handshake then, brother-in-law, and I shall see to it the man is kept at bay for at least two weeks in the West Indies. With the travel time, I'm sure he'll be away long enough for you to conclude your business dealings."

Robert grasped Edmund's hand and enthusiastically shook it up and down.

"Yes, I believe that will give me ample time to conclude my business. Ample time, indeed."

❋ ❋ ❋

A month had passed after Philippe sent his initial report to his investor. He had taken the money and paid off delinquent debts, caught up on past-due payroll to his employees, and began soliciting again for more business. He hadn't, however, expected the surprising instructions recently received by post.

His anonymous investor had been busy at work behind the scenes in his own effort to build the business. A promising prospective customer showed interest in the

Moreau Shipping Company and wished to meet with him. The news would not have been problematic if it was a local client, but the customer's main operation came out of the British West Indies.

Philippe had been instructed, as a further condition of continued support, to travel abroad to negotiate a rather large contract for transportation of sugarcane back to the European market. It could prove to be an extremely lucrative arrangement, which would help him raise enough money to purchase another ship. He frankly despised the idea of a lengthy sea voyage again having had his fill in the French Navy.

Suzette had been rather peeved at Philippe already for hiding the truth about his business woes, but had braced herself for possible changes. Duval's death had devastated her as well, and Philippe believed she had sensed his own loss of a true friend.

As expected, her old insecurities rose from the trials she had endured previously. However, to her immense relief all plans for change ended upon the sudden arrival of an investor. Afterward Philippe spent more time at the office and away from home, which Suzette understood as a necessary requirement. He determined to follow through on the conditions of his investor to make sure all went well.

Once again, when a serious discussion needed to occur, he sought her out and spoke the words that instantly drew a sense of dread.

"I need to speak with you."

"I'm almost afraid to agree to the request," she admitted. "But, of course."

"It's not all that bad, my love," he assured Suzette, as he sat next to her on the settee. "In fact, it's good news again."

"Well, then tell me the good news."

"I have the opportunity to secure a rather large account that will definitely be the feather in our cap, if I can close the deal. When I do, Suzette, you can be assured of our financial security for some time."

"Really?" she asked with keen interest. "What kind of account, Philippe?"

"It's a plantation—a plantation in the British West Indies that needs transportation of its sugarcane crop to European markets."

"You mean sugar? Oh, Robert, that sounds exciting! Have you been in correspondence already with the owner?"

"Well, not exactly. I've yet to speak with them, and that's where I need to talk with you."

"What do you mean?"

"It requires that I travel to the West Indies, Suzette, to procure the deal. There is no contract as of yet, however, my anonymous investor has paved the way and is requiring that I go personally."

"What? And leave your wife and family? Is he insane?" Suzette felt sick inside. "You cannot be serious?"

"I'm afraid I am. I need to go. Our future depends upon it. You'll be fine. The servants are here now to take care of everything; and if you'd like, I'll hire a butler to oversee the household. That should provide you enough assurance with a male presence nearby and a sense of security. Would that help?"

"We can't afford a butler," she protested.

The look in her eyes told Philippe she liked the idea. She had complained beforehand that the house felt overwhelmingly empty whenever he left. She didn't like being alone. Philippe associated her distress with memories of Robert leaving her unaccompanied for weeks on end, while he proceeded with his deception of marriage.

"Don't worry. If I get this deal signed, we can afford ten butlers."

Suzette looked at him in dismay, but he returned her look with determination. She had to agree that it needed to happen.

"Well, then, when are you leaving and how long will

you be gone, Philippe?"

"There is a ship leaving at the end of the week. I should be back within a month or two, no longer."

"Oh, God," she moaned. "I wish you didn't have to go." Suzette reached over and held his hand.

"You'll be all right," he assured. He gathered Suzette into his arms and heard a sigh of surrender release from her lungs.

"Promise me that you'll write and let me know you've arrived safely."

"Of course, my love, but no doubt I'll have returned by the time the post makes it back to Paris."

"Humor me anyway."

He hugged her tightly. "I'll write."

❋ ❋ ❋

The days passed far too quickly for Suzette. When the time for his departure arrived, she insisted on accompanying Philippe to the docks. He had said his goodbyes to Robert and Angelique, telling the lad to be a big boy and watch over his mother while away.

"You're the man of the house now," he instructed with a serious look. Robert readily accepted his assignment, along with the butler's help, of course.

As the carriage pulled toward the docks and came to a stop, Suzette held Philippe's hand tight. She looked at the ship. An ill-omened sense rose in her stomach, and her worry-wart mind played its usual tricks of torment.

"I should go on board," Philippe announced. "It's time." He exited, and Suzette insisted on walking him to the boarding ramp.

"I don't like this," she confessed. "For some reason I just feel like something is not right."

Philippe stroked the side of her face with the palm of his hand. "I'll be back before you know it, Suzette. Don't despair. This is a trip that will bring us prosperity and nothing else."

Suzette couldn't shake off the uncomfortable intuition. Trips across the Atlantic were dangerous. Ships often sank. What if he didn't come back? She'd be left with nothing! The thought brought old insecurities to the forefront, and she quickly wrapped her arms around Philippe.

"Be safe, please," she pleaded. "Come home as soon as you can."

Philippe put his hands on her shoulders and gently pushed her away from his chest. "I promise." He placed his lips on hers and gave Suzette a long, deep kiss. When he finished, he smiled and then turned to board the ship.

Suzette stood silently and watched his departure, shrouded in contradiction. She had convinced herself for some time that she really didn't love him like she had once loved Robert. However, as she saw his departure, she realized that perhaps more attachment existed than she cared to admit. He was, after all, her provider and husband.

Philippe stopped, turned, and waved goodbye. Suzette raised her hand and waved back. She blew him a kiss and smiled. When he disappeared on board, she climbed into the carriage and returned home to spend the next month or two in solitude with her children and worrisome thoughts.

Chapter 12

Marguerite, Edmund, and the children came and went, and Robert became antsy. He had been advised by Monsieur Benoit that Philippe had departed for the West Indies that week. The moment in time neared for Robert to make his move, but one person held him back—his wife.

He thought the best occasion to bring up the subject would be at dinner with his mother and Jacquelyn together, plus a room full of household staff that served the table. Surely, she wouldn't make a scene in the presence of others—at least he hoped.

The soup arrived and they all quietly sipped the liquid with their spoons, enjoying the chicken broth before the main course. For a few moments, he studied the pattern of the plate placed in front of him. All his life, he had never cared to stare at it with any discerning observation, but today it held his attention.

The Spode bone china, which had been in his family for generations, suddenly came alive before his eyes. In the pattern that splashed across the center of his bowl, were tiny lilies sprinkled between the flora. What a strange thing to see at the bottom of his chicken soup after all these years. It gave him the fortitude to lift his gaze, look at his dinner companions, and open his mouth.

"I suppose you two will be redecorating the dining

room next. It could use a makeover, as far as I'm concerned."

Mary looked at him in astonishment. "And when have you ever been interested in decorating, Robert? I thought you abhorred our little hobby."

"No, no, of course not. I just thought since I need to travel to Paris on business tomorrow morning that it might be a good idea for you to pursue another project during my absence."

"Paris? Why do you need to go to Paris? We just came back a few months ago," his wife demanded.

Robert braced himself, but kept his voice calm. "Jacquelyn, I need to go on business, and frankly I need to go alone. I won't be gone long."

"What kind of business?" she flung in irritation. Jacquelyn dropped her spoon into her soup plate. "There is only one type of business I'm aware of that you pursue while in Paris."

Robert pulled his eyes away from her glare, cussing at the woman inwardly. It was obvious, Jacquelyn wanted to pick a fight with him in front of his mother and everyone else in the household. He had to put a stop to it.

"It's business," he said, emphatically. "The trip is not up for discussion."

The room's atmosphere grew thick. He could hear the server behind him shuffle his feet. Robert refused to look at his wife or mother while he continued to finish his soup in the lily-patterned bowl. He pushed the plate away and looked up.

"Next course, please."

The servant took his soup bowl away, and a plate of roast duck landed in front of him. He couldn't believe the coincidental menu choice for the evening. Robert methodically picked up his fork and jabbed at the meat like he had five years ago. It had to be some kind of omen. Perhaps this trip would prove fruitless. He honestly didn't know, but he'd never rest until he pursued the truth.

He carved a piece of breast and took a bite. Suddenly, his wife's voice returned to taunt him. Robert swallowed and lifted his eyes in displeasure.

"What do you think, Mary," Jacquelyn inquired with a sarcastic tone to her voice. "Shall we redecorate the dining room while His Grace takes care of *business*?"

Mary cleared her throat over the snide remark by her daughter-in-law. She glanced at Robert, who shot her a look of anger in her direction. Mary dabbed her lips with a napkin and placed it back on her lap. She turned to Jacquelyn.

"Men have their business; women have their decorating. I dare say, though, we need to ask Robert for a much larger budget this time as compensation for his absence. Don't you think?"

Jacquelyn smiled. "You can afford to give us a rather large allowance, my dear, can't you? After all, I'm sure your business trip will be profitable."

Robert saw the glare in her eye. "Of course," he conceded. "Whatever you need. I'll be departing in the morning, so do as you please."

After the comment left his lips, he put down his fork. The announcement had not been easy, nor would eating the rest of his dinner while he stared at lilies and ducks. Things couldn't be more uncomfortable.

"I'm afraid I haven't much of an appetite. I need to speak with Giles about packing my bags, anyway."

He pushed his chair back, set his napkin down next to his plate, and left the room.

❋ ❋ ❋

Giles traveled with Robert at his request. The following morning his trunks were loaded upon the carriage to the train station, where he'd travel to Dover and then transfer by ship to Calais. After another rail journey to Paris, he would arrive. He did not care to open up the townhouse and bring back a full complement of staff just for his use, so he decided to stay at the Hotel de Louvre instead.

He planned to leave early in the morning to forego goodbyes to his wife. Unfortunately, that well thought-out plan failed. She had knocked on his door at morning's light, just as he had finished dressing.

"Robert, let me in."

He did so and found her standing on the threshold in her bathrobe. "I'm about to leave, Jacquelyn. Make it quick."

"Quick? Like you are with me?"

"Have you come to say goodbye or have you come to bitch at me about something?"

"No, I've come to ask you to visit my bed when you return from your trip. I promise to try and fulfill my wifely duties in a more enthusiastic approach."

Shocked at her statement, Robert stared at her in disbelief. He hadn't been to her bed since the night of their argument. She wanted his seed. Either that or she surmised he headed to Paris for one thing and nothing else.

"We'll discuss it when I return," he stated, in a non-committal tone. He pulled out his pocket watch from his vest and noted the time.

"I need to go. The train leaves within the hour."

Jacquelyn grasped his forearm and flashed him a mocking look. "Don't over exert yourself too much, my dear. Come back rested so we can have our private times."

She turned and sauntered down the hall and closed the door to her bedchamber. Robert called for Giles.

"Let's get the hell out of here."

"Of course, Your Grace. I'll have the footmen load the luggage on the carriage."

Robert took hold of his coat and trotted down the stairs toward the door. He couldn't remember a time that he felt such a need to escape. Unsure of the future, he could only hope it that it included Suzette and his son.

❋ ❋ ❋

Jacquelyn had returned to her room. She watched out the window of her suite as the carriage pulled away and headed down the long pebble path to the main road. By tomorrow, he'd be in Paris and up to something. It irked her not knowing what and decided that the time had arrived to snoop around and find out.

She wrapped the sash of her robe tightly around her slim waist. Only the housemaids were up, cleaning the ashes out of the fireplaces from the night before. They usually took no notice of her actions, and frankly she didn't care whether they noted her whereabouts or not.

Mary often slept in much later, enjoying mid-morning breakfasts on the veranda during nice weather. At six o'clock in the morning, she'd be fast asleep.

Jacquelyn made her way downstairs and walked the long corridor that led to Robert's study. She had never dared to enter his private domain, but desperate women had their vices. She arrived at the door and saw it open. The housemaid knelt in front of the fireplace brushing the last bit of ash into her bucket.

"Leave," Jacquelyn ordered.

The maid jumped to her feet, curtsied, and did as told. "Yes, ma'am."

Jacquelyn waited for her to retreat down the hallway, then stepped inside and locked the door behind her. Not quite light enough in the dark mahogany study to see well, Jacquelyn lit the oil lamp on the corner of Robert's desk. The action reminded her that she wanted to upgrade their estate to the new electric lights, which would be the next order of business upon Robert's return.

At first, Jacquelyn really didn't know what to look for in her husband's study. Clues. She needed some idea of what deceit he was up to. Since he spent most of his time inside this room, certainly there must be some answer for her to discover.

She flopped herself in Robert's overstuffed leather chair and eyed all the papers on his desktop. Very carefully, she lifted and returned to the same place each document she examined, worried that if she shuffled them too much, he'd realize someone had been snooping around.

Nothing of interest satisfied her curiosity, and then she decided to try the drawers. She opened and examined the contents in each, which only revealed boring information about tenants on the land they owned.

As she pulled the last drawer handle, she discovered that it had been locked. She tugged on it for some time, but it would not budge open. Her tenacious determination would not discourage her from discovering the contents.

She took a long hairpin from her up-swept hair and poked one end into the keyhole. Jacquelyn fiddled with it for some time, moving it back and forth until she heard a click. Ecstatic that she had gained entrance, she slowly pulled the drawer open and began rifling through its contents.

An envelope with a return address from a Monsieur Girard, Solicitor, in Paris caught her eye. It immediately piqued her interest, so she pulled out the contents, opened the letter, and read the correspondence. The name of Philippe Moreau met her prying eyes, the man who Robert told her was an old acquaintance. Why had he sought more information about him?

Jacquelyn read the investigative report slowly and took particular notice of one paragraph.

As far as his personal life, Philippe Moreau married a Camille Rousseau in November of 1878, two children have been born of the marriage. Robert Philippe Moreau, birth date May 2, 1879, and Angelique Juliet Moreau, born March 21, 1884. His wife and children currently reside at his current residence of 82 rue Charbonneau in Paris, France.

Jacquelyn read the words over again until finally she understood their meaning. "He said that she died. Is she not dead?"

She laid the letter down on Robert's desk in an attempt to make sense of what she had just read. The dates were confusing. She had given birth to that little boy in May of 1879. Jacquelyn had married Robert in October of 1878. She picked up her hand and began to count the months backward on her fingers—April, March, February, January, December, November, October, September, August.

"August," she said aloud. She paused for a moment until the revelation unfolded in all its horror. "Oh, my god!"

She jumped to her feet and stepped back from the desk. Robert's emphatic statement in the gardens filled her thoughts.

"That's enough, Jacquelyn. There is nothing there besides a young lad named Robert—a common name and nothing more."

If that were true, why did he request an investigation of some man he supposedly knew? The suspicion she entertained when she saw the little blond-haired boy with blue eyes returned to torment her tenfold. Did the boy belong to Robert? Had he gone to Paris to search them out?

Afraid to discover what else lay in the drawer, Jacquelyn eased herself back down into the chair. More papers caught her attention in the bottom, which contained a series of letters to another solicitor by the name of Benoit. With each envelope she opened, the puzzle became more convoluted. Robert had invested in Philippe Moreau's company too, but why?

The last letter, however, revealed more than she cared to know. Philippe Moreau had agreed to travel to the West Indies. The dates were obvious. He had left Paris over a week ago, and Robert had gone to Paris during his absence.

"Bastard," she seethed in anger. "My husband is an

unfaithful bastard!"

Jacquelyn resisted the urge to crumble the letter she held in her hand. With great difficulty, she folded it and inserted it back into the envelope. Each were cautiously replaced just as she found them. When through, she closed the drawer but could not relock it with her hairpin.

Frustrated, she left it open, convinced Robert would think he had forgotten to lock it. She glanced at the clock on the mantel. Almost an hour had passed. For a moment, she regretted searching out matters in her husband's office. The upsetting evidence sickened her heart. It appeared as if he had an illegitimate child.

A child. The thought repeated in Jacquelyn's mind multiple times, until the hurt festered unrestrained. Her eyes filled with tears. If it were true, her womb held the blame. The fault lay not with his seed, but with her body.

Jacquelyn brought her hand to her throat. Her misery choked the breath from her lungs. The cruel reality of the reason behind her barren state tore through her soul like a blade.

Barely able to move, she stumbled toward the door and then wandered back up to her bedchamber. Once inside, she fell upon her bed and sobbed until her eyes were swollen and red. When she had released her despair, she emerged a different woman. A strange, cold emptiness possessed her core.

"My lady, are you all right?" Dorcas called to her from the other side of the door.

"Yes, I'm fine. You may enter."

Jacquelyn stood to her feet. "I want a bath this morning, Dorcas."

"Yes, ma'am, but are you all right, my lady? You look as if you've been . . . crying."

"Nothing of consequence, Dorcas. It's nothing that I can't handle on my own."

Jacquelyn felt a chill go down her spine. The emptiness

she had felt only moments before seemed to be replaced with a hard coldness. Never again would she cry over her barrenness. Never again would she trust her wandering husband. She would harden her heart toward everything and everyone and shield herself from further pain. No one would hurt her again.

Jacquelyn slipped under the readied bath water. This time she instructed Dorcas to pour in primrose bath fragrance. The aroma soothed her tension.

Finished with her duties, Dorcas turned to leave and Jacquelyn protested.

"Sit with me, Dorcas."

"Sit with you?"

"Yes, pull up a chair and sit with your mistress. That is what I've asked."

She noted the confused look on her maid's face, but she obeyed as commanded and pulled up a chair next to the tub.

"Hand me that bar of soap and cloth."

Dorcas did as told and watched her as she foamed the bar of soap into bubbles. Jacquelyn began to wash her body methodically limb by limb.

"Sometimes I envy you, Dorcas," she began casually. "You seem to have such a simplistic life just caring for me. No worries. No family. No husband to give you grief."

"My life is nothing to envy, my lady. You have everything riches could offer. The title of duchess, money, a beautiful home, and a handsome husband. Why would you want my life, for goodness sake?"

"Oh, I have my reasons. Just because I'm a duchess, it does not mean that I am a happy woman. Do you think the duke makes me happy?"

"Oh, my lady, I cannot speculate on such a private matter."

Jacquelyn accepted her honest response. "Well, I assure you, he does not."

She continued to wash, symbolically rubbing away her past life. In a few more minutes, she would allow it to slip through the drain by her toes and disappear forever.

"You see, I was born to be a duchess."

Jacquelyn moved the washcloth down her slim legs, and conveyed to Dorcas her fate in life.

"My mother bred me to be a proper lady. My father was determined that I would marry well. I was well educated. Preened. Taught impeccable manners. My voice was trained to sing, my fingers trained to play the piano. I speak German and am articulate in the French tongue. I have all the qualities of being an excellent wife, and that is all I wanted to be in life—an excellent wife and mother."

She finished washing her legs and then wrung out the cloth and laid it over the edge of the tub.

"You see before you a complete failure, Dorcas. I have done none of these things. I am not, in my husband's eyes, a good wife in bed. He married me because his father told him to do so, not because he loved me. I cannot produce an heir, and he beds other women and probably has produced a child with one of them. Isn't that the mark of a complete failure?"

She heard Dorcas gasp and then turned to look at her in the eyes.

"I . . . I don't know what to say, my lady. I do not see you as a failure. You are a beautiful woman and a kind mistress to me."

Jacquelyn could see that her truthful confession had made her lady's maid feel extremely uncomfortable. Her eyes glassed over with tears. *How touching*, she thought, that her maid held compassion for her plight.

Strangely, Jacquelyn's admission flooded her with a sense of freedom. She had in essence dispelled her parents' expectations and her husband's disappointments in a morning bath. Jacquelyn Spencer-Holland no longer needed to be a proper lady. She could be anything she wanted! No longer did she need to be a failure of a wife and mother. In fact, she could be as good or evil as she wished to be. Other women were vindictive, so why couldn't she embrace those qualities? Any woman spurned by a man she adores has the right to react as she chooses.

Jacquelyn leaned her head back against the rim of the tub and looked up at the ceiling once more. Her heart welled with emotions that she sought to suppress and damn to hell.

Yes, she adored Robert, from the day she met him during a dinner party. He had looked at her with his blues eyes, and she drowned without resistance in the ounce of affection he gave her. Surely, their entire courtship had been feigned merely to marry for her dowry, good breeding, and family.

Jacquelyn's heart ached for him, but no more. Her calling would be whatever she chose, and if it led her down a path of perdition, so be it. She could be weak and broken, or strong and determined. Jacquelyn decided to choose the latter version from hence forward.

"Hand me a towel, Dorcas."

She stood to her feet and took it from her maid's hand.

"Ready my clothes for the day," she instructed. "I have an urge to shop."

Chapter 13

Robert settled into his room at the Hotel de Louvre. He rented a small suite on the upper floor and spent a few days biding his time. Now that Philippe had left the country for a few months, he only had one goal—to see Suzette.

Shortly after his arrival in Paris, he hired a hansom cab and drove past Suzette's residence multiple times like an obsessed lover. It surprised him to find an upper class dwelling in a nice area of Paris. The discovery convinced him that he had done the right thing to invest in Philippe's defunct business. In doing so, he ensured that Suzette and his son would continue to live in some semblance of comfort.

Now that he had discovered her whereabouts, a large obstacle loomed before him. How could he regain entrance back into her life? He had no intention of being audacious by knocking on the door. When their reunion occurred, it had to be on his terms and in a private setting.

Robert had no idea how to produce such a state of affairs, so he instructed Giles to hire a private carriage and discreetly observe her comings and goings. Perhaps he could ascertain if she routinely left the estate, with or without child, on a recurring errand or walk. He hoped for some patterned routine that he could innocently use to cross her path.

Giles maintained a long, boring vigil from a carriage window parked a few houses away. After the passage of ten days, he finally reported that Suzette did undertake a regular outing. It appeared that on Monday and Thursday, at 10 o'clock in the morning, she took a cab to the Père-Lachaise Cemetery. There she would proceed to the ossuary where the bones of exhumed bodies were kept and would keep vigil and leave a bouquet of lilies. When Robert heard of her practice, immediately he knew the purpose behind it—she visited her deceased father.

"Thank you, Giles, for your keen and diligent observation. It's very helpful, though you must have been terribly bored watching for days on end."

"You are quite welcome, Your Grace. I should add that she spends quite a bit of time at the cemetery." Giles paused for a moment and added in reflection, "It is a rather sad location, don't you think? So many bones—so many bodies dumped into one pit. They are poor souls indeed with an unusual resting place, I think. How can a person properly honor a deceased love one when they cannot visit an individual's grave?"

"I have no idea, Giles. It is a strange practice." Robert felt saddened over the grief that Suzette still carried for her deceased father. "At least we bury our dead underneath the earth in solitary graves in England rather than desecrating bodies and dumping them into heaps of bones. The French are strange in their burial practices, I will admit that."

"Will there be anything else?"

Robert looked at Giles. He had been remarkably trustworthy in this situation, in spite of his unusual request to follow the woman he had taken to England with him years ago. Though he never spoke of their affair to his personal assistant, Giles knew of his ways with women. However, to his credit, he always held that knowledge discreetly.

"No, I don't think so. Just have a carriage ready for me

Monday morning at 9:30 a.m. I'll instruct the driver to follow her at a respectable distance."

Robert struggled with strong emotions over his imminent return into Suzette's life. When he thought of what lay ahead, he felt tormented rather than hopeful over the future. How would she react to seeing him once again? Would she spurn him or embrace him?

Just the thought of looking into her eyes, touching her skin, and smelling the fragrance of her body, drove him to thoughts of folly. The days could not pass quickly enough. He pulled out his pocket watch and counted the hours until the next visit to her father's remains.

❋ ❋ ❋

Suzette struggled with loneliness after Philippe departed for the West Indies. Time dragged onward in his absence, and she found little satisfaction being alone.

Philippe had hired a butler, as he promised, bringing a male presence into the home. Monsieur Leroy seemed to be a godsend. A middle-aged man, prematurely graying, and very tall, he emanated an air of confidence that calmed all the women in the household.

After her return from England, Suzette had on occasion returned to the common gravesite that held her father's decaying corpse. As it approached the fifth year of his death, she happened to discover upon her weekly visit that the site had been excavated. The remains of the decomposed bodies, which now only represented bags of bones, had been relocated to the ossuary that literally housed a million others.

Though her mother's grave remained as it had been in the respectable plot of perpetuity, her father had been thrown into a pit to mingle among the boney torsos and limbs of others. It so grieved her, that she felt compelled to visit the ossuary to pay her respect and leave flowers.

Occasionally, she would visit her mother's grave, though she felt little attachment having lost her at an early age. Suzette's father, on the other hand, had been her world for a long time. She continued to struggle with the immense void his death created in her life.

Suzette made a practice of pouring out her soul each time she came to the stone monument. It gave her a sense of strange comfort to think that her father could hear her speak to him of her hopes, dreams, and disappointments.

She had acknowledged her weaknesses of succumbing to the temptation of the brothel, after his unexpected death, and relayed to him her transgressions with Robert. A strange sense of peace filled her spirit during similar confessionals. Suzette found them to be therapeutic and healing in their own way, especially when mingled with prayer.

When Friday arrived, she felt a deep-seated need to speak to her father of her fears and loneliness. Though little Robert seemed to be taking the entire matter of Philippe's absence in stride, Suzette, on the other hand, was not. Her thoughts were still plagued with Robert and whether he suspected the boy to be his son. Though she had been assured that he had left for England and his townhouse remained closed, she could not shake off a sense of foreboding that followed her like a menacing cloud.

"I wish to wear my dark blue hat and knit shawl today." She watched in the mirror as her chambermaid, Rachel, combed out her long hair and pin it up in the latest style.

"It's a gloomy day outside. You should take your parasol in case it rains."

"Yes, it is gloomy outside isn't it?"

"Do you think you should forgo your visit due to the inclement weather?" her maid suggested with concern.

"It can't be any gloomier than that hole they have thrown the bones of my father into," Suzette remarked in sadness. "I so abhor the place. Have you ever seen it?"

"No, I have not. Is it horrifying?"

"Horrifying isn't the word I'd use to describe it. No, it's more disturbing. There are carved figures all around the entrance. Two naked lovers stand at the doorway with their backs to onlookers, while they look into the dark abyss of death. Other figures in agony and ecstasy are carved alongside the doorway. I can barely look at their faces, but I'm often intrigued over the man and woman walking together into eternity—even if eternity's resting place is not the most pleasant of places to lay one's bones."

"Oh, my," her maid gasped. "How terribly romantic—in a strange sort of way, isn't it?"

"Yes, I suppose." Suzette took assessment of her appearance one last time in the mirror. "I should be going. Help me pin my hat on and grab my shawl. You can let Monsieur Leroy know that I shall return within a few hours after my weekly visit to father."

"Yes, ma'am," she replied, with a quick curtsy. Suzette encircled her shoulders with the blue knit wrap, picked up her parasol, and headed downstairs. Before leaving, she retrieved her bouquet of cut lilies taken from her garden an hour earlier. Carefully, she tied the bunch with a ribbon and wrapped the stems in paper to keep them from drying out.

She climbed into the hansom cab after giving the driver orders to take her to the cemetery only a few miles away. Upon arrival, she somberly proceeded past the display of ornate gravesites and sculptures.

Père Lachaise portrayed a picture of beauty amongst grief. Its multiple crypts, gravestones, and carved figures of the dead and angels from heaven were extraordinarily bizarre. The dark and gloomy day shrouded the scene in a sorrowful aura. Puffy gray clouds swirled overhead, and a chilly breeze rustled the leaves of the trees.

After a few minutes of wandering through the pathways of the dead, she arrived before the ossuary and stopped. Each time she looked at the dark entrance that led to the pit below that housed her father, her chest tightened in anguish.

The dreaded reality that his flesh had rotted away to skeletal remains tormented her with grief. His skin, hair, and organs were decomposed and now dust. Suzette rubbed her cold hands together while she pondered her own mortality and the harsh reality of life and death. The struggles of humans seemed so unfair to her, only to be rewarded at the end of life with a cold, lonely grave.

Certainly, there must be something beyond this pit—a Heaven or Hell to welcome or damn our spirits, she thought to herself. Suzette shuddered.

"Oh, Papa," she muttered, "I do so miss you."

She walked to the base of the ossuary and placed the lilies on the ground. Other bouquets rested against the stone entrance. Suzette stepped back and stood quietly. She inhaled the residue fragrance of the flowers nearby. The wind swirled around her feet, and an urge to speak her woes poured forth from her lips.

"Papa, I miss Philippe. It's hard not having him to turn to when I feel lonely and need to talk, but you know how he is. He's such an intense man, I often wonder whether he hears or understands me at all. Philippe has never been intimately involved or interested in my feelings like Robert had once been."

A chill grasped Suzette's body when she felt a few scattered drops of rain splash upon her cheeks.

"Robert looks more and more like his father every day, Papa. I'm so proud of him. He's such a good boy, though he does have a bit of a temper. I suppose he'll grow out of it."

Suzette chuckled when she recalled the blocks he had scattered across the room in a frustrated tizzy when they wouldn't do his bidding.

"I still worry about him and whether he will ever know his real father. Part of me wishes that one day he could know the truth; but if he does, he'll know what a terrible person I had become. I don't want him to think of me as a whore. I'm not a whore, I'm his mother. I loved the man who gave him to me. When I think of him, I still feel love."

Suzette paused for a moment listening to the leaves rustle in the trees where she stood. She wondered if it was the spirit of her father passing by to let her know he heard her words.

"I'm afraid, Papa, one day Robert will find me. What will I do? I don't . . ."

"Suzette."

Her discourse abruptly halted. She stood rigid like one of the stone statues of the cemetery.

Perhaps an apparition knows my weakness and has come to torment me, she thought. *Surely, the voice did not belong to Robert!*

"Suzette."

The unmistakable and recognizable velvet-toned voice spoke her name again. The blood drained from her face, and she felt a weakness flow through her legs. She quickly spun around to face her tormenter, hoping it was nothing more than a mere ghost.

Suzette's hand flew to her mouth in bewilderment. She gasped at the sight of Robert Holland, who stood only a few feet away.

"Oh, my God," she cried aloud, in soulful anguish. "Robert what—what are you doing here?"

Chapter 14

Robert had prepared for Monday morning as best he could, though he tossed and turned without a wink of sleep the night before. He knew that his heart still clung to the memory of Suzette, but he didn't realize how tenaciously those recollections of their past affair had woven themselves into every fiber of his soul. For five years, he had nursed his regrets and kept alive his desires for one woman. Although now she belonged to another, today he would claim his right to be in her presence.

His carriage arrived promptly at 9:30, and Robert instructed the driver to proceed to Suzette's residence and stop a few houses before the address and wait. Precisely at 10 o'clock, a public cab arrived. Robert caught a glimpse of his petite French mademoiselle when she climbed inside. The expanse between them made it impossible to see her facial features, but the sight of her brought a smile to his apprehensive face.

As her driver proceeded toward the cemetery, they followed behind at a reasonable distance. Robert instructed the driver to pass Suzette's cab, which had stopped at the entrance. They turned the corner at the next block. He waited a few minutes and gave Suzette time to exit and proceed toward the ossuary. A nearby groundskeeper pointed him in the right direction, and he made his way along the same pathway.

The day, overcast and gray, added to the ominous atmosphere of the cemetery. It reminded him of his father's death, which brought a fleeting emotion of buried grief to the surface. He eyed the lavish statues and crypts that lined the lane. It appeared quite unlike English cemeteries that were adorned with simple grave markers.

Robert slowed his pace as he approached the ossuary off in the distance. His eyes fell upon the woman he loved who stood before the sad tomb. Suzette, clothed in a dark blue gown and wrapped in a knit shawl, wore a hat that set off the color of her unmistakable auburn tresses. He stopped for a moment and feasted on the vision of her form. Powerful emotions of affection resurfaced from deep within Robert's heart.

He heard her speak, then slowly and quietly inched his way closer until he stood twenty feet behind her body. Robert strained to hear every word that proceeded from her lips, which conveyed her deepest thoughts to her dead father. His intrusion over the moment of private intimacy between a father and daughter pained him. However, when he heard her confessions about their son and that she had loved him, Robert could no longer remain silent.

Her name slipped from his lips practically in a whisper; but as soon as it did, he knew that she heard him. Her voice halted, and her figure did not move. He said it again louder, and then she spun around to face him and gasped at the sight.

Robert took one step forward and stopped abruptly. In desperation, he attempted to restrain himself from the urge to embrace her body.

"Oh, my God," she cried aloud, clearly in shock. "Robert what—what are you doing here?"

"What am I doing here?" he repeated. "Oh, Suzette, my darling. I came to see you."

Suzette stumbled in her stance. Robert quickly stepped

forward and gently, but firmly, grasped her forearm to steady her balance. The blood drained from her face.

"I don't mean to upset you."

She grasped his arm in return and clung to him for stability. Her shock pained Robert, but even more so as he saw something in her eyes—a sad resignation.

"Are you all right?" He tilted his head and looked to her for affirmation that her heart still beat, worried that she would faint.

"Yes," she sputtered, "I'm fine. You just surprised me, Robert. I wasn't expecting to see you here of all places."

Robert lifted his hand and let his knuckles slide down the smooth surface of her right cheek. At first she flinched at his touch, but as he continued to graze along the line of her jaw, she closed her eyes.

"I thought you died." Troubled, he pulled away from her flawless complexion, but still held her arm tightly. "Your husband told me that you had died; and when he did, I died."

Suzette lifted her eyes and looked at him with remorse. "Robert, I . . ."

"Not here." He stopped her words with the touch of his index finger on her lips. "I don't wish to talk here among the dead, Suzette. My carriage is waiting just outside the entrance. Will you come with me so that we can talk?"

"Come where?"

"To a place more private."

"It wouldn't be proper for me to leave with you," Suzette objected. "I'm a married woman and you a married man."

Robert dismissed her reasoning. "And you are the mother of my son. Let us not talk about what is proper, Suzette."

A tiny teardrop trickled down her check, mingled with the rain that had begun to fall more intensely. Her eyes begged him not ask, but Robert intended to seek out the truth, even if she insisted on silence.

"Please," he persisted. He ran his fingers down her forearm to her hand and grasped her flesh in his. "You owe me the truth."

The touch of her bare skin, when they united palm to palm, ignited the flames of his love. With a slight tug of her hand in his, he took a step away from the ossuary.

"Where are we going?"

"A place where we will not be seen or heard, I assure you."

Robert took another step. Suzette resisted, then relented and followed him as he led the way. With a firm grip on her hand, Robert looked into her frightened eyes that were so reminiscent of the first time they met.

"I'm not angry, Suzette. I won't hurt you. I promise."

"You have every right to be angry with me," she countered, as she lowered her head.

Robert said nothing, but led her in silence to his waiting carriage outside the cemetery entrance. He helped Suzette inside and then gave the driver the destination.

"Pull in through the alley in the back and drop us there," he instructed.

Robert climbed inside, closed the door, and sat in the seat across from Suzette. The coach jerked forward. Suzette sat awkwardly across from him avoiding his eyes.

"It's been a long time, Suzette. It is so good to see you." He paused and then leaned forward in his seat and grasped both her hands in his—they were like ice. "You have no idea the grief I felt when Philippe told me you were dead. Why would he do such a thing?"

Suzette finally lifted her head and looked forlornly into Robert's eyes.

"Philippe only wished to protect me. He is, after all, my husband and feared for some time that our paths might cross one day."

Robert let go of Suzette's hands and leaned back into the seat. He had hoped that upon their reunion, she would display more affection toward him. Instead, she defended her husband. Robert hated the crude reminder of her matrimonial bond. Had she not just confessed to her dead father that she had once loved him? Had the flame died in her heart? The thought cloaked Robert in anguish.

The carriage slowed as it turned in behind a row of expensive townhouses and then came to a stop.

"Where are we?" Suzette peered quizzically out the window.

"This is my townhouse."

"Your townhouse? Robert, you cannot be serious! What if someone sees us together? Don't bring me into your home!"

"There is no one there, Suzette. I'm staying in a hotel right now, and the townhouse has been closed for months. My family is in England, and I am here alone. The servants have been let go for the season, as well."

The driver jumped down and opened the door. Robert exited and paid the fare. "Return in one hour to pick us up, and I'll give you an extra tip."

"Thank you, monsieur. One hour," he repeated, as he tipped his hat.

Robert offered his gloved hand and carefully assisted Suzette out of the carriage. "Come with me, sweetheart."

The horses trotted away, just as the heavens opened and a downpour of rain fell upon their heads. He quickly opened the wrought-iron gate into the back gardens and led Suzette to the servant's entrance. After a quick insertion of his key into the lock, he pushed open the door and held out his hand for Suzette to enter before him.

"As you can see, everything has been closed for some time. The furniture is covered, and the drapes are all drawn shut. I apologize for the cold chill and dark surroundings."

They walked down a hallway and turned to the left. Robert opened two French doors that led into a large parlor. He went straight toward the window and shoved open the heavy brocade draperies. The scant, gloomy light from outdoors lightened the room. The sky had opened its floodgates, and heavy beads of rain pounded against the glass with a *tap-tap-tap*.

"Are you warm enough, Suzette? I could start a fire."

"No, I'm fine. I have my shawl." She pulled it around her shoulders tightly.

"Then at least let me get you a drink of brandy to warm you up. I'm sure I can find some glasses and spirits in the kitchen. I'll be right back."

Robert saw that Suzette looked like a lost puppy, afraid to move about in her unfamiliar location. He realized her uneasiness, but couldn't take the risk of being seen together at the hotel. If he escorted a married woman to his room alone, it would certainly cause a stir should either of them be recognized. In contrast, his closed townhouse, through the servant's entrance, would carry little risk of discovery. Most of the residences in his neighborhood were temporary townhouses for aristocrats who came to Paris on holiday.

"Make yourself at home."

He turned and headed to the kitchen and found two glasses in a cupboard, along with a bottle of brandy. Robert poured a liberal amount of the libation and returned. When he entered the parlor, he saw Suzette looking at an oil canvas on the wall by Pierre-Auguste Renoir. The recent painting of a mother and her little girl, entitled *On the Terrace,* had been purchased by Robert for his wife. His townhouse had also felt the decorating hand of Jacquelyn, with its expensive fine art and furnishings.

"My wife is particularly fond of that scene." His comment ended the uncomfortable silence between them.

Suzette turned around and looked at him. "I've heard of Renoir, but have never seen his work. It's quite stunning. The colors are so brilliant."

"Here." He handed her a glass, which she quickly took from his hand. Robert walked over and pulled the white sheet off of the divan and flung it onto the floor.

"Come and sit with me, please." Robert patted the seat and waited for her to sit next to him.

Suzette studied him closely. She appeared to be taking the opportunity to observe how the years had changed him, as well. His roguish boyhood was gone, and Robert knew that she saw more of a man before her now. Life had altered both of them. Even Suzette looked more mature and womanly in her demeanor.

Robert smiled. He tried to soothe her nervous tension, but found it impossible to delay his curiosity.

"You must know that I want an answer about the boy." He hesitated for a moment while he looked intently into her eyes. "He is my son, isn't he?"

Suzette's eyes darted away, and she hesitated. It disturbed Robert that she did not immediately respond.

"Don't lie to me. I've seen his birth record. The boy was conceived before Philippe took you from me."

She nervously fidgeted with the glass in her hand. "He didn't take me from you, Robert. I left you. Don't you remember?"

"How could I forget? The words you spoke pierced my heart, but I did not believe them. You lied," he emphasized sharply, to impart his pain. "You didn't love him. Admit it, Suzette."

"What does that matter now, whether I loved him or not? You were married to another and didn't even tell me! I felt betrayed and used by you when Philippe revealed to me your marriage. Did you ever stop to think of that?"

Suzette's face contorted into a hurtful pout. He had never seen her in such a state, as their emotions clashed against each other like the waves of a stormy ocean that beat upon a rocky crag. The raw wounds that had festered for years beneath the surface reopened.

"When I came to see you the last time, it was for the single purpose of releasing you from your obligation to me.

I would have gladly kept you by my side, Suzette, through eternity had it been in my power to do so."

He reached over, picked up her soft hand, and stroked it ardently. "I came to tell you the truth, because Philippe had demanded that I let you go. He said you deserved a life of respectability, and I could not deny that was true. I told him then that I loved you, as I love you now."

He squeezed her hand in frustration. "But all the while he demanded I release you, he knew that you carried my child! Don't talk of betrayal to me," he heaved. "I've suffered at your hand, as well."

Robert dropped his tight grip, then brought his drink to his lips and downed the liquid. It streamed down his throat in one burning gush. He didn't care, for his declaration of love had burned his soul when it left his lips. He studied Suzette for an ounce of remorse, but could not discern anything from her pale and unresponsive demeanor.

"I loved you, Suzette, but it was too late for me to do anything about it. I was bound by my promises to my dying father to marry another. Now, I am trapped in a loveless marriage, while I languish every waking moment over what I lost."

He closed his eyelids and inhaled a deep breath before he continued to pressure her for a confession. "At this instant, speak to me the truth. No more lies. Tell me that boy is my son. I want to hear the confirmation from your own voice."

Robert saw Suzette's old nervous habit of her bobbing knees reacting to the strain of the moment. Her hands started to tremble, too, but her silence persisted. Finally, Suzette's lower lip quivered and she spoke.

"Yes, he is your son. You have a son—Robert Philippe Moreau."

"You mean Robert Philippe Holland," he corrected her, sternly.

"What does it matter? Surely, by now you have children

of your own?"

"I have no children," he painfully replied. "My wife is barren. I have tried to impregnate her, and for five years she has failed to produce."

"Oh, Robert, I'm so sorry. Your wife must be heartbroken," Suzette whispered, compassionately.

"My wife?" Robert stood to his feet, irritated that Suzette felt an ounce of sympathy for his wife. He walked to the window and paused momentarily, while he considered what to reveal to Suzette about his life. After a few moments of reflection, he turned to face her and released a long, drawn-out sigh of disappointment.

"My wife is not the woman I love. She never has been. She never will be. Our marriage is one of convenience for our families. I hold no endearment toward her or any passion, though I am disappointed she has not given me an heir."

"Is that all you care about, Robert, producing an heir?"

The comment burned. He looked at Suzette in disbelief that she had accused him of being shallow and heartless. Did she not know him?

"He's my son. I have a right to know and love my own flesh and blood."

Suzette jumped to her feet, clearly agitated over his claim. "And had I told you that I was pregnant, what would you have done? Send me away? Send the baby away to be raised by another? Would you have acknowledged a bastard son in your lineage?"

"I don't know what I would have done," he admitted. He took a few hasty steps in her direction and then stopped. "You made the decision for me, Suzette, and that was wrong." He paused realizing it probably hadn't been entirely her decision. Her conniving husband had clearly influenced her actions.

"Philippe told you to do it, didn't he? He promised to marry you to save you from the shame of being an unwed mother and convinced you that it was the best course action. The ideal deception on his part and retribution in his mind for my taking your virginity. I took what was his; now he has taken what is rightfully mine!"

Robert looked at Suzette with deep longing. He eased forward until he stood a mere foot away from her face. Immediately, the aroma of her perfume wafted up his nostrils, igniting the remembrance of her scent. It had not changed. Suzette's auburn tresses were hidden beneath her hat. Her shawl had slipped from her left shoulder and drooped down to her waist. She shivered before him in anger and cold.

The rage drained from his body, and in its place ignited irrepressible love. Gently, he reached down to the fallen edge of her shawl and lifted it up to her shoulder. His eyes lazily crawled across her swan-like neck, up her jaw line, and rested on her quivering lips. He wanted to kiss her, but instead he gazed affectionately into her eyes and lost himself in the woman he loved.

"Do you remember the first time I kissed you?" he asked, in a tender velvet tone. "How sweet and perfect our lips formed to each other?"

Suzette rapidly lowered her gaze from his, clearly distressed over the closeness of his body.

"Yes, I remember," she exhaled, softly in return. "I have never forgotten you were my first, just as you asked."

Suzette looked back into his eyes, and he saw in them her own repressed affections. Robert lowered his head in response and molded his mouth upon the soft flesh of her lips. At first, she resisted his advances and balled her fists against his chest. As the kiss progressed, Suzette weakened in his arms, unable to fight the inevitable. The longer he drank of his beloved, the more she responded until her arms reached around his neck. She clung to him tightly and kissed him passionately in return.

Robert released her lips and entreated her passionately.

you still love me, darling. Tell me the words I ear." Before she could answer, he kissed her ssed his body flush against her warm and me.

to take her like he had done so many times before. It would be easy to scoop her up in his arms and carry her to his suite upstairs. There, they could rekindle the fire and passion of their lovemaking, which he sorely hungered to regain. He ached for her flesh. His body throbbed and demanded release. In a moment, he'd lose all sense of decency if he didn't stop his desperate pursuit.

Robert freed her and stepped back to put distance between them. "Tell me," he begged. "Tell me you love me still." Never before had he felt such desperation of soul. The deep need to hear her confession of love overwhelmed his emotions.

Suzette slowly lifted her eyes and looked at him in return. "You know I love you. I've never stopped loving you, but I'm married, Robert. What future is there for the two of us? You are bound; I am bound. Our lives are forever separated by civil and religious laws over which we have no control, nor any way of breaking."

She paused and then cried her remorse. "I cannot and will not return to being your mistress and be unfaithful to Philippe. It's wrong! Do not ask me to do such a thing. We must think of little Robert. I cannot bring such shame upon his life." Suzette gasped in a soft sob that broke Robert's heart.

He reached out and cupped her face in his hands, wiping her tears away with his thumbs. She leaned her right cheek deep into the palm of his hand and rested it there for comfort.

"I would not ask you to be my mistress, Suzette. However, I do not know what tomorrow will bring to either of us. Divorce is difficult for me to obtain, even in my station of life in England. The laws of France are no different for you. Adultery is the only way to break the bonds. Either we commit it together, or our spouses must commit it, so that we have grounds for cause. I doubt my wife would stray from our marriage bed. She only wants one thing of me—my seed."

Suzette continued to cry. Robert reached into his pocket and pulled out his handkerchief and wiped her tears.

"I cannot leave Philippe. I just bore our daughter, Angelique! She is but two months old!"

"No doubt she looks like her beautiful mother," Robert comforted.

Suzette inhaled a deep breath in an attempt to control her emotions. "I'm sorry for being so emotional. Seeing you has resurrected so many things in my heart, Robert. I will be ruined forever because of this."

"No, no," Robert consoled. "Let us hope only good will come of it, though I dare say I have no answers."

Suzette calmed, and Robert dared to ask. "May I see him?"

"You mean our son?"

"Yes, I wish to talk to him and know him, Suzette. Please."

"I cannot," she replied, with indignant protection. "Philippe would forbid it."

"But Philippe is gone for two months. He'll never know. Besides, he's my son—not Philippe's.

Suzette's brow furrowed over Robert's comment. "How do you know he's gone?"

"Because I sent him away," he confessed, displaying an audacious air. "I am the anonymous investor that saved his business from bankruptcy."

"That was you?" Suzette pulled away from Robert in astonishment.

"Yes, of course. Who else would have rescued you once again from destitution? I could not see that happen to you or the lad. It angered me that your husband could not provide, so I stepped in and did so myself."

"I never thought you a manipulative man, Robert Holland, but now I see who you really are."

"Suzette, I don't understand your anger toward me. I thought you would at least be thankful."

"Thankful? Did you wish me to be indebted to you once again for my life, so that you could take advantage of me and my son?"

"*Our* son," he corrected her once more, with a scowl on his face. "You seem to forget that the boy is as much mine as he is yours."

"Take me home!" Suzette demanded.

"Not until you agree to allow me to see Robert. I have my rights as the boy's father."

"No. I will not until I have discussed it with Philippe."

"Suzette, you are being unreasonable. Don't force me to take steps to assert my authority. If need be, I will, no matter what the cost to me personally or socially. You need not tell the boy I'm his father, if that's what you're worried about. Since we've already met, you can just say I'm an old friend."

"It's not that simple," she protested.

"It's very simple." Robert firmly grabbed her hand. "Don't deny me."

"Don't threaten me."

Exasperated, Robert quickly released Suzette's hand. He struggled with her unexpected stubbornness. Truth be told, she had changed—the naïve woman he had met five years earlier no longer existed. Time had tremendously changed her. Headstrong and determined, Robert did not know how far he should push the matter. If he needed to, he could write to Edmund to give directions to his land manager to stall the deal as long as possible. It would be easy to keep Philippe out of the picture indefinitely, to bide time to woo Suzette back into his life.

Another obstacle loomed before him though—that of his wife. He had told Jacquelyn that he would not be in Paris long. If he delayed, she could very well complicate or muddle his plans by posting a demand he return home.

"I had thought a few moments ago that we still shared the same sentiments, Suzette. My confession of love to you is quite real, and you have confessed to me that your heart remains mine. Why must you deny me?" His face flashed his disappointment. "I only want to see him, and then I'll return to England. Will that make you happy?"

Suzette appeared to struggle over his plea, and Robert prayed inwardly she would relent.

"All right," she finally responded. "If Philippe finds out, though, I shall pay for it dearly."

"He need not know. I'm sure you can counsel little Robert into some deception, since he already played along with his stepfather in the ruse of telling me that you had passed away."

"How awful I must seem to you, Robert—a liar, deceiver, and thief, for that matter."

"And I to you, Suzette—a manipulative man who would do anything to be with the woman he loves and the son she bore him. I'm not without my own faults."

Robert pulled her toward his body and tenderly embraced her once again. It felt glorious to have her in his arms, but disappointment shrouded his heart. He had set his expectations far too lofty, believing their reunion would be far more glorious than it had been.

Since the day they parted, he had fantasized about Suzette, worshipped her in his dreams, and longed for her in his soul. Their moments together were strained and emotional. A future together seemed impossible. Why had he pursued it thus far? Robert questioned his wisdom. Perhaps he should not have involved himself in her life again. It was underhanded, but he could not turn away from pursuing the truth about his son.

"I should be going home. The staff will worry over my delayed absence."

Robert released her from his embrace. "Yes, of course, I understand."

"I was thinking, Robert, that perhaps we can arrange to meet in the gardens for a walk. We could make the encounter look innocent enough by bumping into each other. I do not think little Robert would see it as something planned or worth mentioning to Philippe upon his return. Would that suffice?"

"Yes," he enthusiastically replied, with a broad smile on his face. "When shall we meet?"

"Would 11 o'clock tomorrow morning be agreeable?"

"I'll be there. I'll walk through the west entrance toward the fountain and shall look for you there."

"Your son loves the fountain, so I'm sure he'll be delighted." A warm smile spread across Suzette's face.

Robert relished the moment. He would see her again and spend time with his son. The thought thrilled his soul to think that soon he would look upon the lad once more and know that the boy belonged to him. He had an heir.

The carriage returned, and Robert accompanied Suzette back to her residence. As she climbed down with the help of the driver, he looked upon her with love. Abruptly, the front door to her residence swung open, and a man stood in the entranceway. His face appeared delighted over the return of Suzette, and Robert surmised it must be the butler.

The man glanced curiously at the carriage. Robert hastily grabbed the door and slammed it shut. He sat back in his seat, hopefully unnoticed. Tomorrow he would see Suzette again and gaze upon his son. Joy flooded his soul.

Chapter 15

"Madame, we were quite worried about you!" exclaimed Monsieur Leroy, as he held open the door.

"You shouldn't have been," Suzette replied, with a slight hint of irritation. She heard the carriage behind her leave, but did not turn around, afraid she'd cause undue suspicion. "I was fine. It just took me a bit longer when I got caught in the downpour of rain."

"Yes, it was coming down quite hard," he agreed. Before he closed the door completely, he glanced at the departing growler. "You seemed to have found shelter," he added.

"I did, as a matter of fact." She said nothing more to continue the conversation and turned around to walk upstairs. "I'll be in my room. You can tell the cook I'm not hungry for lunch today. Just make sure Robert eats."

"Of course," he replied.

Suzette briskly climbed the stairs and headed toward her bedchamber. She couldn't wait to lock herself behind a closed door and release the repressed emotions about to burst from her soul. Suzette pulled her shawl off her shoulders and flung it over the back of a chair. She fiddled with the pins of her hat until they finally released their secure hold in the braids of her hair.

For a brief moment, she didn't know what to do. After eyeing the bed that seemed to invite her arrival, she walked over to it and sat on the edge. Suzette noticed a lingering tremor in her body movements from the shock of seeing Robert. She swung her legs onto the bed and laid her head on the pillow. Her hand shook when she brought the back of it up to her forehead and covered her eyes. As soon as she did, her mind sank into an ambiance of memories.

She could not believe her eyes when she had spun around and saw Robert only a few yards away. There had been a repressed hope in the back of her mind that one day he would find her alive. Suzette did not realize how unprepared for such an event she had been, until that moment. The sight of him sent a rush through her veins like hot oil. She felt her body weaken in his presence, and thankfully he had rushed to her side to help her remain upright. Robert—the man she had loved more than life itself—had returned.

Suzette could not be sure that her decision to follow him to his residence had been the right choice. What if someone had seen them enter into the empty townhouse hand in hand? How inappropriate the entire course of action had been, but she wanted to speak with him too. The cemetery did accentuate the thought of death, and leaving the morbid surroundings had been the right choice.

"Oh, Robert," she longingly breathed his name.

He had changed in appearance and demeanor. His face appeared fuller, and the young man who had rescued her had turned into a responsible duke. The burdens of his duties were clearly etched in the lines of his expression, as well as his personal unhappiness.

Though he had lied to her about his marriage after its occurrence, she had somehow always pictured them as a happy couple. Never once did she consider any misery on his part. His wife, in her eyes, had been the luckiest woman in the world to have captured his hand in marriage. Had it all been just a matter of convenience, as he stated? If that were the case, Suzette could only mourn over his misery. His declaration of undying love had been spoken with such conviction, that Suzette could not deny he meant every word.

She turned over on her side and hugged a pillow. When she did so, she thought of her marriage bed. Philippe had always shared her bed, unlike others who slept in separate rooms. She struggled to find in her heart the love he deserved from her as his wife.

When she married him, she did so to save her reputation. Even though he forgave her, Suzette's heart still belonged to Robert. As the years passed, she thought she had put that all aside and would grow to love Philippe once again. However, no love bloomed—only gratefulness. She constantly compared the two, and each time, Philippe came up wanting.

Suzette realized that as a young woman she'd merely had a crush upon him. He looked so handsome in his uniform when he had joined the French Navy and had left to make his livelihood. Like a fairytale story, Suzette had thought of him as her prince charming. The fact of the matter remained, after maturing through her own struggles, they really had nothing in common.

The contemplation of Philippe's lovemaking turned her head from the pillow and back to the ceiling. He always sought his own physical release and not her pleasure. How often had she looked at the fabric overhead in their canopy bed? She fixated upon it until he released his seed. Did he ever consider that she would appreciate anything in return? Robert always had her interests at heart before his own.

Suzette closed her eyes and breathed in and out slowly, trying to make sense of everything that had transpired. Her thoughts were suddenly interrupted by a persistent knock at the door.

"Mommy, are you in there?"

"Just a minute," she called out, as she climbed out of bed and walked over to the door to greet her son.

"Mommy, you're home!"

"Yes, I'm home, sweetie," she replied. Suzette stroked the top of his head with the palm of her hand. "I'm glad you came to see me, because I have an idea I want to share with you."

"What is it?"

"How would you like to go for a walk, with just me tomorrow, to the gardens and see the fountains? Since spring is here, they have turned them on and the water is splashing high into the air. Would that be fun?"

Robert's eyes grew round as saucers, and a boyish grin spread across his face.

"Can we go today, instead?"

"No, not today. Mommy is tired, but I promise tomorrow in the morning after breakfast, we'll take a walk to the gardens—just you and me."

"Let's bring bread too, so we can feed the ducks. Daddy always does and that's fun. I like to feed the ducks."

"Of course," Suzette smiled, "we will bring some bread. Now, you go along and tell Madame Dubois to make sure you have some lunch. Mommy isn't going to eat today. She's feeling a little tired."

Suzette gave him a kiss and sent him on his way. The remainder of the day she spent counting the hours before her secret rendezvous.

❋ ❋ ❋

Antsy over the morning meeting with his son, Robert found it impossible to sleep the night before. Giles had provided ample spirits to ease him to sleep, and he even suggested a trip to the brothel for relaxation. Robert would have none of it. The thought of another's bed distressed him, as he once again felt bound to Suzette in some kind of ritual of fidelity. Instead, he lay in bed tormented by the past and an uncertain future. His body grew fatigued, but his troubled mind refused to rest.

When morning finally arrived, he hurried to the entrance of the gardens well before the meeting time. He had wanted to stop at a toy store and buy the young lad something as a token of his affection, but restrained himself from doing so. The encounter had to occur by chance and not look planned. Perhaps, next time it wouldn't appear inappropriate if he brought a small token of his fondness.

He wondered if Robert would recognize him from their previous encounter. Convinced he probably would not, his thoughts turned to his rash promise to Suzette. He really had no intention of returning to England after seeing the boy. How could he possibly meet the lad once and then leave him behind?

As the hour neared, Robert strolled around the fountain several times. The rainy weather had passed, and a glorious sunny day arrived in its place. The sun's rays danced off the fountain, and its cascading water looked like a thousand stunning diamonds sprinkled from Heaven. The slight breeze sent a misty spray on Robert's face when he walked in front of the fountain at a certain angle.

Robert counted each time he circled, and when he had reached the eighth round, he finally saw Suzette approaching with his son. They strolled together holding hands. She was dressed in a stunning dark green gown, with a matching feathered hat, which blended well with the garden and the flowering plants. Robert thought she looked like an entrancing fairy in the woods. The sunshine danced off her auburn tresses, and he wished to run toward them and scoop each into his arms.

Finally, she approached and stopped. He took off his top hat and greeted the couple. "Madame, what a surprise it is to see you!"

When he looked at the two of them, Robert realized the culmination of his dreams. There before him stood Suzette and his son, who for all rights and purposes, were his family. The sight burned into his heart like an etched picture—a masterpiece of fulfillment.

"Why, Monsieur Holland, it is good to see you," Suzette responded with a sparkle in her eye. "May I introduce you to my son, Robert."

"Very nice to meet you, young man." Robert offered his hand. His son didn't immediately respond. Instead, he looked up at Suzette.

"It's all right, Robert. The polite thing to do is to shake the monsieur's hand in return."

Robert smiled and grabbed his son's hand, shaking it heartily up and down. When their flesh touched, it took considerable restraint for Robert not to cry. He had never experienced such completeness in his entire life. His earnest longing for a child had been fulfilled. Robert held his own flesh and blood within his hand, and the heir to his name and fortune.

"Didn't I meet you once?" Little Robert asked with a confused look upon his face.

"I think you did, young man. You were with your father, and I was with my wife."

"Oh, yeah," he blurted out in return. "Now I remember Daddy said Mommy passed away, but she's here now."

"Yes, indeed, she's here now." Robert looked at Suzette with a comical grin. She merely nodded in response. As much as he hated to do so, he let go of Robert's hand and stood upright.

"I was just taking a walk. Would you and your son care to walk with me?"

"Yes, of course, I don't think my son would mind."

Little Robert grasped Suzette's hand again and then reached over and put his hand into Robert's palm. "We can all walk together," he said, innocently.

Robert knew then he had reached the pinnacle of life. The three of them strolled down the pathway through the gardens holding hands. He had tasted Heaven itself.

"So, Robert, what are your favorite things to do? Do you ride?"

"You mean ride a horsey?"

"Yes, a horse."

"No. We have none. Do you have horses?" His quizzical head and eyes tilted up toward Robert.

"Why yes, I do, in fact. I have a very nice pony that would do well for a young lad like yourself."

"Well, I don't think little Robert will be riding any time soon," interjected Suzette, with a slightly annoyed look in her eyes. "We have no place to keep a horse, Monsieur Holland."

Robert hadn't entertained that thought as he merely envisioned his son riding the pony next to him at his estate.

"Are there other things you like to do?" Robert asked, changing the subject for Suzette's sake.

"I like blocks. I like to build with blocks. Daddy plays with me, and we build castles and forts and all sorts of things."

"Well, that sounds like fun," he replied, with little enthusiasm. Robert didn't care to know what Philippe did with the boy. His son's upbringing had been in the hands of his rival, which infuriated Robert.

"Robert, do you want to walk over to the lake and feed the ducks?" Suzette asked as they neared a body of water.

"Yes, Mama, can I have the bread?"

"Sure, sweetheart, just be careful and stay away from the edge of the lake." She handed him a small paper bag.

Robert ran up ahead and stopped. As soon as he tossed pieces of bread into the water, ducks congregated in front of him.

The ducks quacked, and Robert quacked in return. His father chuckled at the simple-minded joy that a child could

vorld. The innocence of life, and all that was n the universe, was embodied in the small ined himself by the water's edge.

already," Robert confessed. He stood and y move with adoration. "He's a fine young Suzette. He's our son!"

Robert repeated the words again and allowed the reality to sink into his soul. He was not childless after all. All of his prayers had been answered in the form of a five-year-old boy, who quacked like a duck a few feet away.

"I want us to be a family, Suzette. You, me, and Robert. I want it more than the air I breathe."

"You shouldn't say such things!"

"Why not? Cannot a man dream to comfort himself for his losses?" He reached over and touched Suzette's hand gently, but did not grasp it for fear others would see. "I love you, Suzette. Last night I didn't sleep a wink thinking of our predicament and planning for our future. I beg you to tell me that you want a future with me."

"You're being irrational, Robert Holland. There is no future for us. I am married. I also have a daughter. Have you forgotten that? Is she also to be part of our family?"

Robert hadn't considered the baby that she had borne to Philippe. Why did she have to defy him and dash his hopes?

"No, I haven't forgotten you have a baby," came his words of disappointment. "If you love me, Suzette, then tell me you wish for a future together. I have no idea how, but do not deny my hunger for such a life, or I shall surely die for want. I cannot bear such an anguished thought of not living the remainder of my days with you and our boy."

"You must bear it," Suzette replied in resignation. "I do not dream any longer, Robert. I take what comes my way and pray for grace to endure my sorrows." She turned and looked at him with forlorn.

"If I could, I would leave with you this very moment to

begin our lives together. But I have a daughter and a husband; and you a wife and duty. We must find comfort that we shall always be bound together as one in Robert, though we must remain apart from one another. That must be our solace alone for his sake and that of my daughter. Don't you see that?"

Robert's joyful countenance faded over Suzette's insistent thoughts of doing the right thing. "No, I do not see it," he sputtered in exasperation. He pulled his eyes away from her gaze and placed them back on his son.

"You can be assured as the sun rises and sets every day that I shall not rest until I find a way to bring us together as a family. I swear to you upon my honor that we shall be husband and wife, raising Robert together."

"I don't understand you," she replied, painfully. "Is it not enough for you to know my love? I cannot give you anything more."

Suzette stepped briskly away and walked to her son's side at the lake's edge. She pulled a piece of bread from the bag, and began to tear it, angrily tossing pieces into the water. Robert stood and watched. Her staunch refusal to believe in a possible future together broke his heart.

He stepped up next to her while she flung the crumbs into the lake. Every duck within a mile radius seemed to have arrived for the free feeding. Little Robert giggled over the noisy quacks. As Robert glanced over at Suzette, he saw a tear trickle down her cheek. He touched her arm gently, and she turned and looked at him.

"Years ago, I would have gladly married you Robert Holland," she whispered. "You were the love of my life, but you chose another. Now, you wish to bring me back into your life when I belong to another? You torment me," she cried. Suzette turned her face away, so her son would not see her tears.

"I'm afraid to believe, Robert. I cannot bear the disappointment of losing you once again to circumstances I have no control over. Please understand," she pleaded.

"Mommy, can we go now?" Little Robert tugged on her sleeve, and Suzette sniffed a few times. She pulled out her hankie and quickly wiped her nose.

"Are you tired, sweetie?"

"All the bread is gone," he pouted.

"Okay, then in a minute. Mommy needs to say goodbye to Monsieur Holland. Do you wish to say goodbye?"

"Goodbye," he quickly responded, with little interest in any further interaction. He tugged on his mother's sleeve again.

"It seems I have a little boy who wishes to go now."

Robert knelt down in front of his son on one knee and looked him straight in the eye. "It was nice to see you again, and you remember if you ever come visit me, there's a little pony waiting just for you." He stood up and looked at Suzette who gave him another disapproving glare.

"Will you return to England now?" she quickly queried.

Robert peered soulfully into her eyes. "Not yet. I am not ready to leave my family."

He tipped his hat. "It was nice seeing you again, Mademoiselle. Perhaps another time we shall see each other again. Good day."

Robert turned away and strode toward the exit of the gardens. His heart lay within his chest like a heavy stone. It felt dreadful to leave behind all he loved. He had searched for truth and had finally found it. If he could just seal it with Suzette and his son, he'd be satisfied. Whatever the cost to fulfill his dreams, he would gladly pay.

Chapter 16

Suzette left the park with little Robert and hired a cab to return them to her residence. His little face appeared somber, and Suzette found it troublesome.

"Did you have fun?" She reached over and patted his knee.

"Yes, but next time we need to bring more bread. Daddy brings a lot more than you did," he retorted, with a scowl.

"Well, I'm sorry. I didn't know, since it's always you and your father . . ." Suzette stopped mid-sentence and gasped. The remainder of her words wouldn't come out of her mouth. The declaration of *father* resonated so powerfully, that immediately she saw Robert's face and not Philippe's. "Oh, dear," she mumbled, as she looked at her son.

"It was nice to bump into Monsieur Holland, don't you think?" Suzette felt the urge to pry into Robert's thoughts about their meeting.

"I suppose so." A gigantic smile spread across his face. "I like that he has a pony. Do you think we could visit him some day so I can ride the pony, Mommy?"

"I don't know, Robert. He lives very far away in England and only occasionally visits Paris."

"Oh," he replied, sadly. His smile faded. Robert turned his interest to the passing scenery. Suzette heaved a sigh, thankful he asked no more. She had no idea why Robert had seen fit to bring up the subject of a pony to tease a little boy's fancy. *He probably just wanted to impress him*, she thought to herself, while she mindlessly straightened her skirt.

"He has blond hair and blue eyes like me," Robert suddenly announced.

His comment astounded Suzette. How could a little boy his age make such an association? She hesitated to respond over his observation, but then made little of it. "Many people have blond hair and blue eyes, Robert."

Suzette sat back against her seat and closed her eyes. Her hands twisted her gloves in worry over what little thoughts twirled inside the brain of a five-year-old child. Surely, the boy had to be too young to put two and two together.

She felt the cab slow and opened her eyelids. The horse halted, and the driver jumped down and opened the door. Suzette and Robert climbed from the cab, and she paid the fare. After they entered the foyer, Robert immediately ran upstairs to his room.

"Madame, I trust you had a pleasant stroll in the gardens," inquired Monsieur Leroy.

"Yes, quite pleasant, thank you." Suzette unpinned her hat and gave it to the maid, along with her gloves.

"A post arrived for you while you were gone," he informed Suzette, holding out a sealed envelope for her taking.

Suzette immediately grasped it and noted that it had been posted from the West Indies. "My goodness, it's from Philippe!" She took the envelope and walked into the parlor, sat down, and ripped it open to read the letter.

My Dearest Suzette,

I have just this day set foot on the isle of Antigua and make haste to write you this letter to let you know that I have safely arrived. It is my intention to post this directly, so that it might reach Paris within the next few weeks.

Please rest assured that I am fine. My meetings at the sugarcane plantation will begin soon. Hopefully, I will be able to procure the deal quickly and return home within a month.

It is quite beautiful here, Suzette. Warm and humid, and the palm trees are indeed quite out of the ordinary to behold. I wish you could see the beauty of the isle.

All my love,

Philippe

Suzette heaved a sigh of relief and folded the letter carefully, inserting it back into the envelope. Palm trees—how odd to think of such exotic plants. She smiled and held the letter in her hand thinking of her husband and their life together.

As her mind wandered through the years they had spent together as husband and wife, she heard a loud thump from upstairs. Instantly, a baby's piercing cry echoed throughout the entire house. Suzette jumped to her feet. The letter dropped on the floor. She stepped upon it when she exited the room and flew up the staircase to the nursery. Abruptly, she halted in the doorway and observed in horror the bassinet laying on its side. Angelique wailed in the arms of her governess.

"What happened here?" she challenged Madame Dubois. Out of the corner of her eye, she saw Robert laughing out loud.

"Your son pushed over the bassinet. Angelique was taking a nap. I left the room just for a moment, returned, and saw him push it over. Unfortunately, I was too far away to catch the poor baby before she tumbled to the floor."

"My God!" Suzette exclaimed in shock. She ran to her daughter and snatched the screaming baby into her arms. Suzette kissed her cheek. "Now, now, sweetheart. It's all right. Mommy is here."

She looked at Robert and glared at him in anger. "Is this true? Did you push the bassinet over?"

To her chagrin, Robert laughed but said nothing. Abruptly, he turned around, ran out the door, and down the hallway. Suzette, shocked over his actions, looked at Angelique. She smoothed her hand over the baby's head and face, but saw no bruising or bumps. Thankfully, the bassinet tumbled upon a thick rug.

"Thank God, she appears to be all right." She hugged her tight and rocked her in her arms. "Shush, little one." After the wailing subsided, Suzette handed her daughter back to Madame Dubois.

"Please, take her, while I take care of something."

Suzette quickly made her way down the hallway to Robert's room. He sat hunched over in the middle of the floor surrounded by his blocks.

"Robert, come here."

He ignored her.

"I said come to me, little man. We need to talk."

Robert, unresponsive to her demands, continued to play, wearing a smirk across his face. Suzette walked over to him and jerked him to his feet. She led him toward his bed, while he resisted and struggled to get away.

Exasperated over his antics, she bent over, picked him up in her arms, and sat him down on the bed. She tried to peer into his blue eyes, but he refused to look at her in the face. His actions pushed her to the end of her patience. Suzette grasped his chin with the palm of her hand and forcibly pulled it upward until they were eye to eye.

"Whatever possessed you to push over that bassinet? I want to know, and I want an answer now!"

Robert narrowed his eyes at her in defiance. He flaunted a smug, rebellious look upon his face. "Because I hate her!"

Surprised over his declaration, Suzette released his chin

from her hand. She knew sibling rivalry could pose problems, but she had no idea that it would raise its ugly head this early.

"Well, you have no reason to hate her. She's your sister, Robert, and you need to treat her with love."

"I do not!" he bellowed, as he crossed his arms in front of him. "Daddy likes her more than me, and I hate her!"

"Daddy does no such thing," she insisted, appalled over his statement. "Your father loves you very deeply."

A defiant "*humph*" left his lips. Suzette made her demands.

"I expect you to walk down to your sister's room and apologize immediately to Madame Dubois and to your sister for what you did."

"No!" He jumped to his feet and ran out of his room.

"Robert, come back here this instant!" Suzette took off after him, but his young legs had already taken him down the staircase. She watched him fly off toward the rear of the residence and out into their small courtyard.

At a loss over Robert's unexpected behavior, she decided to let him calm down before approaching him again about his brash actions. Suzette understood how a young boy could construe a newborn as a threat to his attention. Every young child feels jealousy when a new baby enters the family, she concluded.

It bothered her deeply that her son felt Philippe loved Angelique more. She had never seen Philippe be anything but kind to Robert. He had always shown such love for him in her presence.

Suzette walked back to the nursery and found Madame Dubois in a rocking chair soothing Angelique. "I asked Robert to apologize to you, but he seems to have run off. I'm sure he'll come around."

"Madame, I should have said something to you before, but this is not the first time I've caught the little boy being somewhat gruff with his new sister."

"What do you mean this is not the first time?"

"Well, there have been other instances where he's poked and pinched Angelique. I hadn't thought very much of it and reprimanded his behavior at the time. Children do tend to struggle with jealousy issues when a newborn arrives in the household."

"That disturbs me," Suzette admitted. "I wish you would have told me this beforehand, so I could have dealt with this sooner."

"I apologize, Madame Moreau—an oversight on my part. I assure you that should it happen again, I will tell you straightaway."

"Please do," Suzette replied, in a miffed tone.

She walked downstairs and found Robert, as she suspected, playing in their courtyard uncaring that he had done anything wrong. His attitude saddened Suzette. The young life developing before her had certain personality traits that she worried about often. Where had they come from? Certainly not from her or her even-tempered father. Robert never displayed such anger in her presence either, except for the time he kicked in the door to save her at the Chabanais.

Whatever force drove her son, now throwing rocks in their garden, would need to be dealt with posthaste. Perhaps when Philippe returned home, he would put down a more stern hand and watch Robert more closely. Her son's accusation that Philippe loved Angelique more than him, resonated uncomfortably in Suzette's mind.

She walked to the parlor, but not before asking her maid to brew a steaming cup of tea. As she entered, she found Philippe's letter on the floor. Suzette picked it up and held it in her hand. Everything in her life was being challenged, from her marriage to her children. Exhausted and confused, she flopped down upon the settee.

Robert clearly wanted more than Suzette believed achievable. How could she consider the possibility of divorce? She had a newborn in the nursery. Philippe would never allow her to take the child, nor would the courts grant her custody.

"Oh, the situation is impossible!" she moaned aloud.

"Madame Moreau, your tea."

The maid stood in the doorway with a clear expression of surprise written across her face. Suzette felt a hot flush run up her neck. Clearly embarrassed that her verbalization was heard by one of the staff, she quickly apologized.

"Forgive me."

"Will there be anything else you require?"

"No, that is all." Her maid exited the room, and Suzette felt exposed and ashamed.

She took a sip of tea and tried to relax, her mind filled with thoughts. Robert had departed the park without asking for another meeting. She had no idea what hotel he resided, nor whether he would stay in Paris or return to England. His departing words were troubling. *"Not yet. I'm not ready to leave my family."*

Her emotional bonds between two men pulled at her soul until she felt it would rip her apart. She owed so much to Philippe, yet she owed so much to Robert! In the beginning, all she ever wanted was to be was his wife. After she vowed to be the wife of another man, those dreams perished.

Robert, with his persistent tug upon her heart, had resurrected the love she held for him. She believed it foolish to think they could ever have a life together. What horrible heartbreak would they all suffer?

It's far too selfish of us to pursue our own desires at the price of others, she thought.

A knock came at the parlor door, and her butler entered with an envelope in hand.

"Madame, this just arrived by courier," he announced.

Suzette stood to her feet, worried terrible news arrived from Philippe.

"From whom?" She snatched it from his hand. No return address had been penned in the upper left-hand corner, but Suzette recognized the handwriting immediately.

"Oh, an old friend." She dismissed the sense of urgency as if it were nothing. "No doubt an invitation for lunch." She folded the letter in her hand and discharged her butler. "Thank you, Monsieur Leroy. That will be all."

She waited for him to leave, and quickly closed the door for privacy. Suzette broke the seal and ripped the envelope when she pulled out the letter in Robert's handwriting.

My Suzette,

I cannot tell you the joy that my heart contains having spent time with my son. You must know how deeply touched and moved I am over the life we created out of our love.

Though I must return to England in the near future, I cannot and will not depart without seeing you again. We have much to speak of in regard to our son and future. Do not deny me the exhilaration of being with you once more—I beg you.

On Wednesday morrow, I shall send a private growler to pick you up at your residence. Please, my love, find it in your heart to take the carriage where it will lead you.

I only ask you to believe, Suzette. Just believe.

I am forever yours,

Robert

Suzette's eyes filled with tears as she read his closing. He would not give her up—not now, not ever.

"Oh, Robert, what have you done? I cannot deny you have stolen my heart. God forgive me for loving you."

❋ ❋ ❋

Jacquelyn, impatient and aggravated, waited for the

return of her husband. To pass the time, she had involved herself in redecorating the dining room at his suggestion. However, her heart wasn't into the project. Nevertheless, the wallpaper did need replacement. The pattern had always grated upon her nerves, but not as much as her current situation.

While they held up samples to the wall, she finally spewed out her frustration to her mother-in-law.

"I don't understand why he hasn't returned," Jacquelyn shrieked. "What could he possibly be doing for the past four weeks in Paris? I thought this was supposed to be a quick trip."

She slammed down the sample on the table and started to pace back and forth the length of the dining room.

"You know how he is, Jacquelyn, always busy with the Frenchmen that take him to the casinos and theatre. I had hoped my son would shake off these desires to play, but he seems to be digressing from his duties again. I'm very sorry."

She spun around and glared at Robert's mother. "Don't patronize me, Mary. You know very well you can add to that list brothels, cabarets, and God knows what else. It's a wonder I haven't caught some dastardly disease from all the beds he's visited."

Mary gasped in dismay over her daughter-in-law's scandalous comment. "Jacquelyn, control your tongue! We shouldn't speak of such horrid acts that only happen to those who frequent the gutters of Paris society. I'm quite sure Robert would do no such thing!"

Jacquelyn airily flipped her hand. "You defend him, but you haven't smelled the exotic perfume on his shirts, as I have, after he's returned from a night out with his Parisian friends. I'm no fool. He strays from our marriage bed, while I'm relegated to live here in this cold, damp estate until I've redecorated every room within its walls!" Her chest heaved with anger. "I'm tired of it, Mary. Tired!"

"My dear," she protested. "I implore you not to say such

things."

Jacquelyn ignored her plea and stormed off, determined to take matters into her own hands. It had been exactly one month since Robert left and not a word of his whereabouts or when he would return had arrived by post. He had effectively cut her off, once again, to pursue his pleasures. Jacquelyn would have no more of it.

As she stormed up the staircase to her bedchamber, she screamed for Dorcas.

"Yes, my lady?"

"Get the footman to deliver a trunk to my room immediately. We're packing for Paris."

"Yes, ma'am," she complied, with a hurried curtsy as she left the room. If Robert would not come to her, she would go to him. One way or the other, she'd expose his treachery. Her ranting stirred the entire household, and Mary soon came to her door to investigate the ruckus.

"What are you doing, Jacquelyn?"

"What does it look like I'm doing? I'm going to Paris."

"You cannot do this," she vehemently protested. "Robert will not approve of your traveling alone and showing up unannounced. Have you lost your senses?"

"Indeed, I have." Her words were laced with an ominous air that she knew would alarm her mother-in-law. She picked up a note on the nearby nightstand and shoved it into Mary's hand.

"Read this. It's from our head housekeeper in Paris. I wrote to check on Robert. Apparently, my dear husband is not even staying at our townhouse. She has not heard or seen him, and as far as she is aware, our residence is closed for the season. What do you make of that?"

"How strange indeed," Mary replied, confounded by the revelation. "Perhaps he is not in Paris because he has traveled elsewhere on business. That is possible."

"Rubbish. He's up to something, and I damn well intend to find out what it is."

"Jacquelyn, please, do not do this. It's inappropriate behavior for a duchess to go traipsing from country to country to search out her husband's whereabouts. You must remind yourself of your place in society. How will this look?"

Angered over Mary's scolding, she glared at her wide-eyed. "Just because you accepted your dead husband's mistresses as a way of life, do not expect me to do the same. I will not be treated in such a despicable fashion by Robert. He already has denied me a child. To hell with you, and to hell with him. Now get out while I pack," she hissed through her teeth.

Mary backed out of the room, with a frightened look upon her face, and Jacquelyn turned toward Dorcas.

"Where in the hell is that trunk?" she demanded. Intent on arriving in Paris by the end of the week, she gruffly pulled dresses out of her armoire and threw them on her bed for Dorcas to pack. After she had finished, she turned and glanced at the dresser and her jewelry box. For a moment, Jacquelyn stood thinking of the wealth of diamonds, rubies, and sapphires that had been given to her as family heirlooms.

Thoughtfully, she walked over to the box filled with riches and began picking out the most expensive items. "One never knows when I might need some cash," she mused aloud. While her mind mulled over various ways to punish Robert Holland, a wicked smile spread across her face.

Chapter 17

Suzette agonized over whether to accept the carriage that Robert would send to pick her up. She struggled over the moral rights and wrongs of succumbing to temptation. Prayer did nothing to dissuade her, because she soon learned her flesh ruled stronger than her spirit. Robert had succeeded in awakening the intense desire she always held for him as a man. She could no longer resist and yearned to see him again.

Without a second thought, the day the transport arrived, Suzette climbed inside. When the horses began trotting down the street, she knew their destination headed for Robert's empty townhouse. When they slowly pulled to the back of the residence and stopped, her stomach churned into a ball of nerves. The driver jumped down, opened the door, and waited for her to exit. At first, she stayed seated and stared at the servants' entrance. Robert stood waiting in the threshold.

"Madame, are you getting out?"

"Oh, yes, I'm sorry."

Suzette exited. A moment later, the driver urged the team of horses down the alleyway leaving her to stand alone. Her hesitation continued, and then she guardedly stepped toward the gate. Robert came forward to greet her. "Tell me that no one will see us here, Robert," she pleaded, while glancing around at the surrounding homes.

"It's fine, Suzette. I've checked. My neighbors are away, my servants are on leave, and we are alone and safe."

"But we are taking such risks," she protested.

"Stop worrying," he assured her, as he took her hand and led her inside. He closed the door and locked it, then escorted her toward the parlor. They entered, and Suzette couldn't believe how many bouquets of lilies adorned the interior.

"You're a stinker," she teased. "You remembered."

Robert laughed. "Of course, I remembered. I've not forgotten one moment of our time together or the things that bring you pleasure."

Suzette walked over to a bouquet and bent down to inhale the fragrance. Afterward, she glanced around the room. Robert had removed the coverings from the furniture and brought the room to life with electric lights. A bottle of chilled wine sat in a bucket of ice and two crystal glasses stood nearby.

"Do you plan on loosening me up?" she jested, in a carefree tone. "You know, I don't handle alcohol well."

"As if wine alone could do the trick." He uncorked the bottle and poured two glasses of Merlot. Robert handed Suzette a glass and grasped her free hand, leading her to the divan.

"Sit and relax. You remind me of the first night we met at the brothel."

Suzette obeyed and made herself comfortable.

"You can remove your hat." Robert reached over and pulled out a hatpin, loosening its secure hold upon her hair.

"Robert!" she giggled. Suzette released the second hatpin and then set her hat down on the arm of the divan.

"Finally," he said. His ran his slender finger through the strands of her hair. "I so missed the color of your hair and its scent of perfume."

Suzette looked at him and pondered curiously. Finally,

she asked a question, which had plagued her since he had come back into her life.

"Do you still go?"

"Go where?"

"The brothel."

"Good Lord, I have not set foot inside the door of the Chabanais since the day I took you away. I told Madame Laurent I wouldn't be back; and I haven't."

"I often think about where I would be today if you hadn't rescued me, Robert. I'd probably still be there, selling my body to survive. I will never be able to repay you for your kindness."

"But you did repay me," he said, with his heart bursting in adoration. He looked at her hands and then gathered them into his own.

"Don't you remember?"

"What do you mean?"

"You gave me your virginity, sweetheart. At that moment, I truly believe our souls were knit together."

Suzette shook her head. "You're such a romantic and idealistic man, Robert."

"Don't make light of it," he begged. "You have no idea how consumed my life has been with regret. Now that we are together, even for a brief moment, and I count each passing second as a precious gift."

Suzette's smiled faded. She had jested and made light of Robert's feelings, but she knew she had done so to conceal her own. He asked her to release her heart back into his hands to do with as he pleased, but their lives were bound to others.

"Robert . . ." She grasped his hand tightly in return, "I'm sorry for making light of your love."

As soon as the words fell from her mouth, Robert swooped upon her with ardent kisses to catch her apology between his lips. Suzette clung to her glass and tried to keep the sloshing wine from spilling. He pulled back, retrieved her wine, and set it down next to his.

"Now you have two hands," he said, breathing heavily along her neckline. "Use them."

Suzette felt the warmth of his love flow through her body like an intoxicating drug. His touch awakened the buried passion in her body to such an extent, that Suzette felt her consciousness flow into a blissful state she had forgotten existed. His hands felt like fire upon her flesh. Robert's kisses tasted sublime, and his passion for her body aroused her own aching need.

The realization of where they were headed increased her heartbeat tenfold. She couldn't breathe. Their appetite would soon drive them into the sin of adultery. Suzette wondered if that had been Robert's purpose in bringing her to his townhouse.

His cunning plan to send Philippe away and weaken her resolve for sexual pleasure all made sense. Robert Holland planned to seduce her and take her to the brink of social ruin to make her his own. Suzette choked. She couldn't allow herself to cross the forbidden path.

"Robert," she cried, as she pushed herself away from his chest. "Please, we can't. I told you that I would not be your mistress."

Robert ceased his kisses and caught his breath. His adoring face turned from delight to distraught in a matter of seconds.

"I don't want you to be my mistress, Suzette. I want you as my wife."

"But the road to that end frightens me, Robert. Must I be brought to ruin to attain that position?"

Suzette gasped for air as her throat continued to close with emotion. Her body tingled from Robert's touch, while her soul questioned her principles of right and wrong.

"My love. My sweet, sweet love," Robert whispered. "My heart is in anguish. I do not want to seduce you for my selfish pursuits. I only wish to pour my heart into your spirit and my expression of love into your body."

Robert's frame trembled next to her own. Suzette feared the consequences of relenting to his heartfelt entreaty.

"Do you truly think that our love will only bring you ruin?"

"No," she answered thoughtfully. "No."

Robert slipped the palm of his hand around the back of her neck and drew her back into his lips. As soon as their flesh touched, Suzette's resolve melted like the winter's snow. Her cold fears turned into heated desire. She grew weak as Robert's mouth searched out the depth they had once shared. The ache for his body intensified, and Suzette shuddered while in his embrace.

He stood to his feet, scooped her up in his strong arms, like he had done so many times in the past, and took her up the stairs to his bedchamber.

"Take me," she pleaded. "Take me and let us be one again. I shall be damned for doing so." She rested her head against his shoulder. He took each step up the staircase with determined resolve.

"No one will be damned, my love. Our lives were meant to be one. You'll see. Let us do away with our past regret and mistakes."

He opened the door to a massive suite and walked toward the canopy bed draped in rich maroon material. He set her down on her feet and then assaulted the buttons of her dress. Hastily, he loosened each one and then pulled it down over her shoulders.

Stripped to her undergarments, Suzette turned around to face him. His hand gently fondled her breast through the fabric. Suzette moaned and began shedding herself of her remaining clothes. Robert fingered the laces of her corset and pulled each string through the eyelets until they released the prize underneath.

"This is unfair," she giggled. "You're still dressed."

"Well, do something about it," he teased, as he cupped her breast in the palm of his hand and kissed her.

Suzette felt new life flow through her veins. Her hand pushed off his jacket from his shoulders, her fingers untied his ascot and pulled it off his neck. The buttons of his vest and linen shirt released, and Suzette pushed his clothes away from his firm chest, dragging them down his arms.

Robert could endure the foreplay no longer. He embraced her naked body and lifted it to the bed. Hurriedly, he opened his trousers, released his erection, and lay on top of her with a hunger that needed satisfaction. Suzette spread her legs apart and received him into her body once again.

The feverish moans and cries between two lovers filled the room. Robert had never experienced such passion in the body of a female before. The moment was more than a heated encounter between a man and a woman; it was a reunion of souls and a melding together as one.

Suzette cried her words of love repeatedly, and Robert relished in her confessions. His thrusts of tender love continued until he heard her cries of satisfaction, and then he achieved his own bursting from his loins.

When they had expended their ecstasy in groans and a flurry of wet kisses, the two lay in each other's arms wrapped in blending of entwined limbs.

Their breathing slowed, and finally they lay side by side alone in their thoughts of what had transpired between them. Robert kissed Suzette. She clung tightly to him, coming to terms with the guilt of her unfaithfulness.

"We will pay a price for this, Robert. It was glorious, but our infidelity will cost us dearly."

"Let us hope not, my love. Let us hope all will work in our favor."

Suzette could not think of the consequences. She pushed the thought away, laid her head on Robert's shoulder, and fell asleep. He held her tightly in return and drifted off into a world of satisfied bliss.

❋ ❋ ❋

Since their indiscreet reunion, Suzette had accepted the inevitable. No longer did she fight the inappropriateness of their relationship. She embraced it, trying not to think of the penalties.

Robert had asked to see his son more often, and Suzette no longer refused his requests. Almost daily, Suzette would take a walk in the park, and each day Robert would join them innocently as if he was nothing more than a friend.

Suzette's excitement grew when she witnessed her son begin to bond with him in a special way. Robert had become the assigned procurer of bread for the ducks, and the two of them would feed the mass of birds that joined them at the lake's edge. Robert taught his son how to identify the various species, and little Robert devoured the knowledge like sweet candy.

Of course, the matter of a pony was brought up once more. Robert would tell tales of riding his own horse, which captured a little boy's attention for quite some time.

As often as she could slip from her residence, without gaining suspicion, Suzette rendezvoused with Robert at his townhouse. Their repeated lovemaking sessions had brought Suzette back to the arms of the man she loved. Philippe's continued absence allowed her to release her husband from her thoughts. What guilt she entertained, she foolishly refused to face until she learned Philippe would soon be home.

Suzette had met Robert, as usual, taking the carriage he sent and arriving through the back servant's entrance. He kissed her at the door, and took her hand and walked her down to the parlor rather than upstairs.

"I have something to tell you, love." He sat Suzette down and smiled softly. "Philippe is on a ship heading back to Paris. I'm afraid our time together must come to an end for now."

"How do you know?" she pressed.

"My brother-in-law owns the plantation that Philippe visited. A deal has been struck between Moreau Shipping and Chambers Plantation. Philippe has won the bid, as I instructed, and should be arriving home within a few days."

"A few days! What shall we do?"

"Let everything return as it was before, Suzette. I will return home to England and face my wife telling her of my adultery. Where it leads from there, only God knows. I have no idea how she will react, but I believe she already suspects my former indiscretions."

Robert sighed and lowered his eyes. "I wasn't quite truthful with you about visiting a brothel since we departed. It is true I've never returned to the Chabanais, but I have, when here in years past, sought comfort at another local establishment." He grasped her hand and squeezed it tightly. "Forgive me," he pleaded. "I shall never touch another woman again as long as I live, Suzette. I vow to you my eternal devotion."

His confession did not shock Suzette, as much as she anticipated. He had, after all, been unhappy in his marriage. They had been separated, and he thought her dead. Though it bothered her somewhat, she saw in his eyes the truth of his vow of fidelity and believed him, nevertheless.

"Oh, Robert, I do not blame you. I know you've been unhappy. Shall I be angry with your indiscretions of the past, when here we are adulterers together? I am no less without guilt, for I have broken my vow of fidelity to Philippe."

Suzette leaned in and kissed Robert. "If our time together is to end today, then take me until I can bear no more."

Robert did not give Suzette a moment to speak, but

kissed her deeply and laid her down upon the divan.

"How about someplace different?" he teased in heated desire. "The bedchamber is becoming unexciting. Besides," he said, lifting up her skirt, "We'd never be able to do this with servants around."

Suzette giggled like a school girl and fingered the buttons of his trousers, unfastening them one by one. Her breast had spilled out over her bodice, and Robert began sucking her nipple, knowing it would drive her to a place of pleasure.

"Robert," she laughed, "You're incorrigible!"

She watched his lips encircle her flesh, which sent goosebumps of pleasure coursing through her body. His hand crawled up her inner leg and pulled down her bloomers. Suzette moaned with delight when his fingers reached their destination and started to fondle her intimately. Their sexual playfulness and location screamed outrageous inappropriateness, but she loved every moment of it!

Suzette couldn't help but encourage Robert into a further frenzy by giving him pleasurable touches in return. Lost in the capture of her body by his hand and mouth, her frenzied desire teetered on the verge of an explosive release. Instead of her screams of pleasure filling the room, a screeching female voice bellowed from the entrance of the parlor door. Suzette recoiled in horror, feeling as if a bucket of cold water had drenched the raging fire in her veins.

"You son-of-a-bitch! You damn unfaithful bastard! Get off her!"

Robert stiffened and quickly removed his hand from between Suzette's legs. He released his lips from her fully exposed breast and glanced up. Suzette saw the horror upon his face. Instinctively, she knew it was his wife, who glared at them in revulsion and rage.

Suzette scrambled to push her breast back into her bodice and hurriedly pulled down her skirt. Suddenly, she'd felt doused in disgrace.

"My God, Jacquelyn, what in the hell are you doing here?" Robert roared.

He jumped off of Suzette's body and rose to his feet. Likewise, Suzette stood, mortified as she swiftly pulled up her bloomers. She retreated behind his body to shield herself from his wife's view.

"I'm your wife, this is my home, and I came from London to find out where in the hell you've been! Now, I know. Who's the whore?"

The woman's eyes blazed with hatred, and Suzette cringed. A maid stood behind Robert's wife, viewing the scene with surprised shock. Suzette wanted to crawl into a hole and die.

"Jacquelyn, for God's sake!" he implored, as he quickly fiddled with the buttons on his trousers and tucked in his shirt. "Not now. We'll speak of this later."

"Later? Who's the whore, Robert?"

"She's not a whore." He took an angry step in her direction. "Now go upstairs," he pointed, "and we'll talk later."

Jacquelyn ignored his command. She unexpectedly pushed by Robert in a gruff stride. It caught him off guard, and he failed to block her steps. Suzette shocked that she headed her way, tried to retreat. It was too late. The palm of Jacquelyn's hand slapped her hard across her cheek leaving a distinct red mark.

"Get out of my house you piece of French trash!"

Suzette reeled from the blow and brought her palm to her cheek, now drenched in hot tears. Jacquelyn raised her hand to strike again, but Robert quickly grabbed her wrist.

"Stop now!" he growled. He saw Jacquelyn's horrified lady's maid in the doorway and dragged his wife over to her. "Take her upstairs immediately, and get her out of her before I do something rash," he ordered. "Now!"

"You'll pay for this, you bastard, and so will that whore,"

she spit at Robert. She glared fiercely over his shoulder at Suzette.

Visibly shaken, Suzette sat down on the divan. She thought she'd faint at any moment from embarrassment. As soon as Jacquelyn had reached the top of the stairs, Robert turned toward Suzette and gathered her in his arms.

"My God, Robert. My God!" she wailed. "Your wife, of all people!"

She wept inconsolably on his shoulder, while Robert attempted to comfort her. "Let me hire a carriage to take you home. I'm afraid, Suzette, we'll have to separate for now."

He kissed her on the forehead.

"Will you contact me?" she clamored, in desperation.

"I'll write."

"Oh, Robert, I shall never get over this humiliation. Should Philippe find out, I don't know what he'll do."

"We'll deal with it when the time comes, my love. Now let me get you home."

He walked Suzette to the coach outside being unloaded with his wife's trunk. Robert paid the fare for her return, and then turned to give her further instructions.

"Watch for a package to arrive by courier to your home. It will come from a store, but will actually be from me. When you receive one, you'll know that I am sending you word. Act as if it's simply an order being delivered."

He gave her a quick kiss upon the cheek, helped her inside, and closed the door. His hand banged on the carriage side, and the driver pulled away down the street. Robert turned around. He lifted his head and glanced at the upstairs windows in mortification. Judgment day had arrived.

Chapter 18

Philippe disembarked from the ship and hailed a hansom cab home. It seemed like an eternity since he had stepped on French soil. His skin, tanned and tone, set off his hair that had grown longer than usual. He sported a full beard and wondered what Suzette would think of his appearance after two months of basking in a sun-kissed paradise.

Things were going well. He had won the account. Soon, his ship would transport sugarcane to European ports, making more money than he had in prior years. He felt saddened that his former partner would never know that he had turned the business around. Of course, he owed much to the anonymous investor for saving him from the brink of bankruptcy—that he could not deny.

Confident that Suzette would be ecstatic over his return, he exited the cab and with a joyful step headed for the front door. Monsieur Leroy greeted him with a welcoming smile when he entered.

"Monsieur Moreau, we are grateful for your safe return."

"Ah, Leroy, good to be back."

"Welcome home, sir. It is delightful to see you. I assume you'll be looking for your wife. She's upstairs in her quarters, I believe, and seems to be under the weather somewhat."

"Nothing serious, I hope."

"I cannot say. It seems to be related more to her spirits than her body."

"Well, she's probably been lonely since I've been gone so long," he concluded, as he turned and headed for the staircase. Leroy gave him an odd look, but Philippe shrugged it off for the moment.

Philippe climbed the stairs and knocked on the door to their bedchamber. Finding it ajar, he pushed it open and saw Suzette sitting in the window seat staring outside. She hadn't heard his knock apparently, because she failed to turn her head.

"Suzette, I'm home."

She spun around and looked at him. Her face looked pale, and immediately Philippe grew concerned.

"My God, Suzette, you do not look well. Are you all right?"

"Oh, Philippe, you've returned," she said, with half-hearted enthusiasm.

"And how is my wife?" Philippe strode toward her, then embraced and kissed Suzette. It felt good to hold her in his arms again; but instead of returning any kind of affection, Suzette seemed rigid.

"Is that the way you greet your husband?" He pulled away from her body. "What's wrong?"

"Nothing, Philippe. I haven't been well. I guess, I've just fallen into a state of low spirits since you departed." She reached out and touched his hand. "I'll be better now that you've returned."

Philippe raised his hand and cupped her cheek in his palm. "I'm sorry for having been away for so long. It took forever to close the deal, but I have and quite successfully, I might add. You have nothing to worry about, Suzette. Our future is secure."

Suzette finally looked at his appearance and commented. "You haven't shaved either, I see, and your hair is longer. I must say with that tan, you look like a local islander." She paused for a moment. "Did you enjoy yourself?"

Philippe brought his hand to his chin stroking his new addition with pride. Actually, he liked his beard, because it made him feel like a new man with a new business.

"Immensely! It was such an exotic paradise. I wish you could have been there with me. Perhaps it was foolish not to have brought you, also."

"Well, I certainly couldn't have gone and left Angelique or Robert, now could I?"

"No, I suppose not," he admitted. "Perhaps one day when the children are older, we'll take an exotic vacation, and I'll show you the West Indies. I'm sure you'll love the blue waters and white beaches. It's so different than Paris."

"It sounds quite wonderful."

"I missed Angelique. Has she been all right?"

"She's in the nursery with Madame Dubois." Suzette added with a hint of irritation, "And Robert, did you miss him too?"

"Of course, I did. Behaving I would hope."

"Not exactly," Suzette admitted, in discouragement.

"What do you mean?"

"There was an incident while you were away."

"What kind of mischievous incident?" he replied, making light of the ability of a five-year-old lad to get into serious trouble.

"He pushed over the bassinet and sent Angelique hurling toward the floor. Thank God, she landed on the soft carpeting and sustained no injuries."

"He what?" he howled. His face darkened in anger. "What on earth possessed him to do such a thing?"

"It seems he thinks you love her more. I told him that wasn't the truth, but he's gotten it in his little head. Frankly, I think it's a case of sibling jealousy. A newborn has taken away attention from him. Perhaps it will pass."

Philippe's nostrils flared. "I'll make sure that never happens again!" He turned on his heel and stormed down the hallway toward Robert's room.

"Philippe, where are you going?" Suzette called after him.

Vehement over Robert's actions, he flew into his bedroom and found Robert on the floor playing with toys. Philippe rushed over to the boy and hovered above him with his hands on his hips.

"What's this I hear, young man, about you pushing over Angelique's bassinet?"

"Daddy!"

"Don't daddy me, you . . ." Philippe, tired and enraged, bit his tongue, but could not restrain his outrage over the reckless action that could have injured his daughter. He flipped open his belt buckle and pulled the leather swiftly from its loops.

"Philippe, stop!" screamed Suzette, as she approached from behind.

"It will stop, and it will stop now. When I'm done with the lad, he'll never lay a hand upon his sister again."

Little Robert's eyes grew wide with fear as Philippe's large hand reached out and grabbed his wrist. Suzette continued to shout her disapproval, but Philippe pushed her aside and walked Robert down the hall to another room.

Before Suzette could stop him, he had slammed the door shut and locked it behind him.

"I'm sorry, Daddy. I won't do it again."

Philippe said nothing. Suzette, struck with fear, pounded on the door pleading for him to stop.

As he looked at the little boy that bore the resemblance of the duke, something within him snapped. He flipped the boy over his knee, pulled down his trousers, and laid his first welt upon the white bottom of a five-year-old boy.

"You'll learn never to touch her again."

Whack. Whack. Whack.

Robert wailed in pain. Suzette pounded upon the door, but Philippe ignored her pleas. He hit the boy repeatedly until he had expelled his anger and made his point. After he finished, he shoved Robert off his lap and watched him tumble onto the floor with tears streaming down his face.

"Will you do it again?" he asked sternly.

The boy merely cried.

"I asked you a question, damn you! Answer me. Will you do it again?"

"No—no—Daddy. I promise . . ."

His little voice gasped between each word. Philippe felt vindicated enough to leave him with his wounds and a lesson learned. He had never taken a belt to the boy before, but believed it to be well deserved.

Angelique embodied his flesh and blood. He had waited for her birth to solidify his marriage with Suzette. No illegitimate child would usurp her rights. After today, he would know never to touch his sister again.

Philippe stepped around Robert, who lay crying on the floor, and headed for the door. He flung it open. Suzette glared at him with astonishment and fear. Her tear-streaked face radiated horror, but Philippe felt no need to apologize for his actions.

"I can assure you, he'll never lay a hand on our daughter again."

He walked past his wife and strode down the hallway leaving Suzette behind to tend to her son. Philippe entered the nursery, where Madame Dubois sat by his daughter's bassinet watching her sleep. When she saw him, she stood to her feet at attention, like a soldier responding to her commander.

"How is she?" He glanced down with adoration and amazement over her tiny body.

"She is quite well, monsieur."

"Leave," he ordered. "I want to hold her for a while."

The governess quickly departed. Surely, she had heard what transpired down the hall, but he didn't give a damn.

He slipped his arms underneath Angelique's little body and lifted her to his chest cradling her head in one hand. She looked like a porcelain doll. He turned her to and fro examining her for bruises and found none.

He smiled and kissed her cheek. "Forever my little girl," he fussed. "Forever my little girl."

❊ ❊ ❊

Suzette ran to her son's side. He lay on the floor in a fetal position, with his pants down around his knees. The red welts from the beating appeared sickening. Tears streamed down Suzette's face as she watched Robert writhe in pain.

"Mommy," he moaned.

"There, there, Robert, I'm here," she tenderly consoled. She knelt and stroked his hair wet from tears.

"I'm so sorry, honey."

"I hate him," he blubbered. "I told you that he hated me."

"He doesn't hate you," Suzette corrected him. "He's taken care of you since the day you were born. He's just angry that you hurt Angelique."

Suzette pulled Robert into her arms and began to rock him back and forth to ease him through his tears and pain. When he had calmed down, she took him to the bath chamber and placed a cold cloth on his bottom to help reduce the swelling. With each grimace of pain, Suzette's heart tore.

How could Philippe do such a cruel thing? For the first time in their marriage, she questioned his true feelings toward her son. Had she been blind in believing that he had unconditionally accepted Robert? She had always thought him loving and gentle, but the unbridled anger she just witnessed appalled her to the core. The resentment she thought never existed had finally exposed its ugly head.

She spent the next few minutes cooling and comforting Robert. Suzette walked her son back to his room, put his exhausted body to bed, and tucked him in. His countenance, grim and miserable, worried her. Robert appeared to withdraw into a world far away.

Suzette kissed him tenderly on his cheek to reaffirm her love. "Robert, I will always love you, no matter what you do. Don't ever forget." She sighed and stroked his head. "Try and forgive Daddy, too."

He turned his head away from her and stared at the wall. Angry at Philippe for his cruelty, she rose and left Robert alone, hoping that he would soon sleep. Quietly, she retreated, closed the door behind her, and made her way down the hall.

With each step she took, her heart pounded in resentment over Philippe's insensitivity. She stormed into the bedroom and found him unpacking his clothes. He must have heard her approach, because a snide remark left his lips without giving her the courtesy to turn around.

"No doubt the little lad is still alive, but the point well taken."

"How could you be so physically harsh?" She shoved herself into his face with daring audacity.

"Easily," he spewed. "You think he was not physically cruel to our daughter by pushing over the bassinet and sending an infant tumbling to the floor? What if she had hit her head on an object and died?"

"I reprimanded him over the matter and was going to ask you to speak with him upon your return. I had no idea this would be your response. You've bruised his body in your tyrannical moment of discipline."

"Good Lord, Suzette. I didn't kill the boy. I merely gave him the whipping he deserved. My father whipped me with a belt often as a boy, and I lived. A good spanking now and then will keep him in line."

"You're not to set your hand upon him again," Suzette hissed.

Philippe spun around. His eyes turned dark and stormy. "Don't threaten your husband. I'm the head of this household, not you! Your behavior is unbecoming." He turned away and folded another shirt placing it in the dresser drawer.

"Please," Suzette reiterated between clenched teeth. "Do not touch him again."

"I'll do as I see fit to raise the boy," he tersely replied. He closed the dresser drawer with a slam and turned his attention upon Suzette. For the first time in their marriage, she took a step back from him to put distance between their bodies. It made no difference, because Philippe closed the gap quickly with his long stride.

"I've just returned after months of being away," he spoke softly. "Is a strife-filled argument all you can give me to welcome me home?"

He bent down and kissed her lips, but Suzette found his behavior repulsive. She tried to feign his advances by attempting to return an ounce of welcome in return. Her stomach turned into a ball of knots.

Philippe drew away. "I need your body," he said, lustfully running his palm down the length of her arm. He stopped and placed his hand upon her hip and pulled her pelvis flush to his own. "It's been too long. I need a release."

Suzette's mind panicked. Her thoughts quickly scrambled to think of an excuse. As long as she continued to breast feed, she would have no menses. She wondered if Philippe knew such things about a woman's body.

Appalled over the thought of sharing herself, after having been with Robert, Suzette shrilled out a lie. "My menses returned yesterday. I cannot share your bed."

Philippe's brow furrowed. "I don't understand."

"You know nothing of a woman's body," she cajoled.

"After you have a baby it takes a few months for them to return, and they have." Suzette held her breath as she watched Philippe absorb her lie, praying he was none the wiser.

He stepped back in response. "Fine then," he mumbled, as he shrugged his shoulders. "I shall wait until it passes."

Suzette said nothing more. She almost giggled aloud with nervous relief but suppressed the urge.

"I have business to attend to in my study." He retreated with a scowl upon his face.

Given a slight reprieve from returning to her husband's arms, Suzette watched him leave the room. Her thoughts drifted toward Robert. She wondered how he fared with his irate wife, who frankly had every right to scream at her husband. A brief wave of regret for giving in to her lover's temptation swept over her soul. Her feet felt as if they stood in quicksand, and soon she would sink to the bottom with no one to save her.

She had barely recovered from his wife's embarrassing discovery of them on the divan. She and Robert shared such reckless abandonment in each other's presence when they joined together as one flesh. He had captivated her weakness, but Suzette loved Robert for far more reasons than just the electricity he sent through her body during intimacy.

Determined to stay away from Philippe as much as possible, Suzette wandered down the hall to her son's bedchamber and quietly opened the door. He appeared to have fallen asleep, so Suzette sat in the chair next to his bed to gaze upon his little body tucked safely beneath the blanket.

Being near him somehow bound her to Robert with ties that could not be broken. Suzette could not comprehend why she did not feel the same with Angelique and Philippe. Her emotions could only be justified by her profound and abiding love for Robert.

As she began to think of all the obstacles they both faced, Suzette fell into a deep hopelessness. Almost certainly, Robert had faced hell from a woman scorned, while she spurned her husband. Both of their lives had weaved together into a complicated mess of adultery and deception. She could only imagine the anguish that lay ahead.

❋ ❋ ❋

Philippe wandered downstairs toward his study, troubled over his wife's greeting upon his arrival home. The return of Suzette's menses at least explained her pale countenance and emotional demeanor.

Monsieur Leroy stood in the foyer speaking quietly to a housemaid. Undoubtedly, they had heard the ruckus upstairs. He felt no disgrace over his behavior and glanced away from Leroy's stare. Philippe walked through the door into his study and turned to close it. To his surprise, Leroy followed. He cleared his throat as if he wished to speak.

"I don't care to talk about family matters with the staff," Philippe addressed his butler, with a gruff warning. "Leave me alone."

"I understand Monsieur Moreau, however, I thought that you would want an accounting of the household upon your return."

Philippe looked at his butler's obvious need to perform his dutiful role and relented. "Fine, come in, and close the door. Make it quick, though, as I have other matters to attend to."

He sat briskly in his chair behind the desk and looked up at his butler. "Well, then, give your accounting. Take a seat if you wish." Leroy didn't budge, so Philippe continued. "I suppose I should take this opportunity to thank you for watching over my household, wife, and children during my absence. I had no idea it would take so long."

"That's quite all right, sir." Leroy glanced at the chair, but hesitated to make himself comfortable. "I prefer to stand."

"Very well, then," replied Philippe. He leaned back into the soft leather and folded his arms. "The house looks well kept."

"Yes, I took the liberty to make sure the maids were supervised in their duties. I oversaw the expenses of the food purchases and did make a change as to where your cook procures your meat. I believe it will lead to savings on the household's behalf, without sacrificing quality."

Philippe's brow rose as he listened to his butler droll on about his money-saving accomplishments. He had to admit, Leroy impressed him with his ability to supervise everything during his absence. Definitely an asset, Philippe decided to speak to him about a long-term tenure. Before he could do so, the conversation took a disturbing turn.

"I also took the liberty of watching over Madame Moreau and her welfare. She seemed to be much more secure with the presence of a male in the household to such an extent that she took numerous outings on her own during your absence, sir."

"Outings? What do you mean by outings? Are you speaking of her visits to Père Lachaise?"

"Well, no, Monsieur Moreau," he replied, with a smug look upon his face. "Your wife did make her visits, however, there were other absences where a private carriage would arrive to pick her up. She would leave for a few hours and then return."

Philippe could not believe his ears. Where on earth could she have been going? "I'm a bit confused, Leroy. You mean to tell me a carriage came here to pick her up?"

"Yes, I'm afraid so. I must say that as the frequency continued, I did find it odd. Since you had given me the task to oversee your household, I had some concern as to your wife's whereabouts and safety." He looked away from his employer and glanced at the floor. "Forgive me if I have overstepped my boundaries, but I arranged to follow her in a hired cab on one occasion."

Philippe jumped to his feet and walked around the front of his desk and stood in front of Leroy. His heart pounded in his chest. He didn't know whether to thank the man or fire him on the spot for his impertinence. He abhorred the idea of his staff involved in his personal affairs. The look in Leroy's eyes, however, spoke of information that he needed to hear.

"To where did you follow my wife, Leroy? A friend's home perhaps?"

"I do not know who owns the residence, monsieur, so I merely wrote down the address. Perhaps you recognize the household and its occupants by the location."

Leroy reached inside his vest pocket and pulled out a small piece of paper and handed it to Philippe. He snatched it from his butler's hand, opened the folded note, and read the address. Immediately, his hands shook from the icy hatred that flowed through his veins.

"It appears you recognize the residence," Leroy concluded, after observing his reaction. "Shall I take my leave?"

Philippe refolded the note and slipped it into his trouser pocket.

"Yes—yes, you may take your leave."

Leroy said nothing else and turned toward the door. Philippe stopped him.

"You've done well. I appreciate you taking the initiative to check on my wife's welfare."

"Very well, sir. I'm glad to have been of assistance."

Assistance indeed, thought Philippe, as he watched his butler close the door behind him. He pulled out the note and read the address again. He wasn't hallucinating—Robert Holland's Parisian townhouse sat at that location.

A knife sliced his heart in two over the possible return

of the duke and his visits with his wife. Had she been secretly meeting her old lover during his absence? The veins in Philippe's neck protruded when he thought of the rogue that once possessed her body.

Treachery.

No other word could describe their actions. His jealous thoughts envisioned what possibly could have occurred between the two while he was away. It fueled his unrelenting loathing of Robert Holland.

Visions spun around Philippe's mind like a whirlpool in the ocean. He staggered over to his chair and sat back down attempting to suppress the urge to run upstairs and confront his wife. Had his beautiful Suzette, who he had won back years ago, returned to the mire from which she came? The thought sickened him.

Bide your time, he thought, as he seized hold of the edge of the desk. His nails dug into the wood. *Bide your time.*

A moment later, he released his grip from the desk's edge. Philippe leaned back, closed his eyes, and fantasized choking the life out of Robert Holland.

Chapter 19

"Who's the whore?"

Jacquelyn confronted him angrily, stepping toward him as he entered the room.

Robert looked at Dorcas, who attended his wife by unloading her trunks. "Dorcas, a moment of privacy, if you please. Close the door on the way out."

Dorcas curtsied and bowed her head in response, before swiftly leaving. "Yes, Your Grace, of course."

Robert watched her cast a glance at Jacquelyn that spoke of empathy. His wife had probably painted him as the villain in their marriage. The door shut, and Jacquelyn wasted no time with her assault.

"Bastard," she spit. She strode closer to Robert and lifted her hand to strike him on the cheek.

Robert clamped his fingers around her wrist and stopped her midway before her palm landed upon his face, already flushed with anger.

"No need to get physical," he warned his wife, while he hastily pushed her wrist downward and held it tight.

"You're hurting me. Let go!" she protested, as she wiggled her hand back and forth to break his grip.

"Not until you promise to control yourself, Jacquelyn." He squeezed her wrist slightly tighter until she winced.

"All right, all right!" she relented. She squirmed once

more.

Robert released her and stepped back at the same time to put distance between them.

Jacquelyn rubbed her wrist, glaring at him with eyes full of vile hatred. "I don't appreciate you manhandling me," she complained. "You deserve my hand across your face, just like the whore I struck earlier."

Again, she heaved her question like a dagger in Robert's direction. "Who is she?"

Robert narrowed his eyes and debated how to answer her question. Choosing the exact words were crucial to his future. As he looked at the woman he had married, painful regret choked his heart. He could only think of Suzette and the life he wished to build with her and his son. The words he would speak would undoubtedly strip bare his relationship with Jacquelyn from this day forward.

"She's my former mistress from five years ago. We have a son together, and I love her."

Robert watched Jacquelyn's cheeks turn bright red. Her eyes turned into a wild glare.

"I want a divorce," he said, with authority. "You can divorce me for adultery, if you wish, and feign any lie of abuse you care to choose. As long as I am free of this bondage with you, I am free to marry the woman I love."

Robert hated being so cruel, but he had never coveted another woman as much as he did Suzette.

Covet.

As he stood looking into Jacquelyn's eyes filled with hurt and rage, he remembered a heavenly commandment. *Thou shall not covet thy neighbor's wife.* He should have felt shame. None existed. Robert could not resist the temptation. His need for Suzette coursed so deeply through his soul, that he knew he'd pay the price of eternal damnation to make her his wife.

"I will return to you the value of your dowry," he finally spoke, in a softer tone to lessen the consequences of divorce. "However, your title as duchess will be given to another."

"You son-of-a-bitch! Do you think I'd divorce you after this? I'll go to my grave married to you, Robert Holland, before I give you a divorce. You can suffer the rest of your life separated from your French whore and your bastard son until they put you in a box and nail the coffin shut."

Robert gawked in shock over her response. Jacquelyn's face turned evil as she balled her fists and approached him at full speed, swinging her hands and arms like a maniac. Robert recoiled and attempted to subdue her.

"You bastard!" she railed, while pounding him wherever she could make contact with his body.

Robert attempted to grab her hands again, but discovered he fought against the rage of a woman he had never before confronted.

"You bastard!" she screeched, repeatedly.

Thump, thump. Her fists beat him until Robert finally restrained her fury.

"Dorcas!" he yelled at the top of his lungs. Her lady's maid burst through the door, and Robert pleaded for her assistance.

"Call a physician at once," he ordered. He detained Jacquelyn in a tight hold, which she could not break. Dorcas ran from the room and down the stairs. Robert wrestled with Jacquelyn while she spit her venom, screaming obscenities at him until he could bear no more.

He pulled her over to the bed and pushed her down upon it. When he did so, she stopped thrashing her limbs and fell limp.

"You bastard," she sobbed. "I'll ruin you! I'll ruin you, and you'll damn the day you ever married me."

Tears freely flowed in torrents down Jacquelyn's face. He released her and stepped away from the bed horrified over his wife's reaction. Certainly, he had expected that she would verbally damn him; but her physical attacks and continued threats were like thorns stripping his hope to shreds.

"I've sent for the physician," he announced. "We shall speak of it no more today." Robert turned and left the room and closed the door behind him. Jacquelyn wailed loudly as she lay upon her bed.

No remorse or empathy filled Robert's heart toward his wife. He had been held in a prison of marriage, bound in a loveless existence that he abhorred. Her physical rampage finally confirmed her mental instability. The incident stripped away what few remnants of emotion existed for Jacquelyn Spencer. Now nothing remained.

His heart pounded as he trotted down the stairs. The servants were opening the remaining portions of the townhouse, and taking off the white covers from the furniture. She had apparently engaged the entire staff in anticipation of her return to Paris.

Finally, Dorcas returned with a physician. Robert briefly explained the current state of affairs.

"My wife is in an unstable emotional condition," he explained. "She has become somewhat violent toward me and now lays in a sobbing remorse. I'd appreciate it if you could attend her physically. If you find it necessary, sedate her in some way, so that she can rest."

The physician looked curiously at Robert. "Yes, of course. I shall examine her and see what I can do."

Dorcas led the doctor upstairs to Jacquelyn's suite. Thirty minutes later, he returned downstairs to give his report to Robert.

"I'm afraid your wife is in an extreme mental state of anguish," he reported. "I have found her to be in need of sedation, which I've given to her. She should sleep the night through."

Robert sighed in relief that there would be no further physical encounters with Jacquelyn that evening.

"I appreciate your help."

"Might I ask you a question?"

"Yes, of course."

"Upon my examination, I was concerned over your wife's mental state of mind. Her behavior was irrational, incoherent, and intermingled with intermittent threats toward your person." The physician's brow furrowed even further when he continued. "Has this behavior been prevalent in the past, might I ask?"

Stunned at his question, Robert paused momentarily. He felt compelled to answer truthfully. "My wife has been prone to moods of various degrees. She has been barren for five years now, and I think she often grieves far too much over the situation. She fantasizes about having a baby in her arms, and at times seems to drift off into a place I cannot reach."

"Anything else?"

"Today was the first time she became violent toward me, though I'm sure she had her reasons." Robert lowered his eyes. "We are having marital problems."

"Well, I do find it disconcerting. You may wish to confer with a physician who deals with the mind and its emotions. In addition, you may wish to consider a more advanced treatment of hysteria and melancholic behavior in women, and have her ovaries surgically removed. Once the organs are gone, it produces a calming effect upon the emotions of a woman. If you need a referral for either a psychiatrist or surgeon, I would be happy to recommend."

"That won't be necessary," Robert assured him. "We will return to England soon, and I will pursue the matter there with our family doctor, if necessary."

"Very well. As I stated, she should sleep through the night."

The physician donned his hat, nodded, and left the residence. Robert watched him depart, and then found Dorcas to convey his whereabouts.

"I am leaving," he informed her. "I trust that you will

look after your mistress. Even though the remaining staff has arrived, I am staying elsewhere. If you need me for some medical reason on behalf of my wife, you may find me at the Hotel de Louvre."

Dorcas merely nodded. Robert, spent from emotion, left the townhouse and headed back to his hotel room. The moment he stepped across the threshold, he made a decision. He would not stay under the same roof as his wife ever again.

❋ ❋ ❋

Jacquelyn woke when the sun filtered through a crack in the heavy brocade curtains of her suite. When the rays struck her eyelids, she squinted from the light and moaned in pain from the pounding in her skull.

It took a few moments for her thoughts to clear. Her brain felt clouded and fuzzy—her body weak. She turned her head from the window and rolled over. When she did, a surge of memories and anger flowed through her mind like pins and needles.

Robert's face and words pranced before her eyes, as if he had just spoken the filth to her face.

"I want a divorce."

The reason behind his words came back with rabid torment. He loved his former mistress, not her. They had a son together—a son! The suspicions about the boy in the park months ago resurrected. Certainly, the documents she discovered in his desk revealed a pile of deceit.

Jacquelyn sat up. The room spun around like a Ferris wheel, and she clutched the edge of the bed for support. She remembered the doctor who had come into her room the night before. He gave her something to drink; after that everything went black. No wonder her head pounded. He told her that it would make her feel better and feel better it did. A few minutes later, she had passed out upon her pillow until the sun had intruded her dreams only moments ago.

"Dorcas! Dorcas!"

A moment later, her lady's maid burst through the door and ran to her bedside.

"My lady, are you all right? I've been so worried."

"Yes—yes, I'm fine," she sputtered. "Help me out of bed and draw a bath for me. I have things to do."

"The doctor thought you should rest."

"To hell with the doctor." She looked straight into Dorcas' eyes. "Where's my husband?"

Dorcas glanced away and muttered softly. "Gone, my lady."

"Gone where?"

"Elsewhere. He's not staying here but at a hotel."

Jacquelyn's eyes narrowed as she considered the fact Robert had crawled away like a coward to hide from her wrath.

"Did he say what hotel?"

"Yes, Hotel de Louvre."

Jacquelyn took note. Dorcas fetched her slippers and slip them onto her mistress's feet. "Here let me help you," she offered, as her hand steadied Jacquelyn as she stood. "I'll draw the bath for you now." She sped off and left Jacquelyn to her thoughts and shaky legs.

Vivid memories of the previous day played before her eyes like a risqué show on a cabaret stage. She saw Robert on top of the whore, her breast protruding, her nipple filling his mouth, and his hand up her inner thigh, fondling her to make her ready. Suddenly, the thought of whether they had shared the bed in his chamber flushed her cheeks.

Quickly, she spun around to the adjoining door and flung it open. The curtains were drawn, and the darkness engulfed her with an eerie sense of betrayal clawing at her heels as she reached the window. With a quick thrust, she pushed back the draperies and twirled around to see what the sun revealed. His bed lay exposed down to the sheets, with blankets and pillows in disarray.

"You unfaithful bastard."

Jacquelyn walked over to the bed sheets and began ripping them from the mattress. She filled the room with curses as she envisioned her husband's betrayal.

Dorcas came running toward her Jacquelyn's screams.

"Burn them." She angrily pulled the last sheet from the bed. "Burn them all. I want the sheets, pillowcases, and blankets burned. If I find them back in this house again, there will be hell to pay."

Dorcas looked at the heap of bed linen in the middle of the floor. "Yes, ma'am, I'll see that the housekeeper takes care of it immediately."

Jacquelyn sauntered back into her chamber after carrying out her decree of retribution.

"Is my bath ready?"

"Yes, my lady."

"Good. I plan on having a leisurely bath. I want breakfast ready in the dining room, and then I shall be leaving for a few hours. I have business to attend to. Very important business."

"Yes, ma'am," she answered sheepishly, afraid to cross her distraught employer.

Dorcas left, and Jacquelyn sat down in front of her vanity. She picked up her hairbrush and began pulling it through the disarrayed blond locks cascading over her shoulders.

She looked at herself in the mirror. "Now it's time I paid a visit," she announced to her reflection. "Time to cause some hell in the lives of those who have dared to betray me. Hell hath no fury, Robert, like a woman scorned."

Jacquelyn laughed.

Chapter 20

Philippe left for his office early the next morning. Upon arrival, he began to write his monthly report to his anonymous investor. He felt proud to report the procurement of the West Indies account. Ecstatic over the increase in income, he had begun to make plans to hire a new crew and captain for a second ship.

He picked up the quill, dipped it in the inkwell, and started to write his accounting. Roland, his clerk, interpreted him just as he penned the first line.

"Monsieur Moreau, there is a lady in the outer office who wishes to speak with you."

Philippe raised his head. "Who?"

"She said her name is the Duchess of Surrey, Jacquelyn Holland."

The pen between Philippe's fingers dropped to the paper below making a blotch of black ink where it fell. He quickly picked it up and put it back in its holder, and then scrunched up the ruined sheet and threw it in a nearby waste can.

"Holland?" He attempted to collect his thoughts at the surprise arrival of the duke's wife, speculating about the reason for her visit.

"You may show her in. After you do, close the door behind you."

The clerk nodded his head, and a few moments later Philippe saw the figure of the duchess. She stood in the doorway and glared at him. Quickly, he jumped to his feet in awe of her imposing manner and stark beauty. Her haughty eyes glanced suspiciously at Philippe from head to toe. He wondered if the recent reunion between her husband and his wife had brought her to his office to discuss the matter.

"Your Grace, what a surprise to see you here."

He held out his hand and offered her a seat in front of his desk. She glanced about the room with an air of superiority. Jacquelyn looked at the chair as if it was unworthy of her resting upon. The office, decidedly decorated in his male tastes, did not offer the supreme comforts that a duchess such as herself required.

She wiped her white gloved hand across the bottom of the chair and then looked at her palm to check for dirt. "Very well." Jacquelyn sat down and fixed her gaze upon him.

Not knowing what to do or what to think, Philippe blurted out a nervous greeting. "And what can I do for you?"

"What can you do for me?" she purred, like a stalking cat. "One thing you can do for me is to keep your damn wife away from my husband. That is what you can do for me."

Philippe observed her facial expression of beauty turn frightfully dark.

"So you know," he declared. "Apparently, they have been seeing one another during my absence."

"More than that, I'm afraid. I found your whore of a wife in a compromising position on my divan in my own parlor, for God's sake. Her exposed nipple filled my husband's mouth, while his hand fondled her between her legs to make her ripe for the taking."

An arrogant abhorrence stretched across her face. "Had it not been for my surprise arrival from England, I'm sure that Robert would have taken her then and there." She inhaled a breath and spat the remaining vitriol. "No doubt he's already visited your wife's cunt and taken the prize many times before I arrived. I found evidence in his disarrayed bed."

The duchess' crass comment took Philippe by surprise. Only a hardened sailor would use such language, but her face was contorted with such disgust over his wife's immoral behavior, he understood her anger.

A piece of hair had fallen into one of her eyes, and she flipped it back with her fingers. "You see," she said, with obvious aversion, "my husband is an unfaithful bastard, and your wife is an unfaithful whore."

Philippe's gut tightened as he sat listening to the description of Suzette's body bared to his foe. A heavy blanket of humiliation covered him while he thought of her brazen unfaithfulness. It was sickening, after everything he had done to save her reputation and care for her illegitimate son. He pulled his eyes away from the duchess, and realized that he had balled his fists in response to the pain of betrayal cutting deep through his soul.

"I can see you are surprised, Monsieur Moreau. You should probably know, too, that your son is not yours, but belongs to Robert."

Philippe lifted his eyes. On the verge of tears, he inhaled a deep breath. "I've known all along," he admitted. "Suzette was his mistress five years ago. I won her back from your husband to give her a life of respectability and to save her from the shame of bearing a child out of wedlock. Robert never knew that she carried his child, but I assume now he knows the boy belongs to him." He paused, hesitant to hear the answer. "Am I correct?"

"Oh, yes, you are quite right. My husband's dream has come true; he has a child."

"And you have no child," Philippe spoke, remembering their comment in the park.

"No."

The room fell silent for a few moments. Each drifted into their own bitter thoughts. Finally, Philippe spoke in a raspy voice.

"I was informed last evening of my wife's comings and goings while I was away, but now that I know for sure—"

"And what do you intend to do about it?" she abruptly interrupted.

"I'm not ready to confront her yet."

"Are you a coward?"

"Coward?"

"Yes, a coward. Your wife is an adulteress. What do you intend to do about it? Will you divorce her?"

"You are pressing me for answers I do not have," Philippe protested.

"Well, before you decide what to do, perhaps you should know that my husband wishes to divorce me. In fact, he has asked me to divorce him and to feign other circumstances so that he might be free of me as his wife. And why do you suppose he craves to be free of me?" She glared at him. "Certainly, monsieur, you are no damn fool."

"It's obvious what he means to do. He wants to marry my wife."

"Well," she huffed, in determination. "I'm not divorcing my husband. I told him that he could rot in Hell for all I cared, but I would never free him to marry that whore."

Philippe narrowed his eyes at the term she continued to hurl at him like dirt. He wanted to protect Suzette's honor, but what honor had she left him to defend? Adulteress, yes. Whore? Perhaps a whore, or she would have been at one time since she made that choice years ago in order to survive.

"I cannot tell you what I will do. Perhaps she will come to her senses for the sake of our daughter, Angelique."

"You have a daughter?" she pressed, leaning forward.

"Suzette gave birth to our first child nearly four months ago. We named her Angelique," Philippe replied proudly.

"A baby girl. How sweet. Well, it seems to me that we are of the same mind. Neither of us will allow our unfaithful spouses the satisfaction of leaving us in order to marry."

Philippe shook his head at her suggestion. It made sense. The two of them could prevent their spouses from making a damnable mistake. After learning of Suzette's duplicity, however, he wasn't sure he wished to keep her.

"Are you staying in Paris long?"

"I haven't decided. My husband is not staying at our townhouse. He's apparently taken a room in the Hotel de Louvre. Right now I couldn't give a damn where he lays his head."

Philippe noted the location of Robert's whereabouts.

"There is one other nasty piece of information, I'm afraid, that you may find quite upsetting."

"Really? What could be more upsetting than what you have already told me about my unfaithful wife? Surely, there is nothing that you could tell me to top this betrayal."

"My husband is your anonymous investor. The duke owns half interest in your little shipping business. It was he who sent you away for two months so that he could seduce your wife while you were gone."

The blood drained from Philippe's face. Jacquelyn chuckled over his reaction to the revelation.

"Surely, you must admit, that's the pièce de résistance to the news I bring you today."

"Are you sure?" he demanded, with icy contempt.

"Quite sure. I read the correspondence between my husband and his solicitor having found it in his desk upon his departure here to Paris." She smiled at him. "You must give Robert some credit. He is a sly bastard, is he not? He has weaseled his way into your business and in between your wife's legs. With clever maneuvering, the rogue sent you to the British West Indies, so that he could steal her fidelity while you pursued a deal halfway around the world that was already sealed before you arrived."

Philippe looked at the duchess in shocked disbelief. All he had recently gained happened by the hand of the man he detested. Like a poisonous spider, he had weaved a web of deceit and ensnared Philippe during a moment of weakness. When he lay unsuspectingly trapped by the lure of a bright future, the creature had taken its prey.

"He is most definitely, as I suspected all along, a man without integrity or scruples," Philippe growled.

He stood to his feet and pushed all the papers off his desk in a blind rage. All of his efforts during the past few months had been for nothing. He had wasted his honorable name and time chasing a lie in order to receive money from a scoundrel. His nostrils flared, and his eyes grew dark. He glared at the duchess, who batted her eyelashes in satisfaction. The truth lay before him like a rancid meal on a table.

"How you propose to stay with a man like him is beyond my comprehension," he bitterly confessed. "But I see you wish to keep him away from his desires as a means of punishment."

The thought of Suzette being with Robert intimately continued to poison his soul toward his wife. Perhaps the duchess could remain. At that moment, he didn't know if he had the strength to stay with his wife knowing about her infidelity.

"I cannot promise you anything. At this moment, my soul feels as if it has been thrust into Hell itself. It burns."

"It's understandable, Monsieur Moreau. You have much to consider and think about. I have told you what I intend to do. It's all out in the air now. No more secrets. No more deceit."

The duchess stood to her feet and straightened her skirt. Philippe sensed her outer façade shielded the heart of a broken woman. She had chosen hate to gain strength, rather than love to show weakness.

"I understand," she added, with a tone of sympathy, "that you struggle due to your newborn child. She should, of course, be your main concern. How you deal with my husband's son, is entirely up to you. I'm surprised you don't throw him in the gutter where he belongs with the other illegitimate children of whores."

Philippe's eyes darkened at her cruel comment. "Your bitterness seems to be rooted in the jealousy that your husband has sired a child with another."

Her lips pursed tightly together in response to his comment. "Yes, indeed. His seed seems to plant far better in the womb of other women than it does in mine. Nevertheless, there is nothing that can be done about it."

The duchess stood from her chair and headed toward the door. She stopped and hesitated for a few moments, as if pondering what to say next. Jacquelyn slowly turned and faced Philippe and offered a suggestion.

"Do keep in touch with me. I would be interested in knowing what you decide. After all, this affects us both in many ways. Perhaps we can meet and speak again sometime. Misery loves company, so they say."

"Perhaps," Philippe replied cautiously considering the wisdom of such a meeting.

"I can keep you apprised of my husband's movements, which I would think is valuable information to you. Why don't we plan to see each other again? An innocent meeting in that nice park where we first crossed paths might do. What do you think?"

Philippe's mind tumbled to and fro with thoughts of offense and revenge. He reeled from the revelations and could not focus upon meeting the duchess anytime soon.

"Perhaps. I cannot say right now, but I know where you reside and will send notice should I wish to speak with you."

"A nice walk in the park with your daughter in her baby carriage might do you both well."

Jacquelyn opened the door and exited the room.

Philippe flopped back down into his chair and brought both hands to his face. The shame of Suzette's unfaithfulness poisoned his soul. His hatred toward Robert Holland ebbed into a tidal wave about to crest toward a ruinous end. He would not allow the man go unpunished for his deeds.

His clerk came through the doorway and noted the papers strewn about the floor. "Monsieur Moreau, are you all right?" he inquired. He bent over, picked up the sheets one by one, and replaced them on top of the desk.

"I don't know," he admitted, his voice choked with emotion. "I need some fresh air."

Philippe took his hat and left his office. He flung the door open and ran out into the streets, as he stumbled and bumped into passing pedestrians on the sidewalk. His vision blurred, and his pace quickened. Out of breath and with his heart pounding against his ribcage, he hailed a hansom cab and climbed inside.

"Hotel de Louvre," he ordered the driver. When he settled into the seat, he noticed his trembling hands. His indignation toward Robert burned in his veins like molten lava. Philippe struggled with the need to defend his honor. The heartless rake had ruined his life.

Unsure what he would do upon his arrival, Philippe carefully thought about his plan of action. With Robert owning half of his business, his entire livelihood precariously stood on the brink of loss should he pursue the course that his anger and pride pressured him to follow. Not afraid of the peril he could suffer, Philippe decided justice had to be served or he would never rest.

Chapter 21

Robert woke to a day of worry and frustration. The prior encounter with his wife shook him to the core. Never in a thousand years did he think she would leave England on her own to investigate his absence in Paris. He could not help but wonder if his mother had even tried to prevent her from embarking on such a ludicrous trip.

Jacquelyn had walked in on his playful tryst with Suzette. Mortified that his wife had caught them in the act, burdened his heart. He had subjected Suzette to shame and ridicule, relegating her to the title of whore once more.

The hard slap from Jacquelyn's hand across his sweetheart's face enraged Robert. He had wanted to smack his wife in return. Never had a woman elicited such anger and irritation from him as she had at that moment.

Finally, after Dorcas removed her from his presence and took her upstairs, he gathered a tearful Suzette into his arms to comfort her about Jacquelyn's tirade. He assured her of his protection and that he would shield her from further physical and verbal outbursts from his wife.

Barely able to control her own shame over the situation, Suzette left confused and frightened. He promised her that he would keep in touch, before helping her into the carriage that would take her home. After he watched it depart down the narrow back street of his residence, he turned to face a thorny encounter with his estranged wife.

Robert had decided then and there as he stomped back inside the townhouse that he needed to tell her the truth about Suzette and be done with it. He would let the chips fall where they may, but he had not anticipated that Jacquelyn would fly into an uncontrolled physical rage after his revelation. Perhaps her love ran deeper than he realized, or perhaps the awareness that he had sired a child with another woman had pushed her over the edge.

Convinced it was the latter that took her to the brink of unconscionable behavior, he tried to feel an ounce of compassion for her sorrow and loss. However, he could not bring forth any empathy, for his heart consumed itself with thoughts of Suzette.

Philippe had probably disembarked by now and returned to her side. He couldn't help but wonder what, if anything, transpired between the two. Had she told him of her love or had she hidden the fact they had reunited? Unable to contain his curiosity, he yelled for his assistant.

"Giles!" he called out, as he paced the floor in a worried frenzy.

"Yes, Your Grace, is there something you require?"

"A carriage," he mumbled. "Order me a private carriage. I wish to go out."

Robert decided to drive by Suzette's residence, if only to be near her for a moment and look upon her house. Perhaps she would leave for a walk or to shop, and he could spirit her away to talk.

At the same time he pulled his jacket over his linen shirt, he heard a knock at the door of the suite. With Giles gone to the front desk to procure transportation, Robert answered the door without a second thought, thinking the maid had arrived to service the room.

He grabbed the handle and pulled it open to find Philippe Moreau on the other side. Robert inhaled a surprised breath, immediately struck by the man's agitated appearance. Wrath, written across his face like that of a demon, spoke of one thing—his visit was not a friendly one.

"You son-of-bitch!" He clutched Robert by the throat and pushed him back into the room. "You fucked my wife!"

Robert stumbled backward into his suite, gasping for breath over the chokehold that Moreau had placed around his neck. His footing landed him into a side table, which pushed it on its side and sent a lamp crashing to the floor. Philippe's eyes burned with hatred as his chokehold became tighter.

Instinctively, Robert grabbed hold of the madman's death grip around his neck with both of his hands. A rush of defensive adrenalin shot through his body. At last, after moments of struggle, he pried Philippe's fingers from around his throat and flung his hand away.

"Get hold of yourself, man," he screamed, in a frightened squawk. "Have you lost all senses?" Robert rubbed the base of his neck where the knot of his ascot had been shoved into his windpipe cutting off his air supply.

Philippe's chest heaved up and down in rapid intakes of breath, while his eyes bulged from his head. "I should kill you, Robert Holland. You've stolen everything from me!"

"I suppose I deserve a punch in the jaw," Robert confessed, "However, I doubt my death would solve anything."

"You've soiled my honor as a man. You have stolen my wife and weaseled your way into my livelihood," he railed, eyeing him up and down. "Anonymous investor, I could spit in your face! I deserve retribution for what you've done to me and my family."

Robert dropped his hand from his neck, astonished over Philippe's vile ranting. Had Suzette told him that he had invested in Moreau Shipping?

"I saved your ass from bankruptcy," Robert flung in return. "You should thank me for saving your family from the gutters of Paris." His eyes narrowed as he cautiously looked at Philippe awaiting his next move.

"Your wife visited me this morning," he smugly replied. "She tells me that she will not divorce you. So where does that leave you with my wife, eh? Do you think you can continue to use her as a mistress for your sexual pleasure, as you once did?"

Philippe took a step closer to Robert with clenched fists, and Robert backed up.

"You've ruined me and sullied my honor. I demand satisfaction for you taking my wife behind my back. I want retribution." He pulled a glove from his pocket and threw it at Robert's feet.

The word *satisfaction* struck Robert's gut like a punch in the stomach, as he understood his intent. The thrown glove confirmed the challenge. *The damned French and their code of honor,* he thought with disdain.

"I will not fight you, Philippe, forget it." He kicked the glove aside and walked away from him.

"You will," Philippe growled. "Or I'll make sure you'll never see your bastard son again." His eyes narrowed as he played his ace. "You forget he lives under my roof and under my care. I can send him away where you'll never find him again as long as you live."

Robert's rage spewed from his mouth over the audacity of the threat. "You goddamn maniac!" Robert spun around in anger. "You'll do no such thing! Suzette would not allow it and neither will I!"

Philippe merely smirked in return. "And how will you stop me? One word from me and he's gone." He snapped his fingers. "Your precious little bastard is gone forever." A smug laugh of confidence left his mouth before continuing. "You either agree to a pistol duel at dawn Friday, or I promise you," he hissed like a snake, "your bastard son will wish he had never been born."

Philippe's hand glided across the leather belt around

his waist, catching Robert's eyes and the meaning behind it. Robert's fingers tingled as mortification shot through his veins. The thought to kill Philippe here and now turned his blue eyes into a stormy sea. Everything stood to be lost—his son, his love, his life.

"You're insane," Robert replied, throwing out his last attempt to dissuade him. "Duels are illegal in France, and you know it. Do you think either of us wounding or killing one another will solve anything?"

"I don't give a damn, Holland. I have despised you since the day we met. You are a blackguard with no regard for anyone but yourself. I intend to carry out the duel and be done with it. You will leave either dead or in shame wounded by my hand. My satisfaction will be complete. Then I promise you that you will never see Suzette or your son again."

Robert, cornered and threatened, stood rigid before Philippe. His heart pounded ferociously in his chest. He wanted nothing more than to permanently rid himself of Philippe Moreau, even if it ruined his own name and reputation. His love for Suzette and his son pushed him to accept the challenge.

"Fine," he resolutely accepted. "Friday at dawn. I expect a neutral third party to oversee the match and have the pistols examined and loaded."

"It is done, then. I shall have my representative contact you with the location and exact time." Philippe started to turn and head for the door, but Robert stopped him cold.

"Don't take your leave just yet, you pompous ass. Now I make my demands," Robert said sharply. "If my shot is on target and you are wounded, Suzette and the boy are mine. You will release your hold and divorce her for adultery immediately."

Philippe stopped and turned around. He glared at Robert. "Agreed, but it will never happen," he replied, with confident smugness.

As soon as the words left his lips, he turned around and headed out the door. Giles returned at the same moment with the news of the waiting carriage. Philippe gruffly pushed by him, nearly knocking Giles off his feet. He grasped the doorjamb to steady his footing.

Robert walked over to the side table, poured three fingers of cognac into a crystal glass and hastily gulped it down his throat. His hand, visibly shaking, caught the attention of Giles' surprised eyes.

"Your Grace, what has gone on here?" he asked, coming to Robert's side and watching him drink in a frenzy.

"Despicable things, Giles. Despicable things," he answered, while he choked down the burning alcohol. Robert finished the cognac and then turned and looked at his assistant for support. "I've been challenged to a duel by the chap who just left."

"A duel? Surely, you didn't accept the challenge!"

"Blackmail will cause you to do rash things, Giles—rash things, indeed."

Robert dragged himself to the divan and flopped down. He loosened the ascot around his neck so he could breathe. His Adam's apple still hurt from the pressure exerted against it, and his head felt as if it would burst from stress.

"Your Grace, please tell me that you are not going through with this senseless encounter. Why does the man wish to harm you?"

Giles, faithful and somewhat ignorant of all of Robert's recent activities, stood dumbfounded before him.

"Sit down, old friend, and I'll tell you why. I'm afraid I've not done the wisest of things, since I met up again with my French mademoiselle." He shoved the glass back at Giles. "Get me another, and I'll tell you what has happened and about my son."

Giles took the glass from his hand. "Your son," he exclaimed, dropping his jaw.

"Pour the drink, Giles. You better pour one for yourself."

Giles did as told and came back with two in hand. Robert took the glass, and his assistant sat in a chair opposite his employer eager to hear the details.

Truth be told, he had underestimated Philippe Moreau. In his zeal to win Suzette, he never considered the means to the end. Payback for all of his scheming had arrived. He would be damned, though, if he would allow Philippe to take away his son and not allow him to see Suzette again.

Robert recounted his affairs of the past month and then looked at Giles. "To top it off, I've separated from Jacquelyn and asked for a divorce."

"Oh, no," he moaned, clearly saddened over the news.

"I wouldn't worry, Giles. The woman hates me anyway and has for some time. It is obvious now that the problem of her inability to conceive is not with me, but with her. That fact, in itself, has broken our bond. I've asked her to divorce me for adultery, but she refuses in spite."

"I don't know what to say," Giles admitted, taking a well-needed drink. His face flushed with worry. "Your reputation is at stake should you go ahead with this duel."

"Damn my reputation," he angrily replied. "I cannot let the man take all that I love. There is nothing more to say. Now you know, and now I need your help. The faceoff is Friday morning. I want you there."

"Of course, I shall be at your side. Will it be by sword or pistol?"

"Pistol. Thank God, I am a fairly good shot. I have no idea about Moreau, though, but I suspect he is an expert due to his naval background. The outcome unquestionably will be dire for one of us." Philippe paused for a moment. "I want you to witness the duel, check the pistols beforehand, and assure all is above board."

"I cannot let you go through with this," Giles protested. "Your mother would be appalled that you have accepted this challenge."

"I must. Moreau has threatened that if I do not, he will

send away my son, and I will never find him. Surely," he reasoned, "I have no choice." Robert stopped abruptly making a quick decision. "There is something else you must do, Giles, no matter what the outcome."

"Yes, Your Grace, what is it?"

"You must protect my son. If I am shot, then you must leave immediately and let me bleed and die. Forget the physician. Go, get the boy and Suzette and take them back to England, posthaste. Make sure you arrive at their residence before Philippe has time to return and stop you. I'll make sure that Suzette knows to be ready. I will see a solicitor before Friday and have a new will written that will provide for them both in case of my demise."

Robert reached out and grasped Giles by the arm sternly. "Swear to me that you will do this!"

"Yes, yes, of course, whatever you wish." Giles' face, drawn tight with worry, demonstrated his loyalty to Robert.

"Good. Is the carriage downstairs?"

"Yes, it should be waiting for you."

Robert stood to his feet. He grabbed his hat and headed out the door. "I have things to tend to and will be back later."

He left Giles in the suite and proceeded downstairs to the hotel lobby. His world had suddenly turned into a nightmare from Hades, yet something inside his spirit told him all would be well, in spite of the challenges that lay ahead.

Chapter 22

Philippe tread heavily down the hallway to the staircase that led to the lobby. The hatred he had nursed for years toward Robert Holland had reached its boiling point. His challenge to end things through violence had been bred into his psyche from the many duels he had witnessed throughout his military career. Not a shred of remorse tainted his decision. He would kill the man and be done with it. Then life would return to normal.

Too upset to return to his office, he had decided to confront Suzette about her unfaithfulness. Fueled by the heated jealousy that burned in his veins, he would give her no mercy. He had one goal—to rid her love for Robert Holland from the depths of her heart, even if he had to dig it out with his bare hands.

As the hansom cab rolled toward his estate, he thought of the duchess and her statement that she would not release Robert from his marital commitment. If he aimed his shot to kill, Philippe would simultaneously relieve the scorned woman of her husband and do her a favor. However, he knew if he killed Robert, Suzette would never forgive him. He'd take the risk nevertheless. With the knave dead, her love for him would eventually die, too.

His thoughts drifted toward her son. The affection he once held for the boy seemed poisoned now. His presence in their family ate away at him like lye upon his flesh. If it continued, nothing would remain except hatred. He had cared for the boy for years, provided for him, accepted him as his own; but when Angelique was born, he admitted the majority his affections had shifted toward his daughter. Certainly, a father's love for his natural offspring held precedence. She was his own flesh and blood, not a half-bred bastard from his wife's days as another man's mistress.

The cab slowed, and Philippe's demeanor soured further over the impending confrontation. He paid the driver and entered his residence. As usual, his conscientious butler greeted him at the door.

"My wife, where is she?" he demanded in a gruff tone.

"I believe Madame Moreau is resting in her bedchamber."

Philippe looked up at the staircase. "No matter what you hear in the next few minutes, I do not want any of the staff interrupting me. Do you understand, Leroy? I have personal matters to discuss with my wife, and my staff is not to be involved under any circumstances."

Leroy's eyebrows rose, and he shook his head affirmatively. "Of course, sir. I'll see to it that no one in the household interferes with your private affairs." He bowed at the waist and left Philippe alone in the foyer.

Philippe stepped toward his wife with determination and purpose. He had been pushed to the brink. As much as Suzette had hurt him, he vowed to remain her husband. Her betrayal, though, would reap painful consequences.

More than ready to teach her a lesson, he did not bother to knock upon the door, but pushed through it quickly. He locked it behind him and slipped the key into his trouser pocket. Suzette sat on the window seat looking outdoors, but turned around to face him upon hearing his approaching footsteps.

"Philippe, you startled me."

"We have things to discuss, Suzette."

"Oh? Is everything all right with your business?"

"With my business?" Philippe gave a husky, sinister laugh. "I thought you knew that my business was half owned by Robert Holland. Do you really think everything is all right?"

Philippe watched the color drain from Suzette's cheeks. Her bottom lip quivered when he took a bold step toward her and hovered over her petite body.

"I don't—I don't know what you mean."

Philippe, angry about her answer, grasped her by the upper arm and pulled her roughly to her feet. He stared into her brown eyes and with his other hand toyed with her auburn hair, feeling a sense of obsessive ownership over the woman he had loved for years.

"I always thought you special, Suzette. I redeemed you from the filthy clutches of Robert Holland. Instead of remaining faithful to me, you crawled back into his bed. Like a sow, you returned to wallow in the mire."

Philippe felt the trembling of her body while he held onto her upper arm. His long fingers wrapped around her flesh and squeezed harder as the words hissed from his lips.

"I've learned much today," he continued. "The duchess came and exposed your infidelity to me, along with Robert's conniving claim on my business. What do you have to say for yourself?"

Suzette's body shook violently as tears streaked down her pale cheeks. Her eyes pleaded for mercy, but Philippe, at that point, felt very little except contempt. The more he thought of Suzette in Robert's embrace, the more his stomach grew sour as he pictured their lovemaking without any remorse or regard for his feelings.

"Philippe, I didn't plan for this to happen."

"You didn't do anything to stop it, either," he dismissed.

"Robert came back into my life while you were away and demanded to know his son."

"Did you allow him to see him?" He pressed harder

against her flesh.

"Philippe, you're hurting me!"

"Did you?"

"Yes, yes, I let them be together," cried Suzette, as she tried to slap Philippe's hand away. "Please, you're hurting me."

Philippe released his grip and stepped back. "You bitch! After everything that I have done for you and the boy. This is how you repay me?"

"It just happened. I could not help myself." She briskly stepped back behind a chair for protection. "All the love I thought was buried resurrected in my heart, and I was powerless to fight it, Philippe. I tried—I really did."

"Bullshit," he spat in her direction. "You betrayed me in the worst possible way."

"I'm sorry for hurting you, truly I am. You have every reason to divorce me for adultery. I will take little Robert and leave."

Philippe threw his head back into the air and roared with a guttural laughter. "Oh, my God, you two are pathetic! You think it is that easy to forget the vows that you made to me before God and the priest? You are my wife, and my wife you will be until death we do part. I shall never divorce you, and neither will Jacquelyn Holland divorce your lover. The two of you will stay where you belong."

Suzette gasped. "Philippe, please, I beg you. I am willing to take the shame of divorce. Just free me. Why keep me here as your wife after all I've done?"

"Why keep you? Did you forget in your lust for that man that you and I have a daughter together? We have a bond in our flesh, and she needs you as her mother. You have obligations, Suzette, to me and to Angelique."

Philippe took an angry step in her direction, disgusted that she would so easily leave behind their child.

"Do not set your heart upon Robert Holland, as I plan to cause him great harm in the days ahead. You are never to see him again, do you hear me? Never!"

"Philippe, what do you mean to do?" she cried.

"That is none of your concern. You will stay here in this residence and will not leave until I say that you can."

"You can't keep me prisoner, Philippe. You can't force me to love you!"

Philippe knew that unless he put fear into her heart, she would defy him. With one more aggressive step in her direction, he lifted his hand to strike her across the cheek hard enough to burn his message into her flesh. Suzette flinched, but he stopped short of making contact with her face. He wanted to see her drenched in tears and pain, just like his heart drowned in tears and pain at that moment.

He looked at her in disdain. "As much as I wish to hit you, I won't give you cause to divorce me. Perhaps one day I'll take my own mistress to make up for it."

"How—how could you think of being violent toward me?" she sobbed uncontrollably. "I will never love you! Never!"

"You're my wife, and you will do as I say. If I need to, I'll lay a hand upon that bastard son of yours. Don't tempt me."

Philippe spun on his heel and headed toward the door. He unlocked it and slammed it behind him finding his way downstairs. The household staff that he passed averted their eyes as soon as he neared, and once he found Leroy he pulled him aside to give him further instructions.

"Under no circumstances is my wife to leave this house until I say so. None whatsoever."

"Of course, Monsieur Moreau. I will see to it."

"I will need you to accompany me on business Friday at dawn," he instructed.

Leroy looked at him in confusion but nodded his head in obedience.

Philippe would finally have his revenge. After the match, he would return to his house and reclaim his wife, while leaving Holland to bleed to death in the dust.

❋ ❋ ❋

Jacquelyn sat in front of her vanity mirror, while Dorcas brushed her long blond hair. Her maid servant said little, but she could see in her eyes sympathy for her plight. It made Jacquelyn wonder how far she could take Dorcas down the path that her mind had toyed with and its malicious intent.

She felt smug over the trouble she had caused her husband and his wench by telling Philippe everything. Jacquelyn had returned to her townhouse to wait its poisonous outcome. She knew that she incited Philippe enough to take some sort of action. The ire in his eye spoke of revenge. Jacquelyn smiled. Wherever his heated emotions led him next, it would explicitly prevent their two spouses from pursing a future together.

Jacquelyn believed that after her return to England, she would obtain Mary's compassion in the situation. As duchess, she would continue to live in their estate among the riches of Robert's realm. If he refused to return home and stayed at their townhouse in London instead, so be it. Little would be lost, for he had never been a husband to her while they lived together anyway.

The name of Angelique floated to the top of her memory. Jacquelyn stirred the jealousy in her heart like a witch's caldron when she thought of Suzette's two children. She deserved neither of them, especially the one they had named as though she was an angel in their midst—a tiny newborn. What hypocrisy! It had come from the womb of a prostitute, regardless of the man she had married. She, on the other hand, deserved children far more than her rival did, and God's denial of her one desperate prayer in life remained unforgivable.

Dorcas continued to pull the brush slowly through her hair. Jacquelyn lifted her eyes and studied her plain face.

"Do you like serving me, Dorcas?" she asked in

curiosity.

Dorcas looked at her reflection in the mirror. "My lady, how can you ask such a thing? You know I do. You've been a fair and generous employer and kind to me as well."

Jacquelyn smiled. "I appreciate all you've done for me," she said, in a soft tone. "If I ask you anything, will you do it for me?"

Dorcas tilted her head, confused over the duchess' question. Her words assured her mistress of her continued loyalty. "Of course, whatever you need, my lady, I am here for you."

Jacquelyn lifted her hand behind her head and touched Dorcas' wrist. "I knew I could count on you. I knew it." She dropped her hand, and Dorcas continued to brush her hair.

A knock came at the door.

"Enter." Jacquelyn looked in the mirror and saw her housemaid approaching with an envelope in hand.

"This just arrived for you by courier."

"That's enough, Dorcas, you can stop brushing. That will be all for today."

"Yes, my lady."

Dorcas placed the hairbrush on the vanity and slipped from the room as the housemaid handed Jacquelyn the envelope, then curtsied and left.

Jacquelyn assumed a communication from Robert had arrived, but as she looked at the writing, she could tell it was not from him. She tore the envelope open and quickly slipped out the sheet of paper and read the hastily scribbled words.

Duchess,

I must speak with you regarding a matter of great urgency. Please meet me in the Tuileries Gardens by the gazebo at 9 o'clock in the morning, if at all possible. It's a matter of life and death.

Philippe Moreau

Jacquelyn did not quite know what to make of the few sentences, especially the words "*a matter of life and death.*" Unbeknown to Philippe, he had opened the door to their meeting again, which could only further her fantasies of ultimate retribution for Suzette's sins.

"Very well, Monsieur Moreau, I shall meet you at 9 o'clock in the morning." She mused aloud as she folded the letter, put it back in the envelope, and placed it into her vanity drawer.

Jacquelyn stood and slipped off her robe. After turning off the lamp, she climbed into bed. The darkness engulfed her, as well as an overwhelming sense of loneliness. Taunting spirits returned to her bedside. Every night, voices visited her in the dark, stealing her confidence and threatening to weaken her resolve.

"Failure," they whispered. "You're a barren failure."

"Leave me," she spoke to them. "Leave me!"

The voices laughed and then faded away. She would prove her tormentors wrong one day until they left for good, with their tails between their legs.

Chapter 23

Suzette received the package from Monsieur Leroy with an expressionless face. Numb from the day before from her heartrending encounter with her husband, Suzette felt void of emotion.

"A package arrived this morning, Madame Moreau. It appears to be from the Gibert Juene."

"Ah, yes, it's that little boutique bookstore. I special ordered a novel. Thank you," she said, walking toward the parlor. "I think I'll spend some time reading."

"Very well."

Suzette cradled the book in her arm as she entered the parlor and closed the door. She pulled the string and removed the brown wrapping paper. The volume of Elizabeth Gaskell's "North & South" told her immediately who had sent the package, so she quickly walked over to a chair and sat down.

Robert had devised an ingenious way to correspond in secret. She smiled that he had chosen a book to do the trick and another English love story for her to enjoy. She opened the pages and flipped through the chapters until an envelope fell into her lap.

She picked it up and smiled while ripping it open.

My Suzette,

Philippe is aware of our infidelities, and he has challenged me to a duel to regain his honor. If I do not agree, he has threatened to take Robert from us both and send him away. We shall never see our son again.

Suzette brought her hand to her mouth and gasped aloud. Her eyes filled with tears. Her hands trembled, fearing the words yet to come.

I cannot risk my son or you, for that matter. I am prayerful that all will turn out in my favor, my love. Do not despair. I promise not to shoot to kill, but only to wound to put these hostilities to an end. Philippe has agreed to release you should I prevail, along with Robert, and will grant you a divorce.

However, I must speak with you regarding all outcomes, my dearest. If I am wounded or killed, Giles, my assistant, has been ordered to rescue you and our son immediately before Philippe returns from his victory.

I have made provisions for you, Suzette. You shall not want for anything the remainder of your life, but you'll need to return to England to live in safety. Please pack the few things you can gather and be ready after dawn Friday morning for Giles' arrival should the outcome be dire. Let us hope, however, that it is I who arrives at your doorstep instead to take you into my arms, along with Robert, as a family.

Pray, my love. Pray for God's forgiveness and mercy for our indiscretions, and pray that our love will prevail and we shall be together.

Forever yours,

Robert

Suzette lowered the letter into her lap. Each word cut away every ounce of feeling she once held for Philippe. His egotistical, self-righteous attitude had finally caused the unthinkable. He doubtlessly had already won the duel in his mind and planned to keep her prisoner in their marriage forever.

Terrified thoughts swarmed around Suzette's head like angry bees. Whatever the outcome, she would lose. If Robert died, she would die. Her heart would turn to cold stone in her chest, and she would despise Philippe for eternity. Should Robert win, she would have to leave behind a daughter.

Little Robert, in the entire affair, had become a pawn in Philippe's merciless hands. She wondered what deceit the duchess and her husband had planned. Even if Robert won, how would he do away with his marriage and escape his wife's clutches?

Suzette stood and stumbled as the room seemed to shift beneath her feet. Unable to breathe, she walked to the parlor's double doors and opened them, calling for Leroy.

"I need fresh air," she begged him. "I'm feeling ill. Fetch me my cloak."

"I'm sorry, Madame Moreau." He blocked her way from the door. "I hate to interfere, but your husband has given strict orders that you are not to leave the residence."

"What are you talking about?" she demanded. "Get out of my way." She attempted to push quickly around him. Her orders did nothing to sway the tall butler that stood between her and the door.

"I'm afraid I cannot allow you to do that." Monsieur Leroy snapped his fingers, and the housemaid came to Suzette's side encouraging her to go upstairs.

"You cannot keep me prisoner in my own home! I'll have you fired for this!" she screamed.

"I doubt, Madame Moreau, that by my obedience to my master's orders, you shall succeed in having me fired." He inhaled a deep breath and narrowed his eyes. "I do not wish to get physical with you by escorting you upstairs, so I beseech you by your good nature that you turn around and go to your room."

A sudden panic engulfed Suzette as her thoughts turned to her son. Had Philippe already done the unthinkable and sent him away as further punishment for her sins? She lifted her skirt and ran up the staircase in haste, flying down the long hallway to her Robert's room. Suzette burst through the door, her eyes darting about.

"Oh, my love," she cried, seeing him by his wooden toy box. She scooped Robert up into her arms and began kissing his face repeatedly.

"Mama, don't, that tickles," he protested. He kicked his little legs, squirming for her to put him down.

Suzette hugged him tightly and gave one last kiss. "I'm sorry, sweetheart. I just missed you. Mommy needed a few kisses to feel better."

"Well, I suppose it's all right this time." He crossed his arms in front of him like a little man.

Suzette smiled as her thoughts turned toward Angelique. "I'll let you play."

She walked down the hall toward the nursery. Upon entering, however, she did not find Madame Dubois, as usual, and walked over to the bassinet only to find it empty. "Oh, my God," she gasped. "Where is Angelique?" She fled out the door, alarmed over her baby's absence.

Madame Dubois came down the hallway and quickly took Suzette by the shoulders. "Madame, calm down. Your husband has taken Angelique for a walk in the park. You should have seen them when they left. He looked so fatherly, insisting that he push the baby carriage all by himself. I made sure that she was properly dressed and warm."

"Why?" Suzette did not understand his strange deed. "He's never done that before. Why would he take her?"

"A father's love, I believe, oui? It is wonderful how he fusses over the little one."

Something didn't feel right. The world felt ajar.

Everyone's life hung by a thin thread ready to break or unravel in a thousand directions. Suzette sobbed.

"Madame, why so tearful? Everything is fine. You'll see."

Suzette would not be consoled, and her governess felt helpless as Angelique's mother heaved in miserable worry.

❋ ❋ ❋

Philippe had taken careful thought to cover every scenario thoroughly. He had never played the fool and would not begin now. When dawn arrived, his final triumph over Robert Holland would be complete. However, he had certain fears that grated upon him should, God forbid, the outcome go otherwise. One fear happened to be the welfare of his daughter, Angelique.

He wheeled the baby carriage into the gardens and slowly walked toward the location of the gazebo. As he neared, he saw the duchess standing inside. The early morning hours in the quiet park afforded all the time they needed.

She turned around and quickly stepped down the stairs and headed toward them. Her face beamed when her eyes caught sight of the baby carriage. Each time he looked at her, Philippe felt overcome by her beauty and demeanor. A slight hint of male adoration swept over him, somewhat fueled by his wife's infidelity and his unmet needs.

"Good morning," she cooed like a dove, walking up and bending down to see the angel inside. "I didn't expect you to bring your daughter, Angelique, with you this morning."

Jacquelyn pulled off the white glove from her right hand and looked at Philippe. "May I touch her?"

"Of course," he replied, unconcerned over the attention given to his daughter.

Jacquelyn ran her fingers down the baby's plump cheek. Her lips parted in a half smile, in awe of the softness of the child's skin. "Oh, Philippe, she's adorable! You must be so proud."

"Yes, I am. I love her with all my heart."

He allowed her to fuss over the baby for a few moments and then broke away her attention. "We need to talk, Your Grace. It's important."

"Of course, why don't we walk over to that bench and sit down."

Her heartwarming excitement over Angelique caused him to feel a slight endearment toward her, even though Philippe barely knew anything about the woman. Perhaps their shared sorrow of betrayal and loss had oddly bound them together.

"I must speak with you." Philippe paused wondering how she would handle the impending news about the duel. "Tomorrow at dawn, your husband and I are to meet and settle things once and for all." He paused for a moment, as he studied her face watching for subtle changes in her demeanor.

"Oh, really?" she drawled, with little concern. "Some sort of manly challenge, is that what you're saying?"

"Yes, I've challenged him to a duel by pistols. I felt obligated to inform you in case you wish to see your husband beforehand. The outcome might be less than desirable for your future."

"You seem intent on bodily harming Robert."

"I intend to regain my honor for what he has done to me and my wife, and if bodily harm returns that honor to me, then yes."

"Well, you Frenchmen certainly have a way of settling differences in a rather violent manner," she puffed, with an air of indifference. "If that is what you feel you need to do, then by all means, proceed. You have my blessing."

Shocked by her cold aloofness over his announcement, he pried further. "You must feel very little toward your husband to be so unconcerned for his safety."

"Well, I might say the same for you, since I should warn

you that Robert is an expert shot when it comes to a pistol. I'd be worried, sir, that you could stand to lose more than you think, due to your confident arrogance." Her eyes flashed at him. "If you do lose, no doubt Robert will still attempt to claim Suzette, Robert, and your little angel that you so dearly love." She glanced at Angelique in the carriage and smiled endearingly.

Philippe pondered an alternate outcome. He had already entertained one at length and thought of the possible conclusion, if he should not return. Robert would take Suzette and both his children. He would keep them as his own, even if the duchess never divorced him. Suzette, widowed and without resources to survive, would depend upon him once again to care for her. In return, she would undoubtedly pay him in gratitude with her flesh.

The duchess reached over and picked up Angelique's hand in her own, rubbing her silky skin with her thumb. "She's such a darling."

Philippe engulfed with panic that Robert could possibly become the father of his daughter, went ahead with his plans.

"I've already had that thought," he announced. "And have made alternative arrangements in this matter. I do not wish to have Robert raise my daughter, nor my adulterous wife. Should something happen to me, then it is my will that my sister, Julianne Bordeaux, who in lives Rouen, become guardian. She is married, with children of her own, and will provide a good home."

Philippe looked at the duchess, hoping that she would agree to his forthcoming proposal. "If I die, Robert will return to my home and claim everything. My daughter needs to be taken safely elsewhere until the war between us finally comes to an end." Philippe entreated the duchess.

"Would you take her, Angelique, I mean, back to your residence until tomorrow morning? Should I survive, I will return for her afterward and give you my condolences regarding your husband. Should I perish, then take this letter of introduction and deliver my daughter to my sister in Rouen," he said, pulling out an envelope from the pocket inside his vest. "I want Angelique in protective care and away from Robert, should he try to take her."

His daughter whimpered and began to fuss. Philippe leaned into the carriage and pulled her into his arms comforting the baby.

"You would trust me with such a mission?" Jacquelyn asked, her eyes ablaze with the prospect of caring for an infant.

"Well, yes, of course. I have no doubt that you will treat my daughter kindly while she is in your care. Frankly, there is no one else to trust with this undertaking. We have both suffered at the hands of our spouses. Therefore, I have confidence in you and your good name to help me now, as I would help you in your time of need."

"Then, I am most honored to be given this charge. I shall take care of her this afternoon and evening, and no doubt will have the joy of returning her to your arms in the morning."

Robert handed her the letter of introduction and waited for her to take it before continuing in a sorrowful prose.

"Your Grace, I know my wife stole from you what was yours. I am mournful over her behavior and the harm it has caused you." Philippe choked down a lump in his throat as he continued. "I mean to shoot to kill and should I succeed, I humbly ask for your forgiveness for taking the life of your husband. He has taken my life, business, honor, and my beloved wife. And if given the opportunity, he would rob me of my adorable Angelique, as well. I cannot allow such treachery to prevail."

Philippe lowered his head and kissed his daughter on her cheek. She looked up at him with tiny eyes. He felt the hand of the duchess reach over and touch his forearm.

"Be not dismayed, Monsieur Moreau. I understand what his black, selfish heart has done to us both. I leave the outcome in God's hands; but should he perish, I shall not grieve his loss." Jacquelyn lowered her eyes, sniffled, and then painfully continued.

"You see, I lost him years ago, and have mourned many times over, with grievous tears, the absence of my husband's love."

Philippe handed Angelique into the arms of the duchess, who scooped her up perfectly and held the baby to her bosom. Her eyes brimmed with adoration that calmed any worries in Philippe's soul over Angelique's safety.

"She is yours until the morning. If I do not come to your residence by 11 a.m., you may assume that I have lost. Take my daughter to my sister in Rouen with the letter of introduction. She is a kindhearted woman, who will receive you because of your goodness. My Angelique will be well cared for in life."

"Of course," she answered, her facial expression turning somber. "God be with you." Jacquelyn lowered the baby back into the carriage.

They spoke their goodbyes, and Philippe watched as the duchess wheeled his daughter down the garden lane. "Goodbye, my little one. Daddy will be back to fetch you soon," he called after her. Philippe, convinced he had done wisely, turned and went home to prepare for dawn.

Chapter 24

"Walk away," Giles heartily entreated. "No one will think you a coward, Your Grace. In fact, they will think you a wise man for not resorting to violence."

"I cannot," Robert groaned. He slipped his arms through his white linen shirt and fumbled with the buttons down the front. "Do you forget my son's future is at stake? What if the idiot sends Robert away? I shall never see him again." He finished fastening his shirt and picked up his vest laying on the bed.

"No, no, I cannot—I will not forfeit my only heir."

"I fear for you. The man has a military background. Surely, he is proficient with the weapon—"

"As I am!" he roared, interrupting Giles with his negative ranting. "Enough. Now, fetch me my jacket, and let's get on with it. I want this over, so I can begin my life."

Robert nervously pulled his arms through the sleeve of his black jacket. He had dressed casually for what would prove to be an unpleasant meeting. He grabbed his leather gloves, shoved them into his pocket, and headed for the door.

"Is the carriage downstairs?"

"Yes, Your Grace. We should arrive at dawn at the prescribed location, if we leave now."

"Very good. After we embark on this horrid affair, I

want you to inspect the weapons and make sure all is above board."

Giles nodded his head. "Yes, sir, I will see to it."

"And if it goes not the way we hope, tell me what you will do," Robert pressured him, as they headed out the door and made their way downstairs.

Giles, out of breath trying to keep up with Robert's quick pace, hurriedly answered. "I will depart immediately and proceed to the residence of Monsieur Moreau. I will leave on the ruse that I'm procuring the undertaker to take care of your remains."

"Fine. Thank you." Robert climbed into the carriage. Giles entered and then banged on the roof to instruct the driver to proceed to the destination he had given him.

Robert's instructions were to meet Philippe in a grove in the southern side of the city wall. The location, supposedly secluded, had been often used for such occasions as planned this morning. He glanced out the window, thankful for a decent day. The sky, pink with the colors of sunrise against the billowy clouds, reminded Robert of blood. *This will indeed be a bloody affair*, he thought, as the daylight would soon breach the horizon.

The horses that pulled the carriage increased their gait as they left the city proper and began traversing a country road heading toward their final destination. Robert glanced over at Giles, whose poor face was contorted with worry. He wrung his hands together like a little old woman.

Robert felt odd. Though his soul remained calm, his body began to react to the stress. An occasional quiver rushed through his arms and legs. Whatever the outcome, all would go well. He had to believe for the sake of all he loved.

He would keep his promise to Suzette and would not shoot to kill. A wound to the shoulder would suffice to make his point. Philippe would not die. Then, as agreed to in the challenge, he would leave and get Suzette and Robert and take them back to England.

His mind drifted to Angelique, knowing that if the baby had to be left behind, Suzette would make a great sacrifice to abandon her child to be with him. Philippe would never agree to hand Angelique over, and no doubt the courts would grant him sole custody because of her infidelity. A part of him, felt thankful it would play out, as it should.

The carriage slowed, and Robert's heart pounded against his ribcage, sending blood pumping through his veins. His hands shook, so he clenched them together to suppress the tremors.

Finally, they came to the edge of a wooded glen and stopped. The driver jumped down and opened the door.

"I believe this is the location. There are gentlemen waiting a few yards off to your left."

Robert exited, and Giles followed close behind. A slight breeze rustled the leaves in the trees above, and the sun breached the horizon and filtered through the wooded canopy. The heat of the rays hit the cool ground and produced a knee-high midst that weaved its way across the grass.

A group of men stood waiting near a tree. He looked at Philippe, who stood like a confident jackass. One man held the dueling pistols in a box, and another unrecognizable individual stood by Philippe.

Robert stopped and looked at each of them before speaking. "Gentlemen, let's get on with it."

"Yes, let's," snarled Philippe, as he shot a dagger-like glare in Robert's direction.

"This is my personal assistant, Mr. Giles Woodward, who will be my witness. And these gentlemen are?"

Philippe answered. "Monsieur Pelletier, is the third-party who has officiated over many duels in Paris. Monsieur Leroy is my butler and witness."

"I would like my assistant to examine the weapons,

please, before proceeding," Robert requested.

Monsieur Pelletier replied, "Yes, of course." He walked over to Giles, opened the wooden box, and presented the matched engraved and gilded weapons for inspection. Giles looked at the single flintlock pistols, checked both chambers, noted they were loaded, then concluded they were in working condition.

"Thank you, they look agreeable."

Monsieur Pelletier kept the case open and invited both men to stand in front of him. "Gentlemen, you may choose your weapons. Monsieur Moreau, because this duel is your challenge, you will have first choice."

Philippe studied both pistols and grabbed the gun on the right. Robert reached over and retrieved the gun on the left. Pelletier snapped shut the lid of the case and shoved it under his arm.

Robert's heart pounded in his ears as he waited for the instructions to stand back-to-back with Philippe Moreau and then pace off, turn, and shoot. For a quick moment, he thought himself quite insane for agreeing to accept the challenge. He had put his life on the line to win his cherished Suzette and the son he loved. The stakes were high. In the next few minutes, he could very well be dead.

He held the pistol in his right hand and looked at the maker's engraved name on the stock, feeling the weight, and gauging its handling. Made by a French gunnery, it felt somewhat different than the English pistols he had been accustomed to holding. He prayed the use of a foreign weapon would not hamper the accuracy of his aim, even though he was a first-rate shot.

Pelletier announced the conditions to them both in a gruff, loud voice.

"Monsieur Moreau has requested that the duel be to first blood, in which case the matter will be settled upon one man being wounded. However, if one man is severely wounded, and that wound leads to death, Monsieur Moreau will receive full and complete satisfaction of the disrespect done to his name."

Robert knew then his nemesis intended to shoot to kill. His gut turned into a hard knot as the moments slipped precariously toward battle.

"Gentlemen, please proceed to the clearing, stand back to back, with pistols in hand. I shall count to twenty paces, upon which you will stop upon the number twenty, turn, and fire your weapons. Do you understand my instructions?"

Robert nodded affirmatively. Philippe called out a confident "yes" in response.

"Very well then."

Quickly, Robert glanced over at Giles who stood on the sidelines watching. The man looked pale as the moon, and Robert lifted his lips in a forced smile. He gave him a quick wink for an ounce of reassurance that all would be well.

"One, two, three . . ."

Robert moved his booted right foot in front of him and stepped in cadence with the numbers that were spoken. Twenty paces—it seemed like such a long distance, which would indeed make it a more difficult aim. He wondered why Philippe hadn't chosen a lesser number to do him in at point blank range and be done with it.

"Seven, eight, nine . . ."

Robert faced his countdown to eternity. He focused upon Suzette and his beautiful son, who looked so much like him.

"Twelve, thirteen, fourteen, fifteen . . ."

In a few more seconds, it would be over. One way or the other.

"Eighteen, nineteen, twenty . . ."

Robert turned on his heel, lifted the gun to aim, and heard Philippe's pistol discharge. He pulled the trigger almost instantaneously in return, and waited for the bullet from Philippe's pistol to lodge in his heart.

His eyelids closed anticipating the blow. Then he heard a piece of wood blow off from the bark of the tree behind him, followed by a fleshly thud, a surprised moan, and a body dropping to the earth with such force he felt the tremor underneath his feet.

His eyes shot open. At first, he could not see through the cloud of smoke spewing from the end of his pistol. Philippe lay on the ground, holding his shoulder, and clenching his teeth in pain. Robert lowered the gun and walked over to his wounded nemesis.

"You son-of-a-bitch!" Philippe growled. He impulsively felt the ground for the gun that had fallen from his hand. Once back in his grasp, he aimed it at Robert and pulled the trigger in a desperate attempt to kill him anyway.

"You goddamn bastard!" he roared.

Click.

Everyone stood silently by, watching Philippe writhe to and fro, after his unscrupulous and foolish second attempt.

"Sir, it's only a single shot," Pelletier said, coming up and removing the pistol from Philippe's clutches. Robert reached out and handed the other pistol to him as well.

"Let it be over, Philippe. I promised Suzette I would not kill you, though plainly you had planned otherwise for me. Why you missed, I shall never know, until the good Lord reveals the reason why He spared my life."

"You fucking bastard!" he spit in his direction, with sweat pouring down his forehead. Philippe moaned.

"I've won," Robert reiterated. "Suzette and the boy are mine."

He spun around on his heel and headed toward Giles. Color began to rush back into his assistant's face. He came over, grabbed him heartily, and patted Robert on the back.

"Well done, Your Grace. Well done, indeed."

"Perhaps." Robert ruefully glanced back at Philippe, who had risen to his feet with the help of his assistant. His wound, though painful, appeared minor. He would recover fully within a month or so, after the removal of the bullet.

Robert recognized the painful defeat written across Philippe's sorrowful face. Remorse flooded his soul for what had transpired between the two of them. Yet through it all, he took solace. It could only mean that he and Suzette were meant to be together.

As they strode toward their waiting carriage, Robert wondered if Jacquelyn knew of the morning affairs. If she had, her silence beforehand was understandable. Certainly, she had wished for his demise many times over.

He patted Giles on the shoulder. "Come my friend, and let us retrieve what this day has awarded me."

Giles' face radiated with a relieved smile.

Chapter 25

Philippe lay on the ground, his white linen shirt soiled from grass stains and dirt. The shot hit him with such force, it knocked him off his feet, and he fell hard to the earth. His shoulder felt as though it was on fire with excruciating pain.

As he watched Robert depart the scene with his assistant, his eyes narrowed into dark slits. The pat of camaraderie between the two brought a flurry of curses spewing from his mouth.

"Monsieur, let me help you up."

He held onto Leroy's hand and wobbled to his feet. The movement sent searing pain through his shoulder. Philippe allowed Leroy to pull back his shirt to inspect the wound, grimacing over the slightest touch.

"You are very fortunate," Leroy assured. "There is minimal blood loss. It appears the bullet can be easily removed. It is a clean shot."

"Yes, I'm fortunate, I suppose, to have been only wounded. I would have rather blown the heart out of that bastard's chest instead."

Pelletier walked over and stood in front of Philippe. "My services have been concluded, and since you have already paid my fee and there are no bodies to be removed, I shall take my leave. Good day," he remarked, with no emotion. He tipped his hat and departed.

Philippe gritted his teeth. He hadn't the strength to reply one way or the other.

"Help me back to the carriage." He leaned upon Leroy for assistance. "I need to take care of this arm immediately at a physician and retrieve my daughter the duchess."

"Of course, monsieur, straight away," replied Leroy.

After they climbed inside, Philippe lifted his shirt to view the wound himself. Leroy put pressure against it with his clean handkerchief to stop the blood until they reached the doctor's home. His face etched with concern over his employer's welfare.

Philippe occasionally moaned in discomfort, while he mulled over his defeat. Angry that he lost the challenge, he found the outcome far too bitter to swallow.

He had arrived confident that morning, feeling fearless beforehand. Though his mind had already relished in his victory, subconsciously his body responded to the inherent possibilities of death just prior to the duel. Copious beads of sweat had formed on his forehead before the pace off. By the time they reached the count of twenty, perspiration had trickled downward from his hairline.

The stinging of the salty liquid, as it rolled into his eyes, caused him to blink profusely from the discomfort. He had squeezed the trigger prematurely, sending the bullet to its target before a clear aim had been gained through his blurred vision. Philippe, confident he would hit Robert somewhere on his body, uttered a profanity the moment the projectile hit the bark of the large oak tree instead.

At the same time, the hot, searing arrival of a bullet tearing into his shoulder sent him crashing to the ground. He could not accept the unfinished outcome of Robert's demise and tried to shoot him once again. The moment he pulled back the flintlock and squeezed the trigger, his anger gave way to the reality it was only a single-shot pistol. He felt like a foolish ass for attempting to murder his nemesis with an empty gun, but his point had been made.

Philippe could bear the pain of a fleshly wound, but found bearing the shame of losing face and honor a thousand times more painful. Leroy stayed supportive throughout the matter. Burdened with the heavy weight of failure, Philippe refused to lift his head while the driver sped toward medical treatment.

They arrived and were quickly spirited into the examining room. Since dueling was against the law in France, the physician had agreed, at the price of a bribe, to keep the visit confidential.

"I can see the bullet," he reported, poking about Philippe's wound site. "It's lodged against your upper arm bone. You are lucky it did not break the bone, but it may be chipped."

"Goddamn it, man!" Philippe roared when the physician inserted a surgical instrument into the injury and quickly pulled out the round ball.

"You see?" he said, holding it up proudly. "You will be fit in no time."

The doctor dropped the lead projectile into a metal bowl with a *clang*, and Philippe watched the horrid thing roll back and forth, taunting him over his loss. The gaping wound was stitched closed, and Philippe gritted his teeth through the whole process. After the removal of the bullet and bandaging of the wound, Philippe stood to his feet and slipped his arms back into his bloodied shirt.

"You should wear your arm in a sling, monsieur, to keep it still. Movement will cause great pain for at least the first week, and then you can slowly work it about." He washed his hands in a basin of nearby water and continued giving instructions. "Come back to me if you see any sign of infection around the wound, especially if it turns red or produces puss. Otherwise, it should heal nicely on its own."

"Thank you," Philippe mumbled, grateful the ordeal ended.

"Do you wish to return home and change before picking up your daughter?" Leroy asked, thinking he looked like a fright.

Philippe balked at the idea of returning to his residence where Suzette stood ready to run away with her blackguard of a lover.

"Damn, no. Direct the driver to proceed to the Holland residence, so I can see the duchess."

They arrived at the townhouse a short time later, much to Philippe's relief. Anxious to see Angelique and bring her back into his custody, Philippe pulled his jacket over his soiled shirt and then headed to the door. He picked up the knocker and slammed it a few times, but no one answered. Finally, after a few more persistent shoves of the brass ring, a maid opened the door. She stood in the threshold with an uncomfortable look on her face.

"Philippe Moreau to see Her Grace. Please announce my arrival."

The young maid looked at his bloody state. Her eyes opened wide, and then slowly she slipped her hand into the pocket of her apron and pulled out an envelope.

"I apologize, sir, but I am to inform you that the duchess has left the residence. She asked me to give you this note."

Philippe snatched it from her hand. "My daughter—I'm here to pick up my daughter. I need not speak to the duchess, where is she?"

A fearful look spread across the maid's face, and her voice squeaked out a reply. "I'm afraid that the duchess departed last evening, along with a baby and Dorcas, her lady's maid."

"What?" Philippe cried in a violent panic. "What do you mean they left?"

He pushed his way through the door into the residence and began yelling at the top of his lungs, while he wandered from room to room. "Duchess! Angelique! Are you here?" His eyes scoured the premises in a panic-stricken search for his daughter.

The maid scurried behind him in a frantic state. "Sir, I told you, they left last evening."

Finally, Philippe stopped cold and looked at the envelope in his hand.

"The duchess has probably explained in her note, monsieur. Perhaps you should read it."

His thumb lifted the lip of the envelope breaking the seal and tearing the paper in the process. Philippe pulled out the parchment and read the neatly written pronouncement of fate.

Monsieur Moreau,

I write this letter in the expectation that you have triumphed in your challenge. My desire is that my husband is dead, Suzette is destitute, and your honor has been restored.

In spite of the above, I must confess that I have taken other matters into my own hands. You were quite right, Monsieur Moreau, when you apologized for your wife stealing from me something that I loved. Now, it is my turn to steal from her something she loves.

"An eye for an eye," says the good Book. Life is filled with principles that if one person injures another, that person will receive the same injury in return. It is my pleasure to confer that punishment upon your wife by taking your daughter, Angelique. Hopefully, the pain I cause her through this one act will be sufficient retribution to cause her grief for the remainder of her life.

You, though innocent of your wife's sins, are not without guilt. You took from my husband his son and raised him as your own. As much as I despise the bastard, it is still an offense for which you must pay. Divine retribution is indeed harsh, and I have come to execute it upon you both.

Your baby daughter now belongs to me. By the time you

read this letter, I shall be far away from Paris leaving my past behind and starting anew. I will settle elsewhere, raise Angelique as the child I never had and love her with all of my heart. She will never know her true parents. She'll only know me as her mother and whomever I take as a husband to be her father.

Forget her, monsieur, as if she were never born. It will make it easier for you to deal with the loss.

Jacquelyn Spencer-Holland

"Oh, my God," Philippe cried in anguish. He dropped the note and fell to his knees with a *thud* on the wooden floor, barely able to breathe from the shock. He wailed aloud like a lunatic in an insane asylum.

Leroy ran to his side when he heard his cries from outside the residence. The house maid merely looked at him in astonishment, until Leroy picked up the letter Philippe had dropped and read its contents.

"My dear, Jesus," he muttered. "My dear, sweet Jesus."

He stuffed the letter into his pocket and knelt down besides Philippe and held him by the shoulders, trying to bring him back from the brink of insanity.

"Monsieur, you must contain your emotions and think rationally. Perhaps we should not delay in calling the police. They couldn't have gone too far."

Philippe wiped his face with the palm of his hands and tried to stand upright. He swayed from the awful pain and grabbed hold of Leroy's arm to steady himself.

"Yes, you are right, we should go to the police. Take me—take me now."

Philippe could barely think straight as he exited the residence and made his way back to the carriage. Life had dealt him an unthinkable blow. In a few short hours, he had lost everything of value—his wife, his honor, and his daughter.

❋ ❋ ❋

Jacquelyn woke to the slow, gentle rocking of the train. She had purchased a ticket for herself and her companions on a new long-distance passenger train owned by the Compagnie Internationale des Wagons-Lits and named the Orient Express. She thought the mode of transportation exotic and wonderful. The coach would take her through Strasbourg, Munich, and onward to Vienna. The train turned out to be everything she had hoped for—luxurious, private, and destined to a city that had always captured her fancy.

Jacquelyn embarked on a flurry of frantic preparations the day before. Her first order of business had been to introduce Angelique to Dorcas, who would watch the baby while she went into central Paris to take care of pressing matters.

Thankfully, she had thought ahead and brought with her all the fine jewels given to her as a duchess—family heirlooms of diamonds, sapphires, rubies, and gold, which were part of the Holland fortune. She found a jeweler, who agreed to pay her a high price for a few small pieces and then went shopping.

There were baby clothes to purchase and all the accessories a newborn required for a long trip. The very act of running about procuring the items flooded Jacquelyn with an elation she had never known. She had been rescued out of the pit of despair. Finally, her dream of being a mother had arrived. She was the proud caretaker of an infant girl who would grow up as her daughter.

After she returned to her townhouse with her newly gathered purchases, she gave instructions for Dorcas and the other maids to repack her trunks for a journey. In the meantime, she penned her departing letter to Philippe Moreau. As far as the outcome of the duel, Jacquelyn thought very little of it the entire evening. Whatever happened, she would win either way.

The misguided affection she once felt for her husband, speedily died when he announced his love of the whore. She buried the loss, as one buries a dead pet—with passing grief and a desire to quickly replace her loss with another pet to take its place. It amazed her how stone cold her heart for Robert had become, like a gravestone etched with painful memories and lack of love.

As she lay in her bed pondering her departure, the baby whimpered. Jacquelyn reached over to the traveling carrier she had purchased, and laid her hand upon the soft bundle and smiled. She lifted the baby to her bosom and spent a few moments bonding with the infant.

No longer did her empty arms ache for a baby. The touch of her warm flesh awakened her maternal urges. Jacquelyn gloried in the completion of her womanhood. With a light tender squeeze, she felt the madness that had flowed through her veins melt away like the winter's snow. Spring had finally arrived. She took a deep breath of air into her lungs as a welcomed infusion of new life. No longer would she curse her lonely and meaningless existence.

Jacquelyn studied the child's hair, weaving her delicate fingers through the strands playfully. Angelique had inherited the darker features of her mother and father with her brown eyes. However, her hair displayed a lighter shade of brunette, and her complexion was fair enough to match Jacquelyn's tones. She imagined the child to have been birthed from her own womb. The memory of her former parents would soon drift into oblivion, as the wheels of the train click-clacked on the rails taking them farther away from Paris.

"You're such a sweetheart," she adoringly whispered, kissing her soft cheek multiple times. "I shall love you and give you a wonderful life, Angelique."

Jacquelyn had not the heart to change the angel's first name, for it fit her perfectly. How could one modify the name of a gift from Heaven? "You need a middle name, though, my love," she pondered. "Angelique Jolene. Now that has a ring to it, doesn't it?"

Convinced they would never be discovered in Vienna, Jacquelyn harbored no qualms of taking her mother's maiden name of Bennett. She fully intended, however, to find herself a new husband and would use the ruse of being a widow to obtain empathy. Certainly, she could come up with some type of dastardly story about the loss of a husband to produce compassion from some lonely aristocrat. Men were foolish creatures and duping one into believing a lie seemed an effortless pursuit to undertake.

If they found reasonable housing, the amount of money pocketed from the sale of her jewels would provide for her needs for quite some time. However, a husband would provide for her needs long term, as well as the fine education she planned to give her daughter. Jacquelyn daydreamed that one day Angelique would be the belle of society in Vienna, and she would marry her off to a prosperous and rich man who would love and respect her.

After obtaining forged documents to support her new identity, a past left behind, and a future to build, Jacquelyn embraced the day ahead. Tomorrow, they would arrive at their destination and begin anew. Leaving had been the perfect consequence for all she left behind. Her husband still bound to a wife who abandoned him; a whore bound to her lover without being able to marry him; and retribution for a man who stole a child. Jacquelyn laughed, feeling like an executioner of divine judgment.

Angelique let out a whimpering cry, just as a knock came at the door. "Madame, it's Dorcas. I have the wet nurse with me."

"Come in," she replied, placing Angelique back in her bassinet. Jacquelyn had hired a wet nurse to accompany them until they reached Vienna, having been fortunate to find one quickly through an agency.

Dorcas had been somewhat skittish over the entire matter of her mistress committing a crime, but promised her loyalty regardless. Her sympathies toward her employer remained strong after all the heartbreak she had seen her suffer. Dorcas promised to attend to her needs for as long as she wanted her in life, in return for secure, long-term employment.

"Madame Boucher is ready to feed the little miss."

"Very well." She stood up and put her robe on for morning tea in her cabin. "Take good care of her, Dorcas. She is, after all, the joy of my life and my ultimate revenge."

Jacquelyn smiled.

Chapter 26

Suzette obeyed Robert's instructions. Her bags were packed and placed by the door of her bedchamber for quick retrieval. When she set them down, her hands trembled over the possibility they would not be used.

Her anxiety the morning of the duel had wreaked havoc upon her physical health. She had vomited from nerves and broke out in a rash across her chest and neck. The wait proved intolerably cruel.

To compound the horrid situation, the evening before, Philippe returned home without Angelique. He would not tell her where he had taken her. Instead, he yelled at her to stay out of his affairs. Tomorrow, their daughter would return, and then she would be expected to go back to her duties as a wife and mother.

Suzette thought fondly of her newborn. Each reflection of her little life tore at her soul. She had given birth to a daughter and one whose arrival she had waited upon for many years. Angelique represented God's forgiveness for her past sins. Her price, now steeped in the sin of adultery, would be to leave her behind.

Should Robert prevail and they leave with their son, she hoped to God that Philippe would find an ounce of mercy and allow her to visit Angelique throughout her lifetime. She knew his devotion to their daughter ran deep, and she would bring consolation to him in his loss. Her anguish, however, did not outweigh her love for Robert. What sacrifices she must make to spend eternity with him, she would gladly embrace.

Suzette spent the night behind closed doors. The emotions in her heart, raw and tender, brought tears to her eyes throughout the evening's vigil. It had become impossible to suppress her bouts of sobbing over all that had happened and all that would soon unfold.

Life had taken a turn—a violent turn once again. Only this time, it happened by her hand and none other. She deeply regretted her choice of not telling Robert about their son. He spoke the truth. She had made the decision for him and had not allowed him to accept his responsibility or perhaps make other arrangements.

Suzette refused to ponder what could have happened between them had circumstances been different. The past would never change. All that remained was a terrifying reality at morning's light.

She harbored anger toward Philippe because he challenged Robert and put both of their lives at risk. He had always been an arrogant man driven by honor and more so since his return from the navy. She should have known that he would not have taken her adultery lightly. He would consider her a traitor.

Suzette understood the desperation Robert felt to protect his son and accept the challenge. In doing so, he had risked his life to bring them together. The thought of his death proved far too painful to allow entrance into Suzette's imagination. After the hours crawled slowly through the night and eventually gave way to the morning, she rose to face her verdict.

Finally, an hour after the break of dawn, a knock came upon her door. Suzette jumped to her feet. "Yes?" she called out, afraid that it might be Philippe on the other side.

"There is a gentleman downstairs asking to see you. His

calling card says that he's the Duke or Surrey."

Suzette threw the door open and rushed by her maid in a frantic dash, nearly knocking her over. She picked up the hem of her skirt and ran down the staircase toward Robert, who stood in the foyer. Across the tiled entrance and into his arms she flung herself, causing him to take a step backward to keep his balance. She clutched him tightly in thankful relief.

"Robert, my dear Robert." Suzette trembled against his warm body, and Robert circled his arms around her gently in return.

"It's all right, my love. All is well. You need not despair any longer."

Suzette's cries of relief continued, and Robert stroked her back tenderly with his hands, comforting her as she released the last bit of fear from her soul.

Finally, she pulled away and looked at him with her tear-streaked face. "Philippe . . . is he all right?"

"Philippe is fine, love. A small wound to his shoulder. He should heal and be well soon."

"Oh, thank God," she whispered under her breath. "Thank God." She stepped back and examined his appearance. "And you, Robert, have suffered no harm?"

"None. I'm fine, Suzette. By the grace of God, his bullet hit the tree behind me rather than lodging in my heart."

She looked up into Robert's eyes. "I'm surprised he missed, but thankful," she exhaled, in relief. "I don't know, Robert, what I would have done had you died!"

Robert embraced her while she continued her unrestrained discharge of joy. Eventually, she pulled away, and Robert handed her his handkerchief.

"Blow your nose, then we'll speak of what is to come."

Suzette did just that, flushing in embarrassment over her earlier expressions of relief. "What now? What becomes of us now?" she asked, after she finished drying her eyes.

"If Philippe is a man of his word, as he seems to be a

man of honor, he will file for divorce on the grounds of adultery. I'm not sure what my wife will agree to at this point, but I need you to come back with me to England—you and my son. Are you packed?"

Suzette nodded her head and suddenly smiled. "A flush of memories washed over me when you spoke those words. I remember the first time you told me that I must go with you."

Robert lifted his hand and touched her cheek with his fingertips. "I remember too, like it was yesterday."

"I've not told our son that we are leaving. What shall I say?"

"Yes, what shall you say?" bellowed the gruff voice of Philippe, who stood menacingly in the open doorway. He had entered unseen during their touching moment. Philippe narrowed his eyes and glared at them scornfully.

"Philippe!" Suzette gasped and brought her hand to her mouth. She reached out and tightly grabbed Robert's arm.

Robert looked at him with a challenging glare. "It's over, monsieur; let us not continue the war here. It is done."

"You bastard." Philippe lurched in his direction. "What have you done with my daughter?"

Robert cocked his head in confusion over the accusation.

"If you do not tell me," he threatened, with clench fists, "so help me God I shall find a way to tear your heart from your chest with my bare hands."

Robert scoffed at the allegation and looked at him in utter disbelief. "I have no idea what you're talking about nor do I know where your daughter happens to be."

Suzette's lips sputtered. "Phil—Philippe, what are you saying? Where is Angelique?"

Leroy entered the doorway behind Philippe and stood there with a sorrowful face. Philippe inquired, "Do you have the letter?"

"Yes, monsieur," he replied. He pulled it from his

pocket and handed it to Suzette.

"Your answer is on that sheet of paper. I took Angelique to your wife to care for her until after the duel. We had formed an alliance of sorts," he confessed. "I was concerned that should I lose and you came to take my wife and your son that you would also take my daughter. I wanted her safe, and she promised that if I died, she would deliver Angelique to my sister in Rouen."

Suzette held the letter open, and Robert stood close by her side as they both read the poisonous words. "Oh, my God," Suzette cried. "How could she do such a thing? My Angelique! My poor baby Angelique!"

"Your Angelique?" Philippe spat from his lips. "Is that all you think about is *your Angelique?* She's my daughter too, you whore!"

Suzette's eyes filled with hot tears that burned a trail down her cheeks. "Philippe . . ."

"I'm so sorry," Robert gulped with emotion. "My wife—you should have never trusted my wife. She is of unsound mind and desperate for a child. When you gave your daughter into her arms, she took it to her advantage to steal what belonged to you both."

Robert's voice cracked, and he looked at his poor Suzette, who had turned pale with sorrowful cries. Robert took the letter from her hand, to spare her from reading the hurtful words again. He handed it back to the butler.

Philippe glared at them. His eyes were heavy with pain and grief. "Leroy and I went to the police as soon as I discovered what she had done. They have sent officers to check train stations and directed telegrams to nearby port authorities to be on the lookout. I fear it's too late."

"I promise you that I shall do everything in my power to find my wife and your daughter. You have my word."

Philippe merely shook his head and shot an accusatory glance at Robert. "Your word? I put as much trust in your word as the pot I piss in." He turned away. "Get out of my house—both of you and take that bastard son of yours. Get out and never come back." Philippe stomped down the hallway in the other direction.

Suzette let go of Robert, lurched forward after her husband, and grasped his arm. "Please," she pleaded, "Forgive me, Philippe. Forgive me. I cannot leave until I hear you've forgiven me. I never meant to hurt you."

He stopped, turned, and looked at her fingers wrapped around his sleeve. "I will never forgive you, Suzette." He seized her hand and pushed it off his body, repulsed by her touch. "I will file for divorce quickly, so I can be rid of you. As long as I live, I don't ever wish to look upon your face again."

Philippe pulled away from Suzette, walked into the nearby parlor, and closed the door. She spun around and looked at Robert, who stood silently only a few feet away. His blue eyes dimmed in the sorrow of the moment, and he held out his hand toward Suzette.

"What have we done?" Suzette cried.

Leroy, who still stood nearby, shook his head and walked down the hallway to the servants' quarters.

"We've only followed our hearts," answered Robert. "God forgive me for not being able to live without you."

Suzette looked at the man she loved. Her heart felt crushed under the weight of sorrow, but it struggled to live for the sake of what awaited.

"I'll get our son." Suzette ran upstairs to Robert's room. She slowly opened the door and found him sitting on the edge of the bed with a forlorn look upon his face. He must have sensed something wasn't right in the world around him, because his countenance was filled with apprehension.

"Mommy, is everything okay?" He looked at her with worrisome eyes. "I heard yelling downstairs."

"Yes, honey, everything is all right," Suzette assured him with a calm voice. "You and I are going to take a trip, sweetheart. Give me your hand, and let's go downstairs. That nice man you met in the park is going to take us to his home, and you can ride his pony."

"Really?" He jumped to his feet and grasped Suzette's hand.

"Really." Uncontrollable tears streamed down her face. Suzette walked him out the door. She passed the nursery, and for a brief moment, she stopped and glanced inside.

"I'm afraid your sister won't be coming with us."

"How come?"

"She's gone away for a while."

"Okay," he innocently replied. Robert released her hand and ran down the staircase, oblivious to Suzette's heartache. When he saw the duke standing by the doorway, he ran up to him. Robert flashed a bright smile.

Suzette ordered Leroy to get their suitcases and load them on the carriage. He complied without saying a word. When done, she wrapped a shawl around her shoulders and put on her favorite hat. Suzette, in shock of all that occurred, trembled as she looked at Robert standing in the doorway waiting to depart.

"I think, monsieur, that I am ready to visit your homeland, as is my son."

"Can I ride the pony when we get there?"

Robert bent down and lifted the boy into his arms. "Of course you can, son."

Suzette glanced behind her one more time, reliving in her mind the last time she had left Paris for a new life abroad. Something in her heart told her this time it would be for good. Paris would never be her home again, nor would she ever visit the pit of her father's grave containing his bones.

"I'm ready," she announced, with a bittersweet smile upon her face. "Take us to your home."

Chapter 27

Robert returned to London fraught with worry over what lay ahead. The trip with Suzette, his son, and Giles went well, but his soul agonized over his wife's actions. His suspicions of an unsound mind had been confirmed but at what price? It would have been painful enough for Suzette to leave her daughter with Philippe, but knowing now that she had been kidnapped made the matter far more horrendous.

As the boat traversed the English Channel, Robert tried to think of where Jacquelyn would go and how would she take care of herself. Even more so, he brooded over how he could be freed from their marriage. The prospects were as gloomy as the line of gray clouds over the horizon that threatened rain upon their docking.

"Are you all right?" Suzette asked, leaning into him as they walked the deck. Giles had agreed to watch Robert while they took a few moments for themselves.

"I should ask you that question, love, after all you've been through." He exhaled a long, drawn-out sigh and tugged her closer to his side. "It's my wife." He paused. "God how I hate that word associated with that woman," he moaned. "When I say the word *wife*, I wish to think of you—not her."

"Robert, tell me the truth. Will you be able to divorce?"

"It depends. We'll have to wait first to see if the authorities find her. I'll hire a private detective in Paris to get on the trail as soon as we reach home."

"Home—that sound so strange," Suzette admitted. "Are you going to take us directly to your estate, Robert, or will you—?"

"To my estate," he replied emphatically, interrupting any thought of Suzette's that she would be elsewhere. "I shall not shove the two of you into some hotel to be on your own while I deal with the legal matters. My estate is large, and there are many rooms to share." He paused for a moment, despairing his other obstacle. Robert turned toward Suzette and grabbed both of her hands.

"You'll meet my mother." He hesitated to warn her of the cold reception that she would probably receive. "I'm afraid the introduction may turn out to be quite unpleasant. She was very attached to Jacquelyn, and her acceptance of you will not come easily. In fact, she can be rather vocal when it comes to a disapproving opinion."

"I'm afraid to meet her. She'll hate me, Robert, I'm sure," Suzette assumed. "Does she know anything about me?"

"She knows I've kept a mistress, but I have not spoken your name to her. Hopefully, she'll understand your place in my life, once I introduce our son."

"I don't know if I can handle this, Robert."

"You'll be fine," he assured her, bringing Suzette into his arms. "It will be uncomfortable at first, but by and by my mother will grow to love you both. I'm sure of it. It will just take time."

"Will we ever marry?"

"I will do everything in my power to make that happen, no matter what the cost to me personally, financially, or socially. I promise." Suzette did not reply, and he wondered if she doubted his vow.

"Look, Suzette," Robert pointed ahead. "The white cliffs

of Dover." A smile spread across his face at the sight of his homeland. "We should find Giles and Robert. Soon we'll be docking and catching the train to London."

"Yes, I remember." Suzette squeezed his hand tightly. "I remember how tired I was when we boarded the train. This time, I feel exhilarated, with only a slight bit of trepidation in my soul for what lies ahead."

"Do not fear, Suzette. I told you once before that I would take care of you, and I will never break my promise to you." He squeezed her hand in return. "Let's find the rest of the family, shall we?"

❋ ❋ ❋

Tired from the long trip, Robert was happy when the carriage pulled into the tree-lined lane of his estate. Even though it had only been a few months since he left, it seemed like years. Everything looked different to him, in an odd sort of way. Jacquelyn would not be there to greet him, and he was sure he would never see her again.

"Oh, Robert how splendid your home appears." Suzette gawked at the stately manor and extensive lands that surrounded the building.

"I probably should have told you ahead of time what to expect."

The land of his ancestors and the estate were an integral part of Robert's personality that he had never shared with Suzette before. "The estate residence was built in the 1700's by my great grandfather, Thomas Holland."

He thought of the portraits that lined the walls and their expressions, which might alarm Suzette. "Don't mind the scowls on the painted faces of my family," he warned. "The Holland line has been far too stoic in character for centuries, as far as I'm concerned," he added, justifying his rebellious traits.

"I'm overwhelmed just looking at it," Suzette admitted.

"Where's the horses?" little Robert impatiently queried, stretching his neck in all directions searching for a pony.

Robert chuckled over his son's enthusiasm. "I imagine at this time of the day they're in the stables having oats," he warmly smiled. "Later on you'll see them in the pasture to the west of the house, over there in the grassy knoll." He pointed his son in that direction.

The wheels slowed, pulled up to the front entrance of Robert's home, and came to a stop. Conscientious footmen ran out and opened the carriage door, then stood at attention.

"My staff is uniformed and quite formal," Robert added. "Don't let them intimidate you, sweetheart."

A footman lowered the steps and offered his white-gloved hand to Suzette, who took it and stepped down onto the pebbled drive. A brisk wind swept by, lifting the corner of her hat, and she quickly grasped it with one hand. Her eyes darted about the large stone façade with its metal-pane windows and multiple chimneys dotting the rooftop. On the other side of the carriage, a small pond with a fountain in the center shot straight up into the air and then fell in a beautiful cascade.

Robert stood by her for a moment watching her reaction to his home that had been so familiar to him throughout his lifetime. Suzette appeared awestruck.

"Look, Mommy, ducks!" shouted Robert.

"Yes, I see," she answered. She clung to his hand, so he wouldn't run off.

"Come on, love," Robert invited her endearingly. He escorted her into the foyer. A flurry of servants greeted the group at the door, grabbing coats, hats, and fussing over them like royalty.

Giles ordered the footmen to unload the trunks and luggage, then looked to Robert for directions.

"Put them in the west wing, in the room of suites that face the hills."

"Fine choice." He nodded in agreement.

"What would you like to do?" He turned to Suzette and Robert. "If you need some time to relax and unwind before introductions, that might be a prudent course of action," he suggested. "Giles can show you to your rooms. I'll have a chambermaid assigned to you post haste, and then when you're settled you can choose a new lady's maid if you wish."

"I am tired," Suzette admitted.

"Good, rest and clean up, both of you, and we'll have dinner at seven o'clock. My butler will call for you."

"All right." Suzette answered meekly, looking tired and overwhelmed.

"I should warn you, we tend to dress formally for supper. It's a family tradition my mother prefers."

"We'll be ready," she assured him. Suzette took her son's hand. Bewilderment spread across her face as she glanced about her strange surroundings. She suddenly looked frightened.

Robert hadn't considered the time it would take for Suzette to adjust to his world and his manner of life. They blended so well together in every other way both physically and emotionally. He suddenly questioned if they would blend together otherwise. Hopefully, she would settle in and find her place in the Holland estate, because one day she would assume the role of duchess.

❋ ❋ ❋

Suzette rifled through the few things she had brought with her to England. Finding an appropriate dress for a formal dinner occasion proved quite difficult. Hopefully, Robert would help her rebuild her wardrobe. Already she had begun to feel somewhat overwhelmed and out of place.

Robert's estate turned out to be much larger than she ever imagined. The household staff continually scurried about everywhere. From what she could tell from traveling from the foyer to the west wing, the enormous residence brimmed with family treasures in art and furnishings.

As Robert indicated, his butler by the name of Mr. Winston, came and announced that dinner was served. Appearing to be in his fifties, gray, and stocky, with a serious look in his eye, his announcement slipped through his lips coolly. Suzette couldn't help but wonder if the staff knew what had transpired between Robert and his wife. Would she be getting the cold shoulder from everyone because of her arrival?

"Thank you, Mr. Winston," she replied, holding Robert's hand. "If you would be so kind as to escort me to the dining room, I would appreciate it. I'm afraid I do not know the way."

"Of course," he said, somberly. "I'd be happy to oblige your request."

The formal atmosphere stifled Suzette. *No doubt, she will be ten times worse,* she thought to herself. She followed closely behind the impeccably dressed butler, studying his formal attire and attitude.

"Robert, be on your best behavior," she reminded him, with a squeeze of her hand. "We are guests of very important people, and I want you to make a good impression."

"Yes, Mommy." He turned his head left and right at the portraits lining the halls.

Suzette shrunk under the gazes of Robert's ancestors, who appeared to be following them with their eyes. She wondered if the estate had ghosts.

"Madame Moreau and Master Robert Moreau," Mr. Winston announced, as they came through the doorway.

Robert stood from his place at the head of the table and walked over to greet Suzette and his son. He offered his arm and escorted her to the chair to his left, placing his son to the left of Suzette.

"Mother, I'd like to introduce to you Madame Moreau

and her son, Robert."

Suzette gulped as she eyed the stern dowager duchess, dressed in such finery and jewels that she felt like a pauper in her plain blue evening dress. It suddenly dawned on her that she didn't know how to formally address Robert's mother, so she picked the obvious.

"It is a pleasure to meet you," she offered, with a nervous smile. Suzette curtsied. Upon standing upright, she brought Robert to stand in front of her, bent down, and whispered in his ear. "What do you say to the nice lady?"

Little Robert stood tall, placed his right hand on his stomach, his left hand on the small of his back, and bowed at the waist. "It's a pleasure to meet you. My name is Robert Philippe Moreau." He stood back up and looked at the duchess. A big smile lit up his face.

"Very polite," Robert chimed in, filled with pride. Suzette saw him look at his mother waiting for her to respond.

"Pleasure to meet you, as well," she replied, her lips pursed tightly together. Her eyes and demeanor remained icy and unyielding, which agitated Suzette's nerves.

After everyone sat at the table and the first course arrived, Robert attempted to lighten the conversation with talk of their good trip and his plans to show his guests around the estate. Of course, the matter of young Robert's encounter with horses also became a prime dinner table discussion.

Suzette felt thankful that her son had decided to behave politely, fearing that perhaps he had been overwhelmed by his surroundings. Footmen stood behind them at the table, only stepping forward to serve the multiple courses one by one as they arrived. The place settings and silverware were impressive, as well as the décor of the room. Not wishing to remain silent as a mouse throughout dinner, Suzette offered a compliment.

"The dining room is very beautiful, especially the

pattern of the wallpaper. It's stunning."

Mary lifted her head and looked at Suzette with icy daggers in her eyes. "My son's wife chose the wallpaper," she replied, in snippy arrogance. "Jacquelyn had impeccable taste in decorating. In fact, many of the rooms in our estate reflect her personal tastes, intelligence, and beauty."

Suzette looked at Robert, who gave a disapproving look toward his mother. She merely ignored his disdainful gaze. Suzette's confidence faded away like the evening sunset. The room grew awkwardly silent, with only the sound of the clock on the fireplace mantel ticking away the time. Hopefully, dinner would soon end, and she could return to her room to contemplate her strange and awkward new life.

❋ ❋ ❋

"Over my dead body!" Mary screamed at Robert. "Like hell you'll bring her and your illegitimate son into this household. Your father would roll over in his grave, if he knew to what depths you've sunk."

"I will not argue with you, Mother. Suzette and Robert will live in the west wing in the suite of rooms that are far away from yours. They are empty as a shell, and now they'll be put to good use."

"I cannot believe you, Robert! Have you lost all sense of propriety by bringing your mistress into this house and that—that boy?"

Robert clenched his jaw at the disrespect his mother had shown his son. "Must I remind you that boy is your grandson? He's my flesh and blood and yours too. There will be no heir coming from Jacquelyn Spencer's womb. The woman is barren and always will be."

Mary huffed and walked over to the window turning her back to Robert. Her chest heaved up and down in anger; but somewhere inside of her heart, a tug pulled at her like a tiny child wanting her attention.

"Jacquelyn—do you suppose you'll ever find her?" Mary still upset over the news of her departure and terrible kidnapping of another's baby, thought of her welfare.

"I don't know. I somehow doubt that we will, and that grieves me for many reasons. I will hire private detectives, and I know the Paris police filed charges against her for kidnapping. They're actively pursuing her whereabouts."

"Before she left," Mary confessed, "I tried to dissuade her from going to Paris to search after you. She would not listen." She turned from the window and faced Robert. "Something inside her soul was amiss; and frankly, I believe it was her inability to cope with the grief of being barren and your lack of love."

Mary looked into her son's blue eyes that appeared as troubled as her own. "What she has done is unforgiveable. If she's found, for heaven's sake, she'll spend the rest of her life in prison like a common criminal."

"Perhaps, but I do not think it will come to that. She is a clever woman—cleverer than I gave her credit. I believe she planned to leave me anyway once she arrived in Paris."

"Why? What proof do you have that she premeditated this course of action?"

"The fact that her jewelry box is empty."

"What?" Mary's eyes bulged in horror.

"She knew exactly which pieces to take to allot her the greatest value. I'm sure if they are sold, they will provide her a source of income for years."

Mary moaned and placed her hand over her stomach. "You mean my mother's necklaces, plus your father's family jewels?"

Robert regretfully nodded his head. "I'm afraid so."

Mary backed up into a chair and sat down with a flop. "Oh, Robert, how cruel to take our family heirlooms!"

"I surmise, that in her mind, it was merely another way to punish me for my sins against her."

"It still sticks in my craw that you took a mistress and

have an illegitimate son," she admitted, with a distinct disappointment etched across her face. "But for your sake, I shall try to accept those whom you love." She forced from her lips a small token of compromise. "All I can offer at the moment is civility, nothing more."

"That's all I ask," Robert replied, knowing that his mother's words came with enormous sacrifice. "Civility is a good start, because Suzette is already brokenhearted over many things, Mother. I do not want to add to her sadness."

Robert lowered his head and looked at the carpet beneath his feet, dealing with the guilt of his participation in the agony that had followed everyone's life. His pursuit of Suzette had come at a great price, but the price of love had been unavoidable to obtain the happiness he had always desired.

"Thank you," he whispered. He crossed the room and kissed his mother's forehead.

She released a small grin and placed her hand on his cheek giving him the proverbial pat. Rarely, had she told him of her love in words. Robert knew that through her show of affection, she spoke what she could not articulate.

Chapter 28

"Well," he said, sucking in a deep breath. "I promised a young boy a ride on a pony, so I'd better get to it," he announced to Giles, who had just finished dressing him.

He left his suite and headed for Suzette's, hoping that she had settled in after her first night in a strange location. Robert decided not to visit her bed—at least not yet. Everyone needed to adjust to their rapidly changing lives. Robert had much to investigate, as well, regarding his legal rights.

Suzette made no decision when to tell their son the truth regarding his parentage. That morning, he did ask why his daddy didn't come with them. She painfully informed him that he had been busy with work and left it at that. Robert was thankful that the attention span of a five-year-old child took his mind quickly off Philippe, as he focused on his pony ride instead.

Robert arrived at Suzette's suite and knocked on the door. A chambermaid answered. "Good morning, Your Grace," she said, with a curtsy. "Madame is dressing for the morning."

"And the boy?"

"Oh, he's up. Running about looking for things to do."

Just then his son ran up to the door, and Robert's face

broke into a broad smile. "Well, little man, are you all settled in?"

"Yes, sir. You have a very big house."

"I suppose I do, but now that you're here, it won't seem so empty."

Little Robert's expression turned into one of curiosity. He fixated his eyes upon his father and studied his features with such intensity that it made Robert uncomfortable. He broke the lad's stare with a question that he knew would pique his interest.

"Well, now, do you have any riding clothes, like boots, breeches, and a riding jacket?"

His eyes grew big as saucers. "No, sir. Do I need them before I can ride the pony?"

"Hum," Robert mused, wanting to clothe him properly before letting him crawl upon the back of a horse. "I think it would be a good idea. How about I ask Giles, my assistant, to measure you and go into town and buy the things you'll need. A riding crop would be a good idea too."

"What's that?"

"Well, a riding crop is like a stick with a leather end that you hit your pony with to get him to go faster."

The countenance on Robert's son fell and fear spread across his face. His reaction surprised him, so he knelt down in front of the lad and put one hand on his shoulder.

"What's the matter?"

Little Robert shuffled his feet and pulled his eyes away. "I don't like to hit with a leather stick."

"Why?"

"Because my daddy beat me with his belt and it really hurt."

Robert strained not to curse aloud in his son's presence. Philippe had taken his hand to the boy and placed fear in his heart. It sickened him to the core.

"We don't hit the pony like that, Robert. I'll show you how to use it, but we never hit hard—only touch him a bit to get a good trot."

The answer seemed to appease his son, and the worry faded from his face. "Do I have to wait for all that stuff before I ride the pony?"

"Well, I think it wise, but you can come with me to the stables before your clothes arrive and see my horses. I'll introduce you to Adara, she is father's . . ." Robert's words trailed off, and an embarrassed flush filled his cheeks.

Little Robert looked at him waiting for him to continue. He could barely speak after talking to his son like a father.

"You mean your daddy's horse?"

"Well, not quite, but I'll explain that later. Anyway, you can meet my other horses, and you can pet them too. Maybe I'll even let you brush one this morning."

"Okay!"

"And what are you boys up to? Talking about horses are we?" Suzette's voice came joyously from the door of her bedchamber.

Robert turned and smiled at her. "Well, you know, I have made a promise, and I must keep my promise."

"Now you be careful, Robert, and do everything this nice gentleman says when he teaches you to ride. Mommy doesn't want you falling off and getting hurt."

"Oh, Mommy," he protested, stomping one foot. "I'm big enough to take care of myself."

Robert laughed as he watched his son walk over to the window and look out at the fields below.

"You'll soon find out that this young man has a bit of a temper when provoked," Suzette whispered.

"He's so adorable," Robert declared with pride. "I shall love him forever."

Robert looked at him imagining Philippe's cruel beating. He would never discipline his son in such a manner. He turned to Suzette. "Did Philippe punish him physically? He just told me his daddy took a belt to him."

"I tried to stop him, Robert, truly I did. He came home

from the West Indies and found out that he had tipped over Angelique's bassinet. He lost all sense of control and took him for a beating. He locked me out of the room, and I was helpless to prevent it from happening."

"Bastard," Robert mumbled low enough not for his son to hear. "I'll never beat the child, I assure you."

"Robert, when should we tell him the truth—I mean about you?"

"Well, I almost slipped myself a few minutes ago, but the reference went right over his head, thank God." Robert reached out for Suzette's hand. "In time. Perhaps when we marry, he will be more acclimated to his surroundings and closer to me as a friend. When his memory of Philippe begins to fade away, he will be more amendable to accepting me as his father."

"I'm afraid, Robert, that I will never be your wife."

"Don't be, Suzette. I've already made an appointment with my solicitor to discuss the legal ramifications of my situation. I'm thinking of petitioning the court and even Parliament, if I must, for a dissolution based on her criminal activity and abandonment. I may prevail on those grounds alone, along with the accusation of adultery."

"Do you think it will work?"

"It will be a long and arduous process, Suzette. I will not lie. It could take years."

"Years?" A veil of sadness draped across her face.

"You'll wait for me, won't you?" He flashed a teasing wink.

Suzette giggled. "Do you even have to ask? I'd wait forever, as long as I'm by your side."

Robert smiled. "Well, now, we're off to the stables," he announced. "Oh, and mother would like you to join her for afternoon tea in the rose parlor at two o'clock sharp," he added. He saw panic flash across her face, so he reached out and tapped the tip of her nose with his index finger.

"Don't worry, love. It will go well. Mother is practicing

the art of civility."

❋ ❋ ❋

Suzette nervously entered the parlor and immediately understood why it bore that name. Its décor of a soft red rose hue with gold trimmed furniture looked stunningly beautiful. Red rosebuds in porcelain vases adorned side tables, filling the room with fragrance.

Robert's mother sat on a divan, bejeweled in her finery. Her brunette hair, sprinkled with streaks of gray, accentuated her harsh appearance. Her makeup drew attention to her complexion that resembled granite stone. Suzette, however, could barely look into her eyes, which reflected her deep displeasure.

"Your Grace." She gave a quick curtsy. "Thank you for your invitation to tea."

"Sit," Mary replied. She wiggled her finger at a chair across from the divan where she lounged like a regal queen of the Holland domain. A servant arrived with a silver tray filled with tea and finger cakes for their consumption. She poured a cup for the duchess, handed it to her first, and then turned to Suzette.

"Madame, do you prefer milk and sugar?" She shot a sympathetic glance in Suzette's direction.

"Yes, milk, please. No sugar."

Suzette received the cup in her hand and looked over at Mary, who quickly sipped her tea.

"You may leave, now," she briskly informed her servant. Speedily, she complied and closed the door behind her.

"I assume Robert is off with your son showing him the horses," she began.

It bothered Suzette that she did not acknowledge Robert as her grandson. "Yes, I believe they are. Our son," she corrected, out of irritation, "is quite excited to learn about horsemanship."

"No doubt," she replied, coolly.

It was obvious by the thick atmosphere in the room that Mary's attempt at civility had gotten off to a poor start.

"I apologize," Suzette offered remorsefully, "if our arrival has upset you. I do hope that one day you'll forgive me for intruding into your life through such an unexpected turn of events."

Suzette clung tightly to the handle of the tea cup, instantly regretting her awkward apology. She thought it was prudent to come to the point of matter, for the sake of politeness. Yet when she saw the duchess' displeasure written across her face, she wondered if her frankness had caused more damage than good.

"Unexpected turn of events," she repeated. "Yes, that is one way of describing it, I suppose."

She set her half-empty cup down on the tray and lifted her eyes to Suzette. "You should know that I was quite fond of Jacquelyn. We got along very well. I respected and admired her, though these past few years she fell into deep melancholy over the fact that she could not bear Robert children, as well as his lack of love and suspected infidelity."

"I am very sorry," Suzette offered sympathetically.

The duchess looked at Suzette warily. "I told Robert last eve that for his sake I would attempt to be civil with you, though I don't necessarily approve of this entire situation."

"Understandable," Suzette offered. "I can only assure you that I am deeply in love with your son."

"Love, my dear, may not be enough. Both of you will pay a greater price for your actions as the years progress. Society will look unkindly upon this relationship. I can only hope my son will be able to handle the rebuff that awaits him. There will be an excessive price for love, which neither of you may have considered."

"I've already suffered some of that price myself." Suzette lowered her head trying not to cry as she thought of Angelique.

"You've apparently given to him an heir, which he intends to recognize, so he tells me."

"Hopefully, you will get to know our son better and will love him as we do."

"And what of your daughter?" she pressed with a slight irritation.

"My daughter is in Jacquelyn's care now. I can only hope that one day she'll be recovered."

Suzette's eyes filled with tears even though she tried to suppress the hurtful emotions. She had not forgotten Angelique. On the contrary, every day she thought of the baby she had given life to only a few months prior. A part of her heart contained a very special corner for the little girl she would probably never know.

"I apologize," the duchess offered. "I can see that Jacquelyn's actions of kidnapping your daughter have affected you deeply."

Suzette wiped away tears trickling down her cheek, thankful that a bit of sympathy had come from Robert's mother.

"Thank you."

The two women sat quietly for a few moments. Mary appeared to be pondering the act of civility, and Suzette struggled with the pain of loss. Finally, the duchess presented an offering of gracious acceptance.

"Well, would you like a tea cake?" She lifted the china plate in Suzette's direction. "There's nothing like a sweet, with a cup of tea, to cheer a lady up."

Suzette could tell in her eyes that she offered more than an afternoon treat. She attempted to bestow acceptance for Robert's sake.

"Thank you." Suzette reached forward and chose a lemon bar.

Mary did the same. She took a nibble and looked kindly into Suzette's eyes. "An excellent choice."

No other words came from her lips; but Suzette knew

in her heart that the dowager duchess had just welcomed her into their home.

Chapter 29

Surrey, England – Fall 1886

Robert stood in front of the window dressed in his black tuxedo as he looked out over the gardens of his estate. The round glass, with its intricate panes in silver design, had always been one of his favorite windows in his estate. It reminded him of life. Each panel represented a season that he had passed through to get where he stood at that moment.

In the distance, he could see the tower of the chapel on his estate where he was soon due to arrive. In one hour, he would be married. The decisions he made nearly two and one half years ago, whether right or wrong, had finally led him to this moment of completion. For the first time in his life, he had arrived at a sense of belonging to another human being—one of fulfilled destiny—even though it had come with a great price emotionally and financially.

As he expected, the obstacle of procuring his freedom from Jacquelyn Spencer proved nearly impossible. The legal ramifications of her disappearance and criminal charges had seriously complicated matters. As thorough as the authorities and private investigators had been, as they scoured Europe for her and Angelique, she appeared to have dropped off the face of the earth. It had been two years, and not a word had arrived to Philippe, Suzette, or himself. No one knew where she had gone or what had become of Angelique. It was a sad state of affairs.

The courts rejected his petition, and an appeal was filed with Parliament. They agreed to hear his petition for divorce on the grounds of desertion, but were not inclined immediately to grant his request. His barrister had returned on numerous occasions before his peers to present documentation of the criminal charges filed in the Parisian courts against Jacquelyn. However, they initially refused to recognize the French indictments since she was an English citizen. Old prejudices between the countries still prevailed.

Since that was the case, desertion in itself was not enough to grant a divorce without being coupled with adultery. Of course, Robert had no evidence Jacquelyn Spencer had committed adultery, but wondered if by now she had attached herself to another man.

The doors continued to slam in his face, locking him away from a marriage with Suzette. Every petition his barrister presented had been repeatedly postponed. Finally, after one last attempt, Parliament ruled that an eighteen month waiting period had to be observed before the dissolution of marriage would be granted on the grounds of desertion. Ample time needed to pass in order to establish proof that the duchess had indeed abandoned the union. In addition, Parliament recognized the criminal charges as extenuating circumstances and granted a divorce.

It had come at a great price to Robert, as his status in society had suffered when rumors swirled about Jacquelyn's disappearance, an unmarried woman residing at his estate, and a young boy all assumed to be his son. Acquaintances and alliances slipped away, but Robert still maintained a few true comrades who stood by and supported him in his pursuit of freedom.

If that were not enough, his investment of funds in the

Moreau Shipping business were a total loss. Philippe ran it into the ground, and the company closed in bankruptcy. His attorney corresponded to Robert that he had fallen once again upon hard times due to poor management of assets and employees, along with frivolous spending. Apparently, his mental ability to keep the business afloat, after so many personal losses, had played a large part in the company's demise.

Robert somewhat blamed himself for Philippe's professional failure. In his zeal to assimilate into their lives in order to find truth, his actions had far-reaching consequences. He couldn't help but nurse some guilt over the past two years for destroying Philippe's happiness in order to regain his own. He had been a man on a mission to win what he so dearly loved. How could he walk away from the deepest desire in his life? Casualties were inevitable, and so were broken hearts.

Jacquelyn, of course, had contributed detrimentally to Philippe's mental state having stolen his one remaining joy. The man's brokenness had not been entirely Robert's fault, for which he took some unusual sense of consolation. Nothing could be done about the past, except to let go and focus on the joys ahead. Robert pushed aside the regrets.

"Your Grace, it's time," Giles' voice announced from behind him.

"Time indeed."

Robert turned around sporting a satisfied smile. Giles reached out, straightened his tie, and brushed off his shoulders quickly with the palms of his hands to remove any trace of lint.

"The landau is downstairs waiting to take you to the chapel. The mademoiselle, your mother, and son have proceeded ahead of you."

Robert checked his pocket for the ring to assure himself one more time that it was there. "Well, Giles, this is it. I take the woman I love as my wife."

"I wish you all the happiness in the world."

Robert trotted downstairs filled with an air of contentment and climbed into the carriage. It wasn't long before he arrived, slipped into the side entrance of the chapel, and spoke a few words with the vicar before the ceremony.

The wedding had been planned as a small affair with his family and a few close friends, who stood by him throughout the stressful ordeal. After the cue had been given, Robert walked out and stood in front of the altar to await his bride.

His mother had been escorted and sat in the front row with a smile across her face and a twinkle in her eye. She had finally accepted Suzette and his son, bringing relief to Robert and peace to the household. He attributed her change of heart to her health. Every day she looked frailer, but today she beamed health and happiness.

Marguerite, Lord Chambers, and their two children had arrived to watch the union, as well. His sister supported Robert after learning of the grief caused by Jacquelyn. Happy that Robert had found contentment, Marguerite reached out to Suzette and their son, accepting them wholeheartedly into the family.

The organ played its first chord, and the small gathering stood to their feet. Robert's son preceded Suzette down the aisle with a big grin on his face, his pace nearly skipping like the carefree lad he had become.

A month before the wedding, Suzette and Robert sat him down and told him the truth about his parentage. Now, seven-years-old, a little wiser, and with a pony of his very own, their son embraced his father willingly. The bond between Robert and the lad grew stronger day by day, and his memory of Philippe seemed to evaporate over time. Suzette and Robert found it strange that he never inquired of the whereabouts of his sister. Suzette surmised his current situation had dissolved his need to compete for attention—he had become the center of their world.

As Robert waited for his bride to appear, he felt grateful. Philippe, as he had promised, quickly divorced Suzette. Though she felt some remorse over their adulterous affair, which brought them to this day, she had accepted the painful outcome as the only means to her ultimate happiness.

Everyone had suffered for their deception, and the consequences of former decisions had been reaped. Nevertheless, their love outweighed the sins and suffering. The walls of class and circumstance had been breached, and soon they would be husband and wife.

Suzette appeared to float down the aisle before him, dressed in a stunning ivory gown. Robert insisted that she wear a traditional wedding dress, but Suzette balked in embarrassment thinking she did not deserve to do so. Eventually, he won the battle, hiring the same dress designer he had used when Suzette first came to England. He could tell by the gleam in her eye that she felt pleased with her appearance.

She arrived before the altar, smiling at Robert. Her sheer veil enhanced her beauty, and Robert's heart pounded fiercely in his chest. He reached out his hand and offered it to his bride. Suzette smiled, grasped it, and Robert wrapped her arm around his. They turned and faced the altar and both knelt before the vicar to receive the blessing. In a matter of minutes, they would finally be one in every way—body, soul, and spirit.

"We have come here today to join this man and this woman in holy matrimony," announced the vicar solemnly.

Robert couldn't contain the urge to peek at his bride. He turned his head and looked at Suzette, fighting back tears. At last, his petite French mademoiselle, whose virginity he had claimed seven years ago, was about to become his wife. Robert Holland had found truth and love.

Epilogue

Vienna, Austria – Summer 1887

Count Eduard von Lamberg walked mournfully behind the horse drawn, glass funeral carriage, which carried the remains of his beloved wife inside a polished mahogany casket. Multiple sprays of white and red roses draped the coffin adding a splash of color among the starkness of death.

The procession of mourners included immediate family members, friends, and an entourage of musicians playing a traditional funeral dirge. The count's footsteps met the pavement with a cadence that matched the timing of the sorrowful piece.

The procession meandered through streets that were lined with curious onlookers. Women bowed their heads making the sign of the cross, and men took off their hats displaying their respect. The count, recognized as one of the most influential men in Vienna, received the sympathy of the city for his recent tragic loss.

Funeral attendees kept their gaze straight ahead, each dressed in Vienna's finest fashions of black dresses and suits. Somberly, they marched toward the Zentralfriedhof cemetery to bury Countess von Lamberg. The Vienna news had printed her obituary and funeral information announcing to the city the time and location of her burial.

Eduard held the hand of his three-year-old stepdaughter, dressed in a black taffeta dress, with matching gloves and hat. She walked obediently silent behind her mother's casket. Her hand clung tightly to that of her stepfather, and a blank facial expression mirrored her child-like confusion.

The horses draped in ceremonial black, click-clacked their hooves on the pavement. Upon arriving at the gated entrance to the cemetery, they proceeded down the tree-lined lane to the open burial plot waiting to receive the body.

The ceremony, somber and filled with grief, moved the count to tears. The parish priest conveyed his deep condolences. Eduard grabbed a handful of dirt and let it slip through his fingers onto the coffin. He mumbled his last goodbyes, and then bent down to encourage his stepdaughter to throw a red rose upon her mother's casket.

"Say goodbye to your mother, Angelique. Toss her a rose to take to heaven."

She did as told, and a tiny tear trickled down her flushed cheek. Eduard wondered if she comprehended the finality of the moment.

"I am so very sorry for your loss. If there's anything I can do, Eduard, let me help. I'll stay with you as long as you need me."

He pulled his eyes away from the coffin being lowered into the cold earth and rose to his feet. "That's very kind, Geraldine, but I will be fine. You should return to Berlin to be with your husband."

His sister had been at his side day and night since his wife's death, comforting him at a most difficult time and helping with the care of his daughter.

"I do not see any of Jacquelyn's family here. Did you not write to them about her death?"

"She had no family that I'm aware of, except for her daughter, Angelique." He looked down at the forlorn face of the little girl holding his hand.

"Will you keep her?" Geraldine inquired.

"Of course, I will keep her," he replied, with determination. "She will be my daughter, as she has always been my daughter, since the day I married Jacquelyn. I have every intention of raising her on my own."

"It's a shame that she will never know her mother, Eduard. How awful to have lost a parent at such an early age."

"I will try and keep her memory alive, for the child's sake. She was an exceptional woman, Geraldine, and will be missed."

"Have the doctors shared their findings with you, Eduard, as to the cause?"

"Yes," he said, lowering his voice so that those nearby would not hear. "I was told after the autopsy they discovered that her fallopian tube had ruptured. She was pregnant, but the fertilized egg had lodged wrongfully there rather than in her womb. When it burst, she bled to death. By the time she complained of the pain and the doctor was summoned, it was far too late to do anything about it. A few hours later, she was gone."

"Oh, dear Lord," Geraldine moaned.

"Thankfully, God had blessed her beforehand with this angel." He bent down and kissed the side of Angelique's cheek. "She was a devoted mother, who loved her daughter deeply. I can do no less."

Others began to crowd around the count to express their sympathy over his loss. He continued to hold tightly to his stepdaughter's hand, determined to bring her up for the sake of her dear departed mother.

When it was over, he glanced at the large, ornate headstone that he had commissioned to mark her grave.

"Countess Jacquelyn von Lamberg. Beloved wife of

Eduard, devoted mother of Angelique Jolene."

Tears filled his eyes as the gravediggers began to cover the casket with dirt.

He thanked everyone for their kind words. After seeing the confused and tired look upon his stepdaughter's face, he led her away from the scene of death.

"Come, Angelique. It's time to leave."

"I want my mommy," she began to cry. "I want my mommy."

His heart tore over her plea. "Someday you'll see her again, child. Someday."

Count von Lamberg climbed into a waiting carriage and headed home. Behind in the grave he left the woman whose past he never knew—Duchess Jacquelyn Spencer-Holland, the Duchess of Surrey.

The End

The Legacy Series

The Legacy Series family saga continues into the Edwardian era with The Price of Love. Each character has paid the price for innocence and deception. Now discover the price paid for love.

At the age of eighteen, Angelique Jolene von Lamberg felt secure in life. After all, her stepfather was an Austrian count, and she inherited his wealth and the title of komtesse. But when a letter arrives claiming she was kidnapped as a baby, suddenly everything changes.

Unable to dismiss the accusations, she embarks on a journey to London and Paris to seek out the truth. When she discovers that her life has been played like a pawn in a chess game of deceit, adultery, and vengeance, she decides to take matters into her own hands.

Will she continue to be the victim of the price of love, or will she become the only person able to heal a broken family from the pain of the past?

For more information about the author's other works and to subscribe to updates, visit HTTP://VICKIHOPKINS.COM.

CPSIA information can be obtained at www.ICGtesting.com
Printed in the USA
BVOW04s1540190415

396639BV00001B/91/P

9 780983 295914